# BLOOD

# MARKS

*Also by Bill Crider*

*Professor Carl Burns Mysteries*
 Dying Voices
 One Dead Dean

*Sheriff Dan Rhodes Mysteries*
 Evil at the Root
 Death on the Move
 Cursed to Death
 Shotgun Saturday Night
 Too Late to Die

# BLOOD

# MARKS

## BILL CRIDER

**ST. MARTIN'S PRESS**

**NEW YORK**

Production Editor: David Stanford Burr

Design by Dawn Niles

Library of Congress Cataloging-in-Publication Data

Crider, Bill.
      Blood marks / Bill Crider.
          p.   cm.
      "A Thomas Dunne book."
      ISBN 0-312-05823-3
      I. Title.
  PS3553.R497B57   1991
  813'.54—dc20                               91-7391
                                              CIP

First Edition: June 1991

10 9 8 7 6 5 4 3 2 1

From the *Houston Post:*

A spokesman for the Police Department said today that there are no apparent links in a series of brutal slayings of young women in the Houston area in the past several years. Sgt. D. P. Preston said that although all the women were about the same age, being between twenty and thirty, there is no other connection among them. "They all died in a different area of the city, they all died by entirely different means, and they had absolutely no connection among themselves that we've been able to discover, except of course for the fact that they've all been murdered." The latest murder victim, number nine in the series of unconnected slayings, was discovered two days ago in an apartment on the city's southwest side. Laura Roberts had been living in the apartment complex for approximately two months, and she was known . . .

# BLOOD

# MARKS

# PART ONE

# MISSING

# LINKS

# 1

There's so much blood.

That's what no one understands, how much blood there is.

They watch TV, they see people killed, they think that when you die violently there's maybe this little spurt of blood, or maybe this little stain on your blouse.

They don't know what it's really like.

I know.

I could tell them, but of course I won't. And they'll never get a chance to ask me. I'm far too good for that ever to happen. The cops are idiots. There was an article in the *Post* today that said . . . well, never mind what it said. It was all wrong, though.

All wrong.

But that just goes to show how stupid the cops are and why they'll never be asking me about things.

Back to the blood. Sometimes I get off the subject. It's not that my mind wanders. Hardly that. My intelligence has been measured, and it's very high. My IQ is genius level. It's just that when I'm thinking about one thing, other things catch my interest. I'm a man with a wide range of interests. My mind likes to examine all aspects of a problem, but that leads me to digress now and then.

The blood.

As I was saying, they don't know, the sheep in the streets. They just have no idea.

The cops know, though.

Oh, yes. The cops know.

They've been there after I've gone. They've seen the walls, the floors. Sometimes even the ceilings. The cops know about the blood, all right.

That's all they find, however, the blood and the bodies. They don't find any fingerprints, and they don't find any fibers. No hair, no semen. They don't find a thing to let them know that I've been there.

They never will.

I'm much too careful for that, now. The first time, that was different, but after all, it *was* the first time. Everyone is entitled to a few mistakes, and I didn't even know there was going to be a first time. It just more or less happened.

After that, though, I knew I'd have to do it again, but I knew that I'd have to do it right. I didn't want to be caught. If I were ever caught, then I'd have to stop.

And I don't want to stop.

The only record of what I've done will be kept on this disk, and I'm keeping this because someday I expect to be quite famous. I'll tell the world my story then, and everyone will see just exactly how brilliantly I carried everything out.

There will be movie offers, I'm sure, and the big stars will be fighting to play me. I'd really like for Paul Newman to get the part, but he's too old. It will have to be one of the young ones, maybe Dennis Quaid.

They'll have to get someone young and handsome, and they'll need someone who can show the requisite amount of intelligence. I think Quaid can do it, even if he did play Jerry Lee Lewis.

They'll need someone who can show exactly how clever I was and how I fooled everyone, unlike most of the poor incompetent fools who give my hobby a bad name.

You take Bundy, for instance. He was stupid; he got caught. And then he waited until the last to start talking, so nobody really knew whether to believe him or not. Sure, he got a lot of books written about him, but he never told anyone how it really was. He had the chance, but he didn't know what to do with it.

It won't be like that with me.

In the first place, I won't get caught. And when I decide that the world's ready for the truth, it will all be printed out in black and white. Right now, I'm storing it all on this floppy disk. Computers are a wonderful thing. It won't be as if I have anything written down where just anyone can read it. But it will be there if I decide to let the world in on the facts.

Otherwise, no one will ever know exactly how things happened, how those women died.

I'm the only one who knows. They can guess, speculate, but they can never put it together. I'm the one with the knowledge. I did it. I was there.

I keep forgetting to talk about the blood. I don't know why I keep getting off the track, unless it's like I said: I want to get everything down right, and all these other things keep occurring to me.

There's not always so much blood, anyway, not every single time. It just depends on how you do things. That's one of the reasons I'll never be caught. I don't ever do it the same way twice.

Bundy did. He *thought* he was smart, but he wasn't.

He couldn't help it, I guess, but he went for the same type of woman every time. They even looked the

5

same. I've studied the case and seen the photos in the books; I know. And he used the same approach lots of times, too, before he went more or less off his rocker there at the end.

That won't ever happen to me, either, going off my rocker, I mean.

No way.

If there's one thing I'm sure of, it's that I'm completely sane, a lot saner than most of the people I know.

It's just that I look at things differently, see things other men can't see.

Like the blood marks.

That's what I look for, the blood marks. Very few women have them, but when I see them, I know them.

Other men don't, but I do.

Sometimes the marks might be on their faces, other times in their eyes. I don't know why I was the one chosen to be able to spot them, but I was. There's nothing I can do about it.

Other men may look at the same woman and wonder what she'd look like in a bikini, or what she'd look like in a leather garter belt, or what she'd look like if they stripped her naked. How she'd squirm under them if they fucked her or cry out when she came.

I look at her and wonder how she'd look with her head cut off, or with her stomach laid open, or with her mouth twisted in a scream as I tell her that she's going to die. I wonder how that scream would sound.

It's all in the point of view.

When they've got the blood marks on them, they're just asking for it. Why no one else can see this has always been a mystery to me, but it's probably that you have to be of a higher order of intelligence to notice in the first place. Most men are just dumb sons-of-bitches anyway.

It takes vision to see the blood marks.

**6**

I would never touch a woman without the marks on her. That's what I mean about being sane. Bundy finally went berserk, just breaking into that sorority house and killing randomly. He even bit one of the girls, left his tooth marks, for godsake.

Stupid.

Insane.

And think about Jack the Ripper. He never got caught, so they say, but maybe he should have been. He killed in the same area all the time, killed the same kind of women. Whores, all of them. It's a wonder the Ripper remained free.

You couldn't get by with methods like that today, not at all. You wouldn't have a chance. The cops, as stupid as they are, would be all over you sooner or later.

You've got to be smart. You've got to watch for the women with the blood marks on them, and when you find them you've got to kill them.

But not if they know each other. Not if they're from the same part of town. Not if there's any connection between them at all.

You can't let the cops have a pattern, a clue, anything. Dumb as they are, they'd get you.

The blood. That's all they find after I've been there and gone, and sometimes not even the blood.

There have been nine so far.

There will be more.

No I won't, Howland thought. No one wanted to talk to Romain. "I'll go by today," he said.

"You'll go by this morning," the Chief said. "You'll go by at ten-thirty, to be exact. I had my secretary make an appointment for you."

"Oh," Howland said. "Thanks."

The Chief smiled. He knew that Howland would simply have told him later that Romain wasn't in or that he'd just missed him or that he'd gotten tied up with his paperwork and hadn't had the time.

"Romain's a good man," the Chief said.

"I know that," Howland said. "He's the best." But that didn't make the son-of-a-bitch any easier to take.

# 2

"Goddammit," the chief said. H
be more, too. He could feel it. "Th
nection, Howland. You know it

Howland looked across the
had come to Houston from a s
made his reputation beca
cracked one of the bigge
killer cases ever to splash
nation.

To Howland, a
didn't look like anyt
man with a beaky r
ners of his mout
photo opportuni
blue suit with

Howland
didn't look
and spare,
tended to
brushin
looked

9

# 3

**R**omain didn't care whether anyone on the force found him easy to take. He didn't give much of a shit if nobody did. In fact, he would have preferred it that way. He didn't like anyone that he worked with very much, no one that he could think of, and he thought it was only fair if they didn't like him, either.

Romain was almost six feet tall, thin as a plank, with the kind of face that would make him look youthful even when he grew old. The eyes gave him away, though. The eyes were old already, a thousand years old.

He had sandy red hair, thin and combed back from his forehead, and he wore thick glasses with heavy black plastic rims, the kind no one wore anymore. The glasses served to make his sad eyes look even older and sadder.

The truth of it was, Romain thought most people were shit. There might be one or two of them out there somewhere that were worth something, but Romain didn't know them.

Romain was the way he was for at least two reasons.

One reason was that Romain was a cop, a member

of a profession that was more often than not confronted with human beings at their very worst.

Romain didn't often see the loving father gently changing his baby daughter's diaper and feeding her with a bottle.

What Romain saw was the thirty-year-old man who had snatched his two-year-old girl up by her ankles and whacked her head up against the wall "a couple of times, that's all. Hell, what's the big deal? The little bitch wouldn't stop squalling."

Romain didn't see the couple, happily married for fifty-six years, who still held hands when walking down the street and shared their joys and triumphs in secret conversations.

What Romain saw was the woman whose husband had told her one time too many to "bring me another fucking beer, and get a move on," after which the loving wife had gone in search of her husband's .38-caliber pistol that he kept in a bedside table for self-defense and had then blown the top of the sorry bastard's head off, splattering blood and brains all over the shabby living room, including the TV set that he had watched incessantly.

Romain didn't see the teenage boy who earned his own spending money by doing yard work around the neighborhood and who spent his spare time painting the house of some widowed impoverished grandmother.

What Romain saw was the teenage boy who shot his buddy three times in the face with a .22 rifle and then took the $200 stereo out of his buddy's pickup because "it sounded real good, and I wanted it."

Those were the kinds of things that tended to sour Romain on humanity.

Add to that the fact that Romain was not just an ordinary cop. He was a police psychologist. He had to

**14**

talk to those people, and he had to try to explain them to his colleagues.

It wasn't easy.

Everything Romain had learned about human behavior while working at his chosen profession led him to believe that human beings were basically pretty damned worthless.

For every example of human dignity and worth that a colleague would bring up, Romain would bring up five examples of human greed, selfishness, neglect and callous disregard of the lives of others.

Let someone mention Schweitzer, Romain would bring up Hitler.

For every Mother Teresa, Romain had an Attila the Hun.

Mention a place where human beings were treated with dignity and respect, and Romain would mention Palestinian refugee camps.

In other words, his outlook on life was less than cheerful.

He also smoked like a chimney. His theory was that since he was breathing heavily polluted air every time he stepped out of doors, since he was eating food laced with all kinds of known carcinogens, since he was exposed to all sorts of electromagnetic fields by the computers he used in his work and the power lines strung all over town, since like everyone else in Houston he was in at least some danger of being shot by some random crazy on the street, and since he was also in plenty of danger of being smashed to a pulp in traffic by some drunk running a red light, then it didn't make a hell of a lot of sense to deprive himself of one of life's few pleasures on the off chance that it might kill him. If smoking didn't get him first, one of the other things certainly would, so he might as well enjoy himself.

**15**

Therefore, he was sitting at his desk smoking an unfiltered Camel when Howland came in the door at ten-thirty. Howland was holding some file folders in his right hand.

Romain mashed out the butt in his overflowing ashtray, reached in his pocket and pulled out his crumpled pack, straightened it, got out another cigarette, stuck it in his mouth and lit it with a disposable butane lighter. Only then did he deign to notice Howland.

"Yeah?" he said. He had a raspy voice and habitually sounded rude. He *was* rude. He hoped Howland would go away.

"I have to talk to you," Howland said, obviously regretting it. "I believe the Chief set up an appointment."

"I don't give a shit about appointments," Romain said, which was the truth. In fact, had he actually remembered Howland's having an appointment that morning, he would have tried to find some kind of excuse to be out of his office.

"This is confidential," Howland said. "Do you mind if I shut the door?"

"Go ahead," he said.

Howland shut the door reluctantly. Howland did not smoke.

After shutting the door, Howland sat in the chair across from Romain's desk. He sat without an invitation, because he knew from experience that Romain would never have invited him to sit.

The desk was littered with papers, and most of the papers were spotted with ashes from Romain's cigarettes. There was a computer terminal on one corner of the desk, and the keyboard was in front of it. Howland had seen Romain use the computer, however, and he knew that the psychologist would not leave the keyboard there. He preferred to put it on his lap.

Romain sat impassively, smoking his cigarette, inhaling deeply, letting the smoke trickle out his mouth and nose, saying nothing.

"It's about some murders," Howland said finally.

Romain snorted smoke. "I figured. You're a homicide investigator, after all. I'm not stupid, Howland."

Howland tried not to let Romain's attitude bother him. As much as he disliked the man, he knew that Romain knew his business. He passed the file folders across the desk to Romain.

"I'd like for you to take a look at those," Howland said.

Romain crushed his cigarette and took the folders. Howland saw that the tips of his fingers were stained by nicotine.

For a long time there was no sound except the shuffling of papers as Romain went through the folders.

When he was finished, he put them on the table and lit another Camel and sucked in the smoke.

"So?" he said as he exhaled.

"So I don't like it," Howland said. "There's no connection that I can see between the killings. You've got mutilations, simple bullet wounds to the head, tortures, a stabbing. Different women, different parts of town, no relationship among them. But what bothers me, aside from the fact that they're all unsolved, is that if there isn't a connection, then we've got nine crazy fuckers running loose instead of one or two."

"And you want my help," Romain said. It wasn't a question. He knew what Howland had come for.

"That's right. You went to that conference on serial killers the FBI held at Quantico last year. Maybe you learned something that I can use. Or maybe you can just tell me to forget it, that there's no pattern at all, and that all those women were killed by different people."

Romain had gone to Quantico, all right. He had heard all the experts, and they had confirmed all his worst suspicions about human nature. He had studied the interviews with the serial killers and sexual murderers that the FBI staff had conducted and compiled, and he had not been particularly surprised at anything he read.

Human beings were shit, all right.

Romain had not been any more popular in Virginia than he was in Texas. No one at the conference liked him; they all tended to shy away from him when they passed him in the hall. But they listened when he talked.

The men at Quantico prided themselves at being able to think like serial killers, but they'd never met anyone quite like Romain. He could get right in there inside the killer's mind with the best of them. He knew what made the fuckers tick, knew what drove them. He was so good that sometimes it was almost scary.

And he didn't even work at Quantico.

More than once, his name would come up in conversation, at the breaks when he wasn't around, and the discussion would always be centered on the fact that it was a good thing Romain was on the side of the law. If he were one of the bad guys, he would be hell to catch.

So while no one at the conference liked Romain, they damn sure respected him. Howland did, too.

That was why he sat up and paid close attention when Romain said, "Oh, there's a pattern, all right. You just missed it, Howland."

"All right, then," Howland said. "Tell me what I missed."

So Romain told him.

# 4

Casey Buckner didn't know why she'd ever moved to Houston.

Maybe it was to get as far from West Texas as she could after the Asshole, which is how she would from now on refer to her ex-husband, had dumped her.

She should have known it would happen eventually.

He was fifteen years older than she was. She had been a student in his graduate class on the later Romantic poets, and the way he talked about Byron and Keats and Shelley had made her squirm in her chair with desire.

"'She walks in beauty, like the night,'" he had read soulfully, his eyes looking right at her, or so she thought.

What a crock. Well, at least that's the way she saw it now. At the time, she'd thought she was going to come right there in the classroom.

Anyway, she had fallen hard, and she thought he had, too. Maybe he had. He'd married her, after all, and he hadn't had to do that.

It had lasted for ten years, some of them good, but the only good thing left now was their daughter, Margaret, who had been born early in the second year of the marriage.

Casey had left her graduate studies to stay at home and care for Margaret, and she had never regretted it, even though it meant that she had gotten only six hours beyond her master's, a fact that was making it hard for her to get a job in the competitive field of teaching on the college level.

The Asshole didn't care about that. He had gotten involved with another one of his graduate students, just the latest in a series, as Casey had later found out. This one was the same age Casey had been when she was in his class.

Ironically, it was the same class on Romanticism. There was something about the way the Asshole read Byron, she had to admit it.

He had been "decent" about it, as he had put it, giving her a generous settlement and promising to be faithful in his child support payments. So far he'd lived up to that promise.

But she'd had to get out of Lubbock. The red dirt, the dust storms, the icy winters, though she had become accustomed to them and even enjoyed them, all reminded her of the Asshole now, and she damned sure didn't want to be reminded of him. She also didn't want to take the chance of running into him on campus if she decided to complete her graduate work.

She was afraid she would be tempted to kick the shit out of him.

So she and Margaret were now residents of Houston, Texas, the currently depressed region known as the Oil Patch, sitting right there in Hurricane Alley, and it was worse than she had ever imagined it would be.

**20**

She'd lived in Dallas most of her life, before grad school, at any rate, and she'd only been to Houston once, and that had been during the winter. It hadn't seemed so bad, then.

It seemed really bad now, in the middle of July. It was three o'clock in the afternoon, and the temperature was sitting at 95 degrees. That was a comfortable temperature in Lubbock, where the humidity usually came in at around 30 percent, but the humidity in Houston almost matched the temperature. All you had to do was step outside and you were immediately covered with a slick coating of sweat that wouldn't go away. It just kept getting thicker.

The mosquitos could get through it, however. They had no trouble at all. She swatted at the big one that was humming in her ear as she tried to carry the thirteen-inch TV set from the U-Haul trailer to the apartment she had rented. Thank God, the apartment was on the first floor.

One reason she had been tempted to move to Houston was that, while she could not get a full-time teaching job at a college or university, she had been virtually assured by three different department chairmen at nearby community colleges that there would be part-time openings on their campuses in the fall. They had further assured her that teaching part-time was the best way to open the full-time door.

She was pretty sure that was bullshit. They were all going to exploit her by paying her as little as possible and passing the raises on to the full-timers.

Still, if she could get two courses at all three schools, or, even better, three courses at two of them, she could survive. She wouldn't be making as much as a high school teacher, but she would be doing something she liked and maybe she could even find time to take a graduate course or two at the University of Houston.

She had found an apartment near the Astrodome, just off Stella Link, and she had quick access to Loop 610, so she could get anywhere quickly, or as quickly as was possible given Houston's traffic and the distances she would have to travel. But if there wasn't a traffic jam on the loop, though there often was, she'd be just fine.

Day care for Margaret in the afternoons was going to be a problem, however. Having to pay for it wasn't the trouble; the Asshole was going to take care of that.

It was just that Margaret was used to being at home with her mother, and her mother was used to being there with her daughter, too. Well, life was never stable, and if they could adjust to the climate, they could adjust to day care after school.

Just as she had lugged the TV set almost to the door, a man appeared out of nowhere and asked if she could use some help.

"I live just down the way," he said with a smile. "Seventeen-H."

Casey and Margaret were in 15-G. It was probably all right to get help from a neighbor, though Casey had heard plenty of bad things about Houston. Even the Asshole didn't want her to move there.

"I'm sure it's not safe," he had said. "There are more murders there every day than we have in Lubbock in ten years. I don't think it will be a good place to bring up a child."

"Too bad," Casey had told him, more determined than ever to go. He had given up his visiting rights to Margaret in the divorce, hadn't even seemed really concerned. A nine-year-old would probably have cramped his style with Charlotte, his new love, and the coeds who were sure to follow, so he had absolutely no say in where she went.

She put the TV set in the outstretched arms of her

new neighbor, taking the opportunity to look him over. He was tall, tan, well muscled. His face, while not exactly handsome, was clean-cut, and he had wide blue eyes. He was wearing cutoff jeans and a faded Warren Zevon T-shirt. He looked about thirty, a couple of years younger than Casey.

"I'm Casey Buckner," she said as he took the set.

"Rob Hensley," the man said. His smile revealed white, even teeth.

Casey was suddenly conscious of her own appearance.

She was one of those lucky people who didn't look their age; she was sure she didn't look a day over twenty-five, certainly not old enough to have a nine-year-old child.

She was wearing shorts and a tank top in deference to the heat, and she knew that her legs and breasts were as good as anyone's and better than most. Too bad the Asshole hadn't fully appreciated them. Maybe one day he'd realize what he was missing.

Her blond hair was pulled up and back, caught in a bun at the back of her head, and she smiled at Rob Hensley, who was looking her over just as she was studying him.

"I'll open the door," she said, walking ahead of him to the apartment.

She opened the door and felt the cool air come rushing out to greet her.

Margaret came rushing out, too. She was brown and thin, more like the Asshole than her mother.

"Where's the TV?" Margaret said. "It's almost time for Wapner."

Casey laughed. She had taken Margaret to see *Rain Man* a couple of years ago, and ever since then Margaret had been a big fan of "The People's Court."

"The TV's right here," Casey said. "Mr. Hensley is helping me bring it in."

Margaret looked at Rob. "Bring it in here," she said. "I'll show you where to put it."

Rob laughed good-naturedly. "I can see who runs the show around here," he said, following Margaret.

He set the TV set on a small table when she directed him to it.

"Here's the plug," Margaret said, pointing to the wall outlet.

Rob plugged in the set, and Margaret promptly turned it on and began searching through the channels.

"That ought to keep her occupied for a while," Rob said to Casey. "Can I help you unload the rest of that trailer?"

Why not? Casey thought. He was a good-looking man, it was time for her to make the acquaintance of a man or two. She couldn't brood forever about the way the Asshole had treated her.

"Sure," she said. "If you don't mind."

"I don't mind," he said. "I don't mind at all."

# 5

Howland spent the rest of the day in his office going over the files again. Romain had certainly given him something to think about.

"The pattern is that there is no pattern," Romain had said.

Howland didn't get it. "But why should there be, if there's no connection?" he said. Then he thought of something. "Or do you mean that they all seem to be motiveless? That's certainly true."

"Let me rephrase it so that you can understand it," Romain said, tapping the folders with his stained fingertips. "It's not simply that there's no pattern. There's something that's very interesting about every case you have there, except for one, the earliest one."

"Ellen Forsch," Howland said.

"Yes, Forsch. That one's different. But the others are all the same."

"They're not the same at all," Howland protested. "I just told you that they weren't."

"Oh, but they are," Romain said. "You just haven't seen it yet."

25

And then it dawned on Howland. It was so obvious it practically hit you in the face. How could he not have seen it sooner?

His expression must have given him away.

"I can see you've got it," Romain said. "You should have spotted it immediately, but I can see why you didn't."

"It's like a Sherlock Holmes story," Howland said. "I don't remember which one."

"I don't read fiction," Romain said, his mouth twisting. He got out a cigarette.

Howland brushed his hair back from his forehead. "There's a story, I don't remember the name, where Holmes says that the peculiar thing was a dog that *didn't* bark."

Romain breathed smoke. "Perceptive guy, that Holmes. We could use him on the force here in Houston."

"I think he's dead," Howland said. "He'd be long past retirement age by now, anyway."

Romain shook his head, stirring the cloud of smoke in front of him. "Never mind that. Tell me what you've finally spotted."

"All the killings are the same in one way all right," Howland said. "But it's not what's there that makes them the same. It's what's not there. It's what's missing."

"Correct," Mr. Holmes," Romain said. "And what's missing?"

"Nothing," Howland said. "Or everything, depending on how you want to phrase it."

Romain balanced his still-burning cigarette on top of the pile of crushed butts in his ashtray. "Let's say everything. Everything's missing."

"Or nothing's there," Howland countered. "There's

**26**

not a clue in a single one of those folders. Those are the cleanest crime scenes in the history of Harris County."

"Absolutely," Romain agreed. "What do you think the chances are that nine different killers, or eight, not counting Forsch, would leave a scene like that? One in a million? A billion? Probably higher than that, I would think."

He was right, no doubt about it. It was as if the women had been murdered in an antiseptic environment. It didn't matter what the method was, knife, gun, garotte. There was not, in any instance, again with the exception of Forsch, a single trace of the killer remaining. It was almost impossible that such a thing would happen once, much less eight times.

"We do have something on Forsch," Howland pointed out.

"She might not be part of the group, then, but we might have to think about that," Romain said. "I would surmise that the others were quite likely all killed by the same man, however, someone who knew what he was doing. Someone who is almost as smart as we are."

"'Almost?'" Howland said. "Hell, he's way ahead of us."

"Not as far as he was," Romain said.

"Sure he is," Howland said. He didn't like this a damn bit. "Even if it is the same man, we still don't have a clue as to who he is or when he'll kill again. If he does."

"Oh, he will," Romain said. "There's no doubt of that. No doubt of that at all. They always do."

Howland liked hearing that even less than he liked everything else. Romain was convinced, and so was Howland, now, that they had a serial killer on their hands, one who was sure to kill again. And there was not a single clue as to who he was, not one fucking

**27**

thing. As unbelievable as it was, it was looking more and more as if it were true.

And he was sure to kill again.

"Forsch," Howland said.

"As I told you, she might not be a part of the group. But if she was, then . . ."

"Then I'd better concentrate on that one," Howland said. "If it's the same man, he slipped up on that one."

Romain put his elbows on the papers on his desk and steepled his fingers. "Let me tell you a little bit about serial killers," he said.

# 6

Casey and Rob sat on the couch in Casey's apartment, relaxing in the air conditioning after finishing with the trailer, and sipping Seagram's wine coolers from the bottles. Casey had put them in the refrigerator as soon as she had arrived that morning and they were refreshingly cold. Margaret lay on the rug in front of them, watching *The Princess Bride* with close attention.

"I loved that book," Rob said. "I thought the movie was OK, but the book was a lot better."

Casey was surprised. Rob didn't look much like a reader. He looked more like someone who'd spend his spare time playing volleyball or jogging. She knew that she shouldn't stereotype men, or anyone else, like that, but she couldn't help it. It was a habit she had, and as was often the case, she'd been wrong in her assessment. It was as if she hadn't learned a single thing from her experience with the Asshole, who had seemed like such a classy guy at first.

"I think it's a wonderful book, too," Casey said. "I always wished that Goldman would write another fantasy."

"He did," Rob said. "*The Silent Gondoliers*. It's more like a short story than a novel, though, and it's no *Princess Bride*."

"I never read it," Casey said. "I'd like to."

"I have a copy somewhere," Rob said. "I'll see if I can find it if you'd like to borrow it."

"I would," Casey said.

Rob awkwardly set his bottle on a coaster on the coffee table in front of them. There was something wrong with his arm, not anything really noticeable, not anything that interfered with his being able to lift and carry, but something that just obviously caused him a bit of trouble now and then.

He noticed Casey looking at him.

"Bad break," he said. "I fell out of a tree when I was eight years old. That elbow will never be the same."

Casey, embarrassed that she had been caught in what must have seemed a curious stare, changed the subject.

"I'm sure glad you were here," she said. "I don't think I could have gotten that trailer unloaded by myself. I hope I didn't interfere with your vacation or anything."

"I'm on a permanent vacation," Rob said. "Or that's what a lot of people seem to think when I tell them how I earn a living. I work at home most of the time."

"Oh," Casey said. "What do you do?"

"I'm a free-lance writer," Rob said. "Articles mostly. I'm working on a novel in my spare time, but that's a long way from being finished. I get outside for research, but I can set my own hours."

Casey was interested. As an English major she had a great respect for writers, and she suddenly realized that while she had read books and articles for most of her life she had never actually met a single person who made his living by writing.

"Where have you published?" she said.

"A lot of regional magazines," Rob said. "I did some articles for *Houston City* before it folded, and I had one in *Texas Monthly* once. I've done things for airline magazines, industrial publications, computer magazines, a little bit of everything. I even sold a poem once. I'm not getting rich, but so far I've been able to keep solvent."

Casey told him a little about her own background, glossing over the divorce and concentrating on her study of literature.

"I've never tried to write, myself," she said. "I know what makes good writing, and I can recognize it when I see it, but I've never been tempted to try it. I guess I'm afraid I won't live up to my own standards."

"I'll try to keep my stuff out of your sight," Rob said. "I'm not sure how it would stand up to professional criticism."

"Oh, no. I'd like to read something of yours," Casey said, meaning it. "I'd like to see how a real writer works."

Rob smiled. "Maybe one of these days, then."

On the TV screen, Inigo Montoya was about to extract his long-postponed revenge, to Margaret's evident satisfaction. She was lying on her stomach, her knees bent and her feet in the air. Her hands were folded under her chin as she watched.

"How about a swim?" Rob said to Casey. "The pool here is one of the main attractions."

Casey thought about it. Why not? Maybe all the stories she'd heard about how easy it was to make friends in city apartments were really true. Maybe the move to Houston was going to be the change for the better she'd hoped it would be. She certainly seemed to be getting into the swing of things more quickly than she had counted on.

"Fine," she said. She reached out and touched her

**31**

daughter with the tip of one toe. "What about you, Margaret?"

Margaret didn't look away from the TV screen. "I want to see what happens to Wesley," she said, referring to the movie's hero, who was currently more dead than alive.

"All right," Casey said. "You know where the pool is, and you can come out after the movie if you want to."

The pool had been one of the first things Margaret had checked out that morning. She liked to swim, and she had already told Casey that she wanted to get into the water. She had not had much opportunity to go swimming when they had lived in West Texas.

"OK," Margaret said, not very interested at the present time. Wesley's friend Inigo was suddenly in deep trouble, having just been struck by a thrown dagger.

"Just give me a few minutes to change," Casey told Rob. "I'll meet you there."

"There'll be a lot of people," Rob said. "Everyone likes to go for a dip after work. It relieves some of the tension they build up driving home on the loop." It was clear from his tone that he was glad he did not have to get out and fight the traffic every day.

"Sounds good," Casey said. "I need to meet the neighbors."

"Some of them are pretty strange," Rob warned. "You know what apartment living is like."

Casey really didn't know about apartment living, but she told Rob that she was still interested in meeting everyone.

"OK, then," Rob said. "Thirty minutes?"

"See you there," Casey said.

# 7

**H**owland had read the literature on serial killers, but he'd never heard anyone talk about them at length before, not the way Romain talked.

Romain knew all there was to know, and he could speculate about a hell of a lot that wasn't known. The guy was eerie.

"Let's talk about Forsch to begin with," the psychologist had said. "She doesn't fit the pattern, since there are actually a few clues in her case. Not many, not anything that seems particularly useful, but more than on the others."

Saying there was nothing useful was like saying the Sears Tower was a tall building, or at least that was the way it seemed to Howland.

"So you're saying Forsch's murder is not part of the series?" Howland said.

"No, I didn't say that. It might not be, but it may very well be the most important part. It may be that she was the killer's very first victim, and in that case the most important one."

"You're saying that because hers was the first of the

motiveless murders we've been able to come up with, I guess," Howland said.

"No," Romain said. He leaned back in his chair and reached for another cigarette. Howland wondered what the man's lungs would look like if he were ever autopsied.

"You see," Romain said when he'd lit up, "in many serial killers something serves as a trigger. Something happens that sets them off. They may go for years before they kill their first victim, and all that time something is building up inside them. Then something happens. We don't know what it is, or why, and it's probably different in each case, but eventually they see something, hear something, think something—hell, who knows. Then they kill, and it's almost spontaneous. They don't have the control that they develop later."

"You're saying that after the first time, they plan better."

"That's right." Romain looked at the glowing tip of his cigarette. "The first time is often impulsive. Then they have time to think about it. If they got away with it, they begin to think of how much fun it was, but at the same time they can see all the ways they screwed up."

He drew in a lungful of smoke and said, "They don't want to get caught, you know, not most of them. That 'Stop me before I kill more' stuff, in most cases that just doesn't happen. So after the first murder, they take their time. They set things up very carefully."

"I never thought of killers as being very smart," Howland said.

"That's one of your biggest mistakes, then," Romain said. "It may explain why you didn't notice that the thing tying these killings together was the intelligence of the killer, his complete control of the crime scene from beginning to end."

"Jesus," Howland said. "It's almost as if you admire the creeps who do this kind of thing."

"In a way, I do," Romain said. His gaze behind the thick lenses of his glasses was intense.

"I'm still not sure I agree with you about the intelligence part, though," Howland said. "A lot of these guys seem to get by just on pure dumb luck."

"Some of them do," Romain conceded. "A certain group, anyway. Those are the ones that are usually caught. They don't have any social skills, they're loners, with very few friends, and they're not smart. In fact, they're mostly of below average intelligence. They have sexual problems, too. Women don't like them, don't even like having them around. If they have a job, it's not a good one, not one that pays much above the minimum wage. They move around a lot, some of them anyway, and that helps keep them out of jail. For a while. They're not the kind of guys you'd invite over to meet the wife and family. You wouldn't even want them around you at work."

"But you don't think we're looking for anyone like that, I take it," Howland said.

"Probably not," Romain said. "There's another kind of serial killer, even more dangerous. He's the one who could pass, who *does* pass, for normal in almost any company. He makes a good impression. He's as smart as anyone else, often smarter. Has a good job, works hard, makes plenty of money. He doesn't appear—and let me stress *appear*—to have any sexual problems. He might have a steady girlfriend. He might even be married. And if he is, believe me, his wife would never suspect that there was a thing wrong with him. In other words, he's someone pretty much like you or me."

Like me, maybe, Howland thought. I'd sure never put you down as being completely normal.

"So we're looking for the second kind," he said.

"If there's a serial killer out there, and judging from the reports you've shown me, I think that there is, it's the second kind," Romain said. "No doubt of it."

"When will he kill again?" Howland said.

Romain stirred the butts in the ashtray around until he had cleared a space where he could mash out his current smoke. "No one can tell you that, maybe not even the killer," he said.

"You mean even *he* doesn't know?"

"That's right. The first kind of killer we were talking about more or less does things at random. He'll just kill someone. He gets the opportunity, and he does it. That's what makes him easier to catch. He'll leave clues, and he might even kill in a place where he's known. He might kill someone he knows."

"But not the boy we're looking for," Howland said.

Romain nodded. "Not the boy we're looking for. He wouldn't work that way. He picks his victim carefully, though we may never discover just how. It will never be someone he knows, and he'll never kill near where he lives or works."

"You don't shit where you eat," Howland said.

"Something like that. He may even stalk his intended victim for days, possibly weeks before the murder. That may even be a part of the fun. Sometimes he might kill within days of a previous murder, sometimes within months. It's more often a longer period than a shorter one, however."

"But there's usually a pattern," Howland said. "Bundy killed women who looked alike. The Green River killer went after whores, like Jack the Ripper. This guy"—he waved the folders—"this guy isn't giving us anything!"

"Which just goes to show how smart he is," Romain said. "Assuming that he does indeed exist."

"You mean we might be wrong about this?"

**36**

"Of course we might. As you said, you might have simply nine motiveless killings with no clues at all."

"Pretty damn doubtful, isn't it?" Howland said.

"Pretty damn doubtful," Romain agreed.

A new thought occurred to Howland. "We've been talking about a male all this time," he said. "I guess there's no chance that we're dealing with a woman."

"There's a local saying that covers what you're asking," Romain told him. "It goes like this: 'There are two chances: slim and none.'"

"Why?" Howland wanted to know.

"Because women aren't generally serial killers," Romain said. "Don't ask me why, though."

"Dammit, you're the psychologist."

"That doesn't mean I know everything. Sometimes I think I don't know anything at all."

"You must have an idea."

"Not a one. Oh, there have been cases of women who were multiple murderers, and they've even killed serially in a sense, but it's just not quite the same kind of thing we're talking about here."

"Why not?" Howland said.

"Usually it was husbands, and then it was usually for money. Insurance or an inheritance, let's say. Not for the thrill of it, the power trip, the sexual charge, whatever it is that the man you want is getting."

"That's what I'd like to know," Howland said. "What the hell is he getting? There's no sign of sperm anywhere at these scenes. No rapes, no oral sex. What the hell is going on?"

Romain permitted himself a thin smile. He didn't smile often, not at the office anyway. "That's something you'll have to ask him," he said. "If you can catch him."

"And you don't think I can?"

"You might. Maybe he'll make a mistake. Or

37

maybe you'll spot something in those reports that no one's picked up on yet."

"But you don't think so."

"No," Romain said. "I don't. I think you're dealing with a man who doesn't make mistakes."

"Bundy did," Howland said. "More than one. They caught him more than once."

"This man may be smarter than Bundy."

"And there's the Forsch murder," Howland said. "The 'trigger,' you called it."

"There's that," Romain said. "It may be your best bet. Otherwise, what do you have to go on?"

"Not a thing," Howland admitted. "Not a single goddamned thing."

**And now, looking** back over the folders, Howland could see that there was no reason to modify that statement. He still didn't have a thing to go on, outside the Forsch killing, and the clues in that one were worthless unless he could develop something from them that the previous investigator had overlooked.

Meanwhile, somewhere out there, the killer was getting ready to murder someone else.

Howland put the folders on his desk and put the palms of his hands on them as if he might absorb something from the papers that would help him.

"Not a thing," he said to himself. "Not a single goddamned thing."

# 8

It took Casey a little more than thirty minutes to get ready, maybe because she stood in front of the mirror a little too long as she looked at herself in her new bathing suit. She had bought it because of the move to Houston, knowing that she would be living in an apartment with a pool and that she would be only thirty or forty minutes from Galveston Island and its beach on the Gulf of Mexico.

Now she was wondering if it wasn't a little too much.

Or a little too little.

She hadn't bought a suit in years, since swimming wasn't a big activity in Lubbock, and she hadn't really thought about how revealing the new suits were.

They were pretty revealing, she thought now, as she looked in the mirror and wondered just when it had become all right to show almost your entire ass to the whole world. Still and all, she had to admit that it was a pretty good ass.

She didn't have much of a tan, though. In fact, she didn't have any kind of a tan at all. She looked so pale that she might be taken for the victim of vampire attacks. Well, a few days at poolside would take care of that.

She realized that tanning was now known to be very unhealthy, and she planned to put on plenty of sunscreen—or maybe to let someone else put it on her—but surely a little tanning was permitted. If everyone else was as tan as Rob, she was going to have a lot of catching up to do.

The movie was over when Casey came out of the bedroom, and Margaret had decided that she wanted to go swimming after all.

Casey told her to get ready. "Five minutes. That's all you're going to get. So get that suit on and get out here."

"Right!" Margaret said. She ran into her bedroom, the smaller of the two in the apartment, and slammed the door.

Casey gathered up a towel for herself and one for Margaret while she was waiting.

Margaret was back in less than the allotted time, and Casey wondered how she had done it. She stopped wondering when she glanced into the room and saw the clothes strewn around, the shorts and shoes on the floor, the shirt on a chair, socks on the bed and the panties lying on a bed pillow.

She didn't say anything, however. Margaret was generally a very neat person, and Casey was sure her daughter would clean up the room later.

"Ready, Mom!" Margaret said.

She was enthusiastic about everything, Casey thought. Most of her conversation sounded as if there were built-in exclamation marks at the ends of her sentences.

Some of that enthusiasm came from the Asshole, as much as Casey hated to admit it. He was devoted to his teaching, and he loved his subject. He never relied on the traditional yellowing lecture notes for his courses; every spare moment during the semester and even on his summer vacations he was in the library reading all the latest research and doing research of his own into the Romantic poets. All of them, not just the major ones he taught in his classes.

Damn. In some ways she actually missed him.

"Come on, Mom!" Margaret said, interrupting her thoughts. "What're you waiting for? Everyone at the pool will be wondering where we are!"

Margaret was already browner than Casey would allow herself to get, but her coloring was another inheritance from the Asshole and had nothing to do with the sun.

"Mom!" Margaret said, striking a comic pose with her hands on her slim hips, her right foot tapping impatiently.

"All right, all right," Casey said, laughing. "I'm coming. Can't a mom have a little time to think? You're the one who was watching the movie and not going swimming."

"That was when there was a movie to watch," Margaret pointed out. "It's over now."

"Can't argue with logic like that," Casey said, reaching down for her daughter's hand.

Margaret slipped her own slim hand into her mother's and they went out the apartment door together.

It was after six o'clock, but it was still very hot outside. Daylight Savings Time meant that it would not get dark until nearly nine, so there was still plenty of sun. If Casey and Margaret had not been wearing beach sandals, the sidewalk in front of the apartment would have practically scorched their feet.

41

The humidity was still in evidence, too. If anything, it was worse, an almost palpable presence in the air.

"It's hot," Margaret said.

"Wow, you should be a detective," Casey said. "Don't worry. We'll be at the pool in a minute. Then you can cool off."

The pool was located in a central courtyard in the midst of the apartment complex. They could hear laughter and splashing from where they were, and Casey wondered if there would be noise like that all night. Then she recalled that they had not heard anything from inside the apartment. That meant they had good soundproofing, which was a relief.

They followed the sidewalk to the end of a row of apartments, then turned left and went into the shade between two of the units. They could see the concrete apron of the pool. There were people sitting at tables, others in reclining chairs, and some stretched out on towels beside the pool. Most of them were adults, but there were one or two kids. There was a separate shallow pool for them at the other end of the larger one.

As Casey and Margaret walked back out into the sun, Rob hailed them from a table with an umbrella over it. There were three other people sitting there with him, two men and a woman.

Casey and Margaret started toward them, but Margeret veered away.

"I want to go in the water," she said.

"OK," Casey said. "But just in the little pool."

Margaret turned and made an exaggerated frown. "But that's for kids," she said.

"What do you think *you* are, an old lady?"

Margaret laughed and went on toward the little pool, which is where she had intended to go all along.

Casey headed for the table where Rob was sitting. It was time for her to start meeting people. If Margaret wanted to put it off for a while longer, well, Casey didn't blame her.

She thought for a minute of the friends she had left behind in Lubbock, and there had been more than a few.

The Hansens next door, and Bernie their dog.

The Terrells across the street. They had a son, Jon, about Margaret's age, and the two had been good friends.

Some of the members of the Asshole's department, many of whom had come to visit in their home over the years.

For just a brief moment, Casey allowed herself to be sentimental about what she had left behind her.

Then she thought of the Asshole and his bimbo. To hell with them. To hell with the past. This was the new Casey Buckner. She was going to win friends and influence people.

Feeling a bit self-conscious in her new suit, she walked as confidently as she could across the patio, threading her way between tables, smiling when she received curious looks from the other residents who recognized her as a newcomer.

What was that sappy saying that people embroidered on samplers and framed and hung on their living room walls?

For a second she couldn't think of it, but then it came to her: "Today is the first day of the rest of your life."

Maybe it wasn't so sappy, after all. This was the first day of the rest of her life, and she was going to make the most of it.

Casey arrived at the table and sat in a chair that Rob had saved for her. She hung her towels on the chair back. It had a metal frame and lengths of vinyl strips formed the back and sides. The vinyl was sticky in the humid heat, but the shade of the umbrella helped a little. There were canned drinks, beer and soda, on the table, since there was a prominent sign demanding that residents bring NO GLASS IN THE POOL AREA.

"Let me introduce you to some people," Rob said. "Casey Buckner, this happy couple here is Craig and Tina Warley."

The man and woman smiled. They were both in their midtwenties, maybe a little younger than Rob.

"Hi," Craig said, half standing and making a sort of bow with his hands on the arms of his chair. He had a deep bass voice, a hairy barrel-shaped chest and a dimpled chin that Kirk Douglas might have envied. His already thinning hair was combed straight back off his forehead in a widow's peak, and there was an old scar high up near the hairline.

"Glad to meet you," Craig went on. "Rob tells us you just moved to Houston from somewhere out in West Texas."

"Lubbock," Casey said.

"It's not always this bad down here," Tina said, waving a hand as if to indicate the sun and humidity. "It just seems that way because the weather's so shitty."

Everyone laughed, including Casey.

Tina's name must have been given her by hopeful parents who did not see their hope fulfilled, because Tina was not tiny. She was broad-shouldered and heavy-breasted, with brown hair that hung to her shoulders. She had a wide forehead, big brown eyes and a wide, sensuous mouth.

"Don't let her kid you," the other man at the table said. "It's always pretty bad here."

"And this cheerful fellow is Dan Romain," Rob said.

Romain, older than the others, wearing a pair of thick glasses, was the only one to offer her his hand. "Pleased to meet you," he said.

# 9

**N**o one in the police department was aware of Romain's double life, nor were the people who lived in the apartment complex aware that he was on the force.

That was the way he wanted it. He kept the two halves of his life entirely separate, never socializing with anyone at the office, never telling anyone from the apartment where he worked. He told them he was a psychologist, but that was as far as he went.

He would never tell anyone at the table that only a few hours earlier he had been discussing serial murder with a homicide investigator. It wasn't the kind of thing that tended to come up in conversation, though the murders themselves very well might. It was becoming obvious to nearly everyone that something strange was going on in Houston.

Not that anyone thought there was anything extremely unusual about it. A year or so previously there had been another series of murders, this time of elderly women, mostly black, who lived alone.

At first some people, including some of the police, had thought that a serial killer might be responsible; but as it turned out, the connection among the victims was that because of their ages and living situations they were all especially vulnerable to anyone who wanted to try a quick burglary for dope money.

There were a lot of people in Houston who needed dope money, and the old women had just happened to get in the way of some of them. All the cases that had so far been cleared had different perpetrators.

So it was only natural that people would wonder about the latest killings, wonder if they were merely random as the earlier ones had been or if they were part of a series.

No one at the pool had ever asked Romain's opinion, however, and if they had he would not have given it.

He was more interested in finding out about the new woman who had joined them. She was quite attractive, and Romain found himself getting interested in her.

He had much better luck relating to people outside the department, and though he was not what most men would have considered an outstanding success with women, he did have occasional dates, none of which he ever discussed with his colleagues. Howland would have been amazed.

Casey told them something about herself, glossing over the divorce again, and turned the subject to the community colleges she hoped to get part-time jobs in.

Craig was not impressed. "Community colleges. They used to call them all *junior* colleges, and that's what they are. Not the real thing."

"Don't mind him," Tina said. "The rest of us are used to him, and he does take some getting used to." She looked at her husband with a mixture of affection and exasperation. "He can be a pompous ass, now and then."

46

Craig looked slightly hurt and definitely taken aback. *"Moi?* A pompous ass? You must be kidding."

"Come on, Craig," Rob said. "You know you do tend to make pronouncements about things. You might have hurt Casey's feelings, after all. She's hoping to teach in those places."

"Those places are not for intellectual development," Craig insisted. "They're for baby-sitting."

Romain was accustomed to Warley's manner. It didn't bother him. He attributed it to deep-seated and well-concealed feelings of inferiority which led Warley to criticize everything that was of no immediate interest to himself.

The psychologist wondered whether Casey would bother to defend the community colleges, and he was glad when she did. That told him something about *her* personality.

"Did you ever attend a community college?" she asked Craig.

"No, I never did," he said. "I went to a real school."

"So did I," Casey said. "But I did a little research before I moved here, and I happen to think community colleges perform quite a few valuable services."

She went on to tell him what those services were, mentioning quality education at a bargain price, offering an education to people who might not get to attend a four-year institution, giving technical training to people who would not otherwise be able to receive it, and especially providing small classes and a personal attention that was impossible to find in the larger universities.

Romain was impressed, but not Warley. Nothing impressed Warley. Nothing, that is, that he had not thought of himself.

Romain had wondered more than once why a beauty like Tina had ever married the jerk.

Changing to a more pleasant subject, at least to

**47**

him, Warley began telling Casey what he did for a living.

"I'm an accountant," he said. "So's Tina. We've got our own office not far from here."

"They're good, too," Rob admitted. "They do my taxes. In a way, they're like me. They can do a lot of work at home."

"Thank God for the personal computer," Tina said.

"The greatest invention since the wheel," Craig said, making another of his pronouncements. This time no one bothered to argue with him.

"I'll drink to that," Romain said, picking up a Coors from the table in front of him and taking a long sip.

Rob reached into a plastic cooler at his feet and pulled out another beer, offering it to Casey, who accepted it, and pulled the tab.

They drank their beers and talked for a while about computers, a subject that did not particularly interest Casey. Word-processing programs, spreadsheets, data bases, Mac versus the Big Blue—all of those were beyond her experience. She said if she took any graduate courses, she planned to type her papers on the old Olympia portable typewriter she had gotten for high school graduation.

"You've gotta be kidding," Craig said. "I didn't even know there were any of those things around anymore. It must be an antique."

"I'm not *that* old," Casey said.

"We can see that," Rob said, looking at her appreciatively.

"Craig always likes to have the latest technology," Tina said. "Another one of his failings."

Warley's face reddened. "I don't like to hear so much about my failings."

"Sorry, dear," Tina said. She didn't look sorry to Casey.

"Why don't we go for a swim?" Rob said. "Casey must be really hot, not being used to this weather."

Casey was grateful for the chance to get away from Craig and Tina. Dan Romain seemed all right, but she was not overly fond of the Warleys.

"I'd like to try the water," she said.

"Last one in's an effete snob," Rob said, pushing back his chair and getting to his feet.

Casey followed him to the pool and dived in, feeling the cool water close over her. She didn't know whether anyone followed them.

# 10

She has the marks.

I don't know why no one else saw them while we were sitting there. Or maybe they did. Maybe they're like me and just didn't want to say anything.

But I don't think so. I still think that no one can see the marks but me and that because I can see them, I'm the one who has to do something about them.

To me, they were plain as day, right there on her face, the face that floated above the body she was flaunting in that suit that barely covered anything.

The blood marks.

So she will be the next one.

Casey Buckner.

Blond, leggy, good body as anyone could see, not that any of that matters. The others weren't all like that. Some of them were, but not all. It's not the body that matters, not the hair, the face, the eyes.

It's always the marks.

I don't think I've put anything in here about where the marks are, but that's because they can be anywhere.

Usually they're on the arms or the face, somewhere that's easy to see, and that's the way with this one, too.

The marks are on her face.

They're red, as red as blood, like all the others, but that's the only similarity, because they can have different shapes.

Sometimes they look like a heart, a real one, not the kind you see on Valentine's Day. Sometimes they look more like a bloody puddle, and sometimes they just look like a shapeless red *thing*. Like something that might be able to move and wiggle and crawl right off that face or arm if you stared at it long enough.

The marks can move. They move like something alive there on the face or the arms, and they can change. They don't always have to look the same.

People with things like that on them don't deserve to live.

I never stare, however, no matter how grotesque the marks might appear.

I never give anyone the idea that I'm overly interested in her face, even though I'm pretty sure they don't even know themselves that the marks are there.

I don't see how that can be, how they can't know about them, but they don't seem to. If they were aware of them, surely they'd cover them with makeup. It wouldn't be that hard to do, but I don't think they could hide the marks from me even by doing that.

Somehow I'd know the marks were there.

I'd know because I'm the one that's supposed to see them, and when I see them I know what I'm supposed to do.

This one may be a little more difficult, though. She's too close to home.

The others were women I'd see in malls or on the streets or at a restaurant. I'd have to follow them home, get to know their habits, study them. They were no danger to me because they were always from far away. I had to go looking for them to find them.

And now one turns up right in my backyard. I should have expected it, sooner or later, but somehow it came as a big surprise to me.

Can I kill her here? I don't see how. Far too dangerous. It will have to be somewhere else, but where?

That doesn't really matter, not yet. It's something I can deal with as the plan develops. I never rush into things.

Not since the first time.

Maybe I should explain about that here. I know my readers will be curious about that very first one.

Her name was Ellen Forsch, though of course I didn't know that when I first saw her. She was in line at Egg Roll Charlie's in one of the malls. I'd just come out of the movie when I saw her.

I knew then, instantly, that I was going to kill her.

I don't know why.

I'd never killed anyone before. I'd never even thought about it.

That's a lie. I promised myself that I'd be honest here, because I know the readers of this document will expect that. They'll want to know the whole truth about me. So let me retract that last bit.

I'd thought about it. I'd thought about it a hell of a lot. In a purely theoretical way.

I'd never thought I'd act out the thoughts, however. What I mean is that I'd seen women, not women that I knew but just women that I'd pass in the street or at a mall, and I'd think, Jesus, I wonder what she'd think if I walked over and stuck a knife in her stomach and ripped right straight up to her breastbone?

I guess not everyone has thoughts like that, but I do.

Did.

**53**

I don't have them anymore, now that I know the answer.

OK. I'm getting off the track again. I saw the woman in the line, and I knew that I was going to kill her. Simple as that.

She was standing there, probably trying to decide whether to have shrimp or pork or just vegetables in her egg roll, and I was looking at her and knowing that she was as good as dead.

It wasn't the blood marks. I didn't know about them then. I just knew that she had to die.

As I said, I'd been to the movie in the mall, *Great Balls of Fire*, if you must know, and I'd been alone. I mean I attended the movie unaccompanied, but I don't think there were more than two or three people in the theater aside from myself, either. The movie had been hyped beyond belief, but it was a bomb.

Anyway, I was there in the mall, alone, and she was there, also alone.

I don't know where she'd been, and I didn't care. I knew what was going to happen to her.

She didn't.

Not yet, she didn't. She found out, however.

When she found out, it was far too late for her to do anything about it.

I got in the line. There were two people between us, and I took the opportunity to look her over.

I know what people will say, and that's one reason I'm writing this down. They'll say she looked like my mother, or some such bullshit.

That's all it is, just bullshit.

She didn't look anything like my mother.

My mother was short, kind of dumpy, really. Gray hair that she wore in a bun. She had thick arms and legs, and her face was round and fat. She wore glasses with wire rims.

**54**

I don't know why I got off on my mother. She doesn't have anything to do with any of this.

As I was saying, the woman didn't look anything like my mother. She was tall, nearly six feet, with black hair that hung down past her shoulders. She was wearing a red dress, and she was too skinny for my taste, really. Her legs and arms were very thin. She didn't wear glasses.

I couldn't really see her face from where I was standing, hadn't really had a good look at it yet.

She got her egg roll and went over to a table. The food court wasn't too crowded, so I couldn't very well ask her for a seat at her table after I got my own egg roll without causing her to be suspicious, but I sat as near as I could and still remain inconspicuous.

I wasn't interested in eating. There was a kind of excitement building up in me that I can't explain, not even now. I still feel it, though. Every single time.

It's not like sex, exactly, but then again it is. I've read about some people who kill because they can't have sex any other way. They kill and then they squirt all over the place. It's as if they were waving their dicks like fire hoses.

Not me.

Later, maybe. When I'm thinking about it, thinking about the way they look at me, the way they—

I'm not going to talk about that part yet.

I'm not ready to talk about that part yet.

I'm getting off the track again. Where was I? Sitting in the food court, the excitement building in me, that's where.

I saw her face then. It was a thin face, like I should have expected, having seen the rest of her, thin and kind of pinched. Thin lips, thin nose, sunken cheeks. Her black hair fell forward as she ate.

That's when I saw the blood marks.

The hair couldn't hide them. Nothing could hide them. They were there, squirming on her face like some kind of red living thing.

I had taken a bite of my egg roll, trying to look like anyone else there, and I nearly puked it out on the table. I'd never seen anything quite so awful.

No wonder she had to be killed.

I looked around the food court to see if everyone else was as repulsed as I was, and that's when I got another surprise. No one seemed to have noticed a thing.

Everyone was eating, talking, laughing, just like there was nothing unusual, just like there wasn't some kind of monster sitting right there in their midst with the goddamned blood marks pulsing on her face like some kind of obscene cancerous growths.

And then I realized that they didn't know.

I was the only one, the only one out of that group of blind and ignorant assholes who could see and who knew what he was seeing. I was the one chosen to see, and I was the one chosen to do something about what I saw.

The excitement was still building in me. It was like a keen, high sound in my head by then, a sound that only I could hear, a sound like no one had ever heard before. It was like music, but it wasn't like music. I can't explain it any better than that.

I followed her to her car, a little red Toyota Tercel, which luckily happened to be parked not too far from mine.

(Lucky for me. It wasn't so lucky for *her*, now, was it?)

It wasn't easy following her from the mall, which was near the loop. If you've driven in Houston, you know what I mean. The fucking loop is busy all hours of the day and night, and the people drive like maniacs, changing lanes, zooming across four lanes of traffic to

get to an exit, cutting in front of you if you leav
than ten feet between your car and the bumper
one in front of you.

I managed it, though. She pulled off the loop
the Galleria and drove down Westheimer. Following
was a little easier then, but not much. All the fuck
traffic lights.

She turned off on Gessner and then turned agai
and pulled into an apartment parking lot.

I hadn't even thought about how to kill her.

I'd been so busy with the traffic and trying not to
lose her, I hadn't even made a plan.

It was almost dark, about eight-thirty (this was in
the summer, two years ago, which means I've only
killed nine women in two years, a demonstration of my
restraint if one is ever called for).

The parking lot was deserted. There were cars there,
of course, but no other people.

I parked a short distance away from her. I was getting desperate now. I *had* to kill her, but how?

Then I remembered that I had a tire tool under my
seat. Lots of people in Houston carry guns, but I carry a
tire tool. You never know when some idiot will pull you
over and attack you for some reason, like thinking
you've shot him the finger for his own driving habits or
needing five bucks for another hit at the local crack
house. There are all kinds of maniacs running loose in
this town.

She got out of her car and started toward the apartments, so I reached under the seat and got the tire tool.
Then I got out and followed her.

The tire tool was round, with a flattened tip to
make it easy to pry off the hub cap. That part was about
a foot long, and then it bent off to a shorter part that
ended in the wrench that fit over the lug nuts. It felt
smooth and cool in my hand as I followed the woman.

57

She never suspected a thing.

Most of them never do. They might read stories about people being attacked, mugged in their own parking lots, but they never think it will happen to them.

I was whistling a tune, just walking along, holding the tire tool down by my leg. I was trying to look calm and unconcerned, like I was just another resident of the apartments. As excited as I was, it wasn't easy to appear calm, but I think I managed very well.

I had gotten to within ten feet of her when she opened her door, and when she went through it I was right behind her.

She tried to close the door, but I smashed right into it, hitting it hard with my shoulder. The edge of the door caught her and threw her a few feet into the living room. I barreled in after her and slammed the door behind me.

She was looking at me, her thin mouth open, her eyes getting big. I could tell she was about to scream.

The blood marks were writhing like snakes. Any minute they were going to crawl right off her and try to get on me.

I couldn't let that happen.

So I stepped over to her and swung the tire tool at her face.

# 11

Casey was tired after the swim, but it was late and she and Margaret were both hungry. She fixed Kraft macaroni and cheese out of a box for supper. Margaret liked macaroni and cheese, especially if it had plenty of cheese in it.

"Did you meet anyone in the pool?" Casey asked as they were eating.

"Just some boy named Jack," Margaret said around a mouthful of noodles. And some girl named Sandy."

"Did you like them?"

"I guess." Margaret swallowed her noodles and drank some milk. When she put the glass down there was a white milk mustache on her upper lip.

She seemed notably lacking in her usual enthusiasm when it came to her new acquaintances. "I liked my old friends better."

Casey felt a momentary twinge of guilt. It had been her decision to move to Houston, and she had known all along that Margaret would be more affected by the move than Casey herself. Still, it had seemed like the right thing to do. She could not picture herself living in the same town with the Asshole any longer.

"I'm sure you'll like Jack and Sandy a lot when you get to know them," she said. "As I remember it, you hit Jon in the head with your shovel the first time you played in his sand pile."

"Did not!" Margaret said. She smiled. "I hit him with the pail."

"Oh," Casey said, remembering the incident more clearly, smiling along with her daughter. She was sure Margaret would adjust, probably better than her mother.

They had stayed at the pool for a couple of hours, Casey swimming and talking. The more she had talked to the group at Rob's table, the more she found herself liking Rob and Dan Romain, despite the latter's sometimes cynical outlook on life.

The Warleys were another story. Tina was OK; she had a good sense of humor and knew a little about books and poetry, but she tended to pick on Craig a lot.

Craig did not take the picking very well, either, but Casey thought a lot of it was justified. He did tend to make pronouncements about everything and to believe that he was the ultimate moral authority on almost any question that came up.

They had somehow gotten off on the subject of drugs and prostitution, problems with no seeming resolution. It was Rob's opinion that the police did nothing that really helped.

"They bust the whores on Telephone Road," he said, "or maybe they put on a sting and bust a few of the johns. But what good does that do? In a week or two it's business as usual. The big drug dealers are never touched; they're not even harassed."

"Why bother?" Dan Romain said, never mentioning his connection with the department. "Bust one dealer, and three more take his place."

That was Warley's cue. "Why bother to bust 'em at all? The prisons are so full that they'll be back on the streets in six months so we can put somebody else in the crossbar hotel for half a year. What they oughta do is cut their damn hands off."

"That seems a little harsh," Tina said.

"Hell it is. I read somewhere that in one of those Arab countries they executed a couple of guys for spray-painting a wall. They know how to do things over there. I bet there isn't a hell of a lot of graffiti on the walls over there, what do you think?"

"So you think the fear of really severe physical punishment, like being permanently maimed, would keep people from committing crimes?" Romain said.

"Damn right. Catch 'em and cut their fucking hands off. Or their noses off. That might be even better. You can get artificial hands that work pretty good, but it might be hard to fix yourself up with an artificial nose that looks like the real thing."

"But this country doesn't believe in cruel punishments like that," Casey protested.

"Who says it's cruel?" Warley wanted to know. "Those whores, they don't even stay in the slammer overnight. I bet if you sewed their pussies shut for a first offence, you'd do a lot to cut down the number of ladies of the evening soon enough. Pretty drastically, too."

"It's a drastic punishment," Romain said. "I don't think you'd get the Supreme Court to go along with it."

"Fuck the Supreme Court," Warley said. "Flag burners, the whole bunch of 'em."

It went on like that for a while. Casey came to see that Rob and Dan probably kept Warley around simply for the amusement he provided, but she took him more seriously than they obviously did. She thought men like Warley were dangerous. All the anger they kept building up inside was bound to break out sooner or later, or so it

**61**

seemed to her. Of course, she wasn't the psychologist. Romain was.

She also found that she was definitely attracted to Rob Hensley. He didn't try to put any moves on her, for which she was grateful, but he was sensitive and responsive, the kind of man she thought she needed after her experience with the Asshole.

She wasn't about to think about getting involved at this point in her life, however, not with some man she'd met only a few hours before. There was plenty of time for that later. Right now, all she wanted to do was get the supper dishes done and go to bed.

**"What are you** working on now?" Tina Warley said. She was standing in the doorway of the "study," which was what she and her husband called the smaller bedroom of their two-bedroom apartment. There was no bed in it; instead it contained a desk, two gray steel filing cabinets, a bookshelf, and a computer table.

Craig Warley was sitting at the computer table, his face bathed in the glow from the screen of a monitor. The overhead light in the room was not turned on, nor was the desk lamp.

"Nothing," Warley said, not looking up from the screen. "You can go on to bed if you want to."

"Is it something for one of the clients?" Tina said.

"Yeah. Yeah, it is, but nothing that you're familiar with. I'll be through in a minute or two."

Tina went back into the living room to watch Johnny Carson's monologue before going to bed. She was a little worried about Craig. He was doing quite a bit of work at night lately, sometimes leaving the apartment and going to the office, sometimes preferring to work on their home computer.

The accounting business was going well, and they were making money now, after a couple of hard years at the beginning. They had opened up with the help of a loan from her parents right after they got out of college, though they knew it was a risk to start right off with their own business. That was the way they wanted it, however. They didn't want to have to go to work for someone else.

She and Craig had both passed their CPA exams on the first try, and they knew they could make money, but it had been a struggle in the beginning. They'd opened the office right at the depths of the oil bust, and clients were few and far between.

Now the city seemed to be recovering, and their business was doing well, but she didn't like the workaholic attitude that Craig had developed. He was away from the apartment almost as much as he was there, and the more money they made, the more overbearing he became.

She was doing her share of the work for the partnership, had her own clients, but she lacked whatever it was that drove her husband. There were times when she wondered if somehow she might be at fault, if he was using the work as an excuse to avoid her, but that didn't seem likely.

She sat and watched the TV, and just as Ed was stooging it up and asking Johnny, "How hot *was* it?", she suddenly wondered if there might be another woman in Craig's life. That might explain his absences even better than work, might explain why he was telling her to go on to bed without him. Maybe he didn't want her anymore.

She almost laughed at herself for thinking it. Craig seemed, if anything, more interested in her sexually than ever. Sometimes it was as if he couldn't get enough.

She allowed herself a satisfied smile. There was nothing wrong on that score. If her husband was driven to make money, that was all right with her; there were worse ways for him to spend his time.

**It was an** hour later when Craig shut off his computer. He covered the keyboard and monitor with their plastic antistatic covers. The printer had not been used.

He was getting tired of Tina coming in there when he was working on his private projects. He was going to have to warn her off, maybe keep the door closed.

He went into the bathroom to get ready for bed, thinking about the new resident, Casey Buckner. She was a real piece of ass, and he felt himself getting hard as he thought about her.

It was a good feeling. He was glad he was still young enough to enjoy it. Hell, all he had to do was think about fucking and he got stiff as a board. He'd been talking to one of his clients, Sam Rouster, a sixtyish oil man, who had told him that nothing, not even sex, ever came easy after you hit the big Six-Zero.

"'Bout the only thing does it for me now is the young ones," Sam had said. "Early twenties. They got to have big tits and hard asses, too. Otherwise, forget it. I'm just damn lucky I can afford it. Good thing I didn't lose all my money in the bust."

Craig turned on the shower and stepped in. He was a long way from the big Six-Zero. Tina was going to get a rude awakening if she was already asleep.

He sort of hoped that she was.

**Romain turned off** his surge protector and watched his monitor grow dark. A faint glow lingered for a few seconds after the power was gone.

He rubbed his hand over his face. He hadn't been sleeping well lately. Didn't know why. Maybe too much work at the office.

It could happen that way. You got so involved that

the work carried over, simmering down there in your subconscious, bursting to the surface when you least expected it, waking you every time you were about to drop off into deeper sleep.

There were other things like that, things that boiled around below the surface and burst out unexpectedly in certain types of people. He'd been talking to someone—Howland—about it that afternoon.

And when it did burst out, it could be terrifying, though not always to the person it burst out of.

He wished that Howland would leave him out of things. He didn't like dealing with people at work.

And it wasn't going to help him sleep if Howland kept on pestering him about the serial killer. He almost wished he'd told Howland that he was on the wrong track, that it just wasn't possible for a single person to have committed all the crimes Howland thought were part of the series.

He would have said that, but sooner or later, probably sooner, someone would have noticed the same thing Romain had, that what tied the crimes together was the remarkable tidiness of the crime scenes.

It was beyond the reach of probability that there were several killers on the loose, all of whom could commit such antiseptic murders.

Howland himself would have spotted it, and it wouldn't have taken him much longer.

Then Romain would have been on the spot, a place he didn't like to be. He never liked calling attention to himself in the department.

He didn't particularly like it in social situations, either, though there were times when he was tempted, like today. That Casey Buckner was quite an interesting woman.

She wouldn't have any interest in him, however. He knew that. The women he went out with, when he went, were not like her at all. They were older, and usually a lot more desperate.

He didn't mind, he told himself. He could even understand it. Why would a young, attractive woman want to go out with a skinny, sour guy like him?

Money. That was one reason, but he didn't have any, not enough, at any rate.

Still, looking at her, he was resentful, knowing that even an ass like Craig Warley was more likely to have a chance with her than he was.

It was almost enough to make him angry.

But he wouldn't allow himself to get angry.

That never solved anything.

**Rob Hensley worked** late into the night at his own computer, typing feverishly. He wasn't up against a deadline, but there were some things that just wouldn't wait. You had to get them on paper while you were on a roll, and this was one of those times.

As a writer, he liked the feeling. It was a lot better than those times when things were coming slowly, when it was as if every word were being pulled from his bone marrow with tweezers.

Casey Buckner had inspired him, that was the only answer for the ease with which he was writing now.

It wasn't that he was writing an article about beautiful women or sex; it was simply that he knew he was going to try to spend some time with Casey and he wanted to have that time available.

So he had to get the writing done.

There had been other women lately. He didn't have any trouble in that area, thank goodness, but this one looked as if she might be something special. He hoped that her experiences with her ex-husband, whatever they might have been, hadn't soured her on men.

He found himself wondering about the reasons for

her divorce. She hadn't talked much about that, but there was plenty of time for discussing it later on. He'd find out eventually.

His fingers fairly flew over the keyboard.

The work was going well; it might even be some of the best stuff he'd ever written.

He smiled. He'd stay up all night if he had to, but he had to get it down.

So what if he missed a little sleep? He'd missed sleep before.

He had the feeling it would be worth it.

# 12

**H**owland was at Romain's office early the next morning. He stood in the hallway drinking coffee from a Styrofoam cup while he waited for the psychologist to show up.

Romain didn't look so good when he arrived. He was carrying his own coffee, and Howland could see steam rising above the top of the cup.

"Rough night?" Howland said.

"Rough enough," Romain said, slipping the key in his door and opening it. He didn't look eager for company. Howland didn't care. He followed him into the office and threw his empty cup into the metal wastebasket.

Romain closed the door behind them.

Howland sat down and crossed his legs. He was carrying the files on the killings, and he held them in his lap.

Romain ignored him. He set his coffee on the desk and began pawing through the papers there, apparently looking for something. Whatever it was, he didn't find it. He took a drink of the coffee and folded his lanky frame into the chair behind the desk. Finally he looked up at Howland.

"You still here?"

"Still here. I have a few more questions for you."

Romain sighed. He had known that it wasn't going to be easy getting rid of Howland, but he really didn't feel like dealing with him today.

"What kind of questions?" he said.

"I did a little reading last night," Howland said. "Just enough to get me confused."

"'A little learning is a dangerous thing,'" Romain said.

"Who said that?" Howland asked.

"Alexander Pope."

"Is he FBI? Quantico?"

"Not exactly," Romain said. "What did you want to know?"

"It's about something you didn't mention yesterday."

Romain slumped in his chair, holding his coffee in both hands. "It's hard to tell you everything I've learned in ten years of work in just a few minutes."

"I understand that. What I was wondering about is whether our killer is aware of what he's doing."

Our killer, Romain thought. Now it's *our killer*. He got out a cigarette and lit up. "It's possible that he's not," he said. "It's happened."

"That's what I was reading about. The killer could be someone with a multiple personality, right? The one that's doing the killing might not even be aware of the others, and vice versa."

"What were you reading?" Romain said.

*"The Minds of Billy Milligan."*

"An excellent book. If you've read all of it, you know that what you're talking about is possible. But why were you wondering?"

Howland uncrossed his legs and leaned forward. "I was wondering about the crime scenes. Could a civilian know how to keep them so clean?"

70

"Jesus Christ!" Romain said. He crushed out his half-finished smoke. "You think we're dealing with a cop?"

Howland looked slightly ashamed of even having thought it. "Well, it's possible," he said defensively. "I'm not saying he's aware of what he's doing, though. It could be that the cop part of him doesn't know what's happening, but the killer part has retained the cop's knowledge and knows how to clean things up."

"No way," Romain said, but his voice lacked conviction.

"Why not?" Howland said.

"If we—if *you*—were dealing with multiple personalities, they'd be separate and distinct. It's barely possible that one might be aware of the other, but it wouldn't have the other's knowledge and skills. It doesn't work that way."

"It could, though, couldn't it? Just because it's not in the literature, you can't say it couldn't happen."

Romain took off his glasses and rubbed the bridge of his nose. "Anything is possible. But it's not likely. If that's the best lead you've got, you must really be desperate. You'll have to come up with something better than that."

"It was just something I was wondering about," Howland said, settling back in his chair and brushing back his hair. "You don't have to be so touchy about it."

"A cop," Romain said. "Jesus." He got out another cigarette.

"It wouldn't have to be a cop. It could be anybody with law-enforcement training."

"It could be," Romain admitted. "But if that's the case, the perpetrator is probably fully aware of what he's doing."

"Shit," Howland said. "That's even worse than what I was thinking."

"Did you study the folders some more?" Romain said, changing the subject.

**71**

"Yeah, I looked at them all day. They weren't much help. That's why I was trying to come up with something new."

"What about the first one—what'shername."

"Forsch. It's been investigated thoroughly. Nobody came up with anything."

Romain tried to recall what he'd seen in the folders. "Wasn't there a witness?"

"If that's what you want to call it. One of the apartment residents thinks she saw someone come out of the Forsch apartment that night and get into a car."

"And that's it?"

"That's it. She's been questioned about the car, about the person she thinks she saw, everything. It hasn't helped."

"What about hypnotism?" Romain said. "We remember everything we see, but it's not always easy to recall it. Sometimes hypnotism helps."

Howland looked into the Forsch folder. There was no mention of hypnotism having been tried.

"Nope," he said. "No hocus-pocus."

"It's not hocus-pocus," Romain said. "It's a sound technique."

"Have you ever done it?"

"Several times," Romain said. He added a second butt to the ashtray. Howland wondered how long it would take him to fill it up. Probably not very long.

"Did you ever find out anything important?" Howland said.

"Once," Romain said. "You say the witness saw a car. Did she know what kind of car or the license number?"

"No," Howland said.

"Under hypnosis, she might remember. It's worth a try."

"I'll talk to her," Howland said.

At this point he was willing to try anything.

# 13

It's hard to write about this part.

It's not that telling about it bothers me or that I'm ashamed of it; it's not that at all. I wouldn't want anyone who reads this to get the wrong idea.

It's hard simply because it's hard to put the feelings and sensations into words. I know that's what people will want to know about, and I'm not sure I can get it down right. It's one of those things that you have to experience to understand.

But I'll try to give you some idea.

The woman got her right hand up in front of her face and I could hear the cracking of her finger bones as the tire iron drove her hand back into her face and I could hear the crunch of her nose breaking and the way her scream stopped in her throat and turned into some kind of gurgle.

She went over backward and her head hit the rug with a solid thud. It sounded sort of like a heavy book hitting the floor. There was blood coming out her nose and a little trickle coming out her mouth and she wasn't moving. Her face was a mess. She just lay there and I

73

stood there looking down at her, the tire iron dangling from my hand.

I could still see the blood marks on her face, but they were fading a little and they weren't moving around the way they had been before, not that it mattered.

It was too late for that to make a difference.

I stood there for a minute or two, waiting for her to make a move, hoping she would make one, to tell the truth.

She didn't.

The sound in my head was still going on, louder than ever. It was getting stronger and stronger and it was almost like sex when you reach that point when you're about to climax and you know there's nothing that's going to stop you.

But there wasn't any climax. It just kept building and building. If someone had come in the door of the apartment just then, I doubt that I would have heard them.

My mind was working, though, and it was then that I remembered to lock the door. I was very careless that first time, as I said.

When I came back, she was still lying there. She looked as if she might be dead, and I was afraid for a minute that she was, but I could tell she was breathing. The blood in her nose was bubbling. I was glad of that. I didn't want her to be dead.

Not yet.

I looked at my clothes. I hadn't gotten any blood on them, but that was just luck, not planning. There was a little blood on the tire tool, however. I put it down on the rug.

I went into her bedroom and opened a drawer in her dresser. What I was looking for was right there in the top one.

Pantyhose.

I took two pairs and went back into the living room. The woman was still out, so I tied her hands and feet with the hose. They're pretty strong, even if women are always complaining about getting runs in them. She wouldn't get away.

Then I sat down and waited for her to wake up.

It took a while, about ten more minutes. I didn't mind. There was a TV set in the room, and I picked up the remote and turned it on. By then I was thinking even more clearly and I went back into the bedroom and got a pair of the woman's bikini panties from the drawer. I wiped the drawer handle and the TV remote.

I sat back down and watched TV. I don't remember the show.

When the woman woke up she was scared. You could see it in her eyes. But she didn't scream. Maybe she was hurting too much. She tried to sit up, but she couldn't.

She tried to talk to me then. She said something like, "Please, don't hurt me anymore. I'll give you money. I'll give you whatever you want."

Of course she would. I smiled at her. It wasn't as if she had any choice.

"You don't have anything that I want," I told her.

"Then why—?"

"The blood marks," I said.

She tried to look as if she didn't know what I was talking about, and maybe she didn't. You'd think she could see them in the mirror, see them twisting their way into her flesh, but maybe she couldn't.

I could.

She struggled a little then, trying to get loose, but it didn't do her any good. That was the best part of it, really, the best part of all of them, every single time, as I realized later. *There was nothing they could do.* I was

75

the one in control, in complete control. The noise in my head was building. It didn't seem possible, but it was.

She tried to smile. It made her face look awful, but maybe she didn't know that.

"Please," she said.

"Yes," I said, "Say 'please.'"

Something changed in her eyes when she heard me. The fear was still there, but there was something else there, too. I don't know what it was. Hopelessness, maybe.

She didn't say anything. She just looked at me.

I got out of the chair and picked up the tire iron. "Say it. Say 'please' again."

She struggled with the pantyhose and managed to squirm a little way across the room, trying to twist her way into the bedroom, I suppose. It didn't do her any good.

"Say it," I told her. I was standing over her now, looking down at her, dominating her completely.

"Please," she said. "Oh, dear God, please."

I hit her then. There was a crunching sound, and I kept on hitting her, again and again.

I don't know how many times I did it. My arm was tired when I was through hitting her, and the blood marks were gone because there really wasn't much left of her face, not much at all. I think I was breathing pretty hard. There was blood all over the floor and on my clothes, and I think there was even blood on my face.

The sound in my head had finally stopped.

**It was all** pretty much of a mess. Blood was soaking into the carpet, and when I looked I could see that there was blood on the walls and ceiling. It had gotten there when it came slipping off the tire iron as I swung it up to strike again.

76

That's what I mean about there being so much blood. You have to see it to really believe it.

Now that it was all over, I was suddenly scared. I could imagine some little old lady in the apartment next door sitting in her living room and hearing the sound of the tire iron hitting the woman's head. I could imagine her dialing the cops even as I stood there, the tire iron in my hand, blood dripping from the end of it onto the rug.

I didn't panic, however. I'm too intelligent for that, and I knew that I had to think. I stood and tried to remember if I had touched anything aside from that remote and the drawer handle.

I knew I hadn't touched the door. I'd hit it with my shoulder and come right on through. I didn't have to worry about that, I thought, but then I remembered that I had locked it. I got the panties and wiped the knob, the deadbolt lock, and the wood around it.

There was blood on my shoes, but I wasn't leaving any recognizable tracks. There was nothing else that could identify me, nothing at all. I was sure of it.

I had to get out of there.

I unlocked the door, covering my hand with the panties. There was blood on the panties now and there would be blood on the door, but I couldn't help that. There would be blood on the outside, too, when I pulled it shut. There was no help for that, either.

I was sorry that I'd made such a mess. I was always taught to be a neat person. My mother was always very demanding about that. She was an extremely careful housekeeper, and no one ever messed things up more than once, not without being sorry, and that included my father. We always tried to keep her happy and to keep things in their places, but it wasn't always easy. But I'm getting off the subject again. My mother doesn't have anything to do with this.

It was dark when I got outside, but the parking lot

**77**

was fairly well illuminated by the streetlights and a few auxiliary lights that the apartment owners had put there on poles around the edges of the lot.

I walked straight to my car, no hesitation. Just a man going to the store for a quart of milk and a loaf of bread. I opened the door and threw the panties and the tire tool onto the back floorboard. That was another mistake; there would be blood there, but I didn't think about that at the time. I learned a lot that night. Learning by doing, they call it.

When I got in the car, I could see a woman outside one of the other apartments. She appeared to be looking in my direction, but I couldn't be sure. If she was, there was nothing I could do about it.

I wasn't going to go back and kill her, though I suddenly realized that I would have liked to.

I drove out of the parking lot and went to a service station, where I parked on the dark side, away from the street in the shadows. I went into the rest room and washed my hands, since by that time I realized that I was getting blood on the steering wheel and that I had gotten it on the outside door handle of the car. As I said, I learned a lot from the experience.

When I had cleaned up, I went back and sat in the car. The station wasn't busy, and no one bothered me, but that was another misake—stopping so close to the scene of the crime. Nothing came of it, but I would never do it again.

I had to sit, however; because for the first time the enormity of what I had done was sinking in.

I had committed murder.

And I had enjoyed it.

That was the important thing. I had enjoyed it immensely. As I sat there and thought about it, going over each detail, remembering every second of it, I could feel a tightening in my groin.

It was like sex, but it was better than that. It was like the sound in my head. Only if you've heard that sound can you really understand what it was like, and only if you've ever felt anything like the heat that was building in my groin can you know what I'm talking about now.

I had an erection that you could strike matches on.

I didn't need a woman, however. Conventional sex was as meaningless to me at that moment as dollar bills are to dogs. What I was feeling was far beyond that.

I've had that feeling eight times since that first one, and it never happens when I'm with the woman. I think the blood marks inhibit sex; it must be something like that.

It's only later that the feeling comes, only after the blood marks are put to rest. It's only then that I can experience the ultimate release.

So I felt it then, parked in the shadows beside the service station, felt it building, growing, until the throbbing of my organ was almost unbearable.

I touched the front of my pants, just touched, and then I exploded. Everything pumped out of me then in a thick hot stream that kept coming and coming and coming.

I was exhausted when it was over. If the cops had walked up to the car at that moment and ordered me out, I wouldn't have had the strength to resist. I wouldn't have had the strength even to get out of the car.

I sat there and leaned my forehead on the steering wheel until I recovered. I don't know how long it took. A long time.

Finally I was able to drive home. I didn't try to go back into the rest room to clean up. All I wanted to do was go home.

It was quite a drive, I must say, the bloody tire iron

**79**

and panties in the back seat, my own pants hot and wet and sticky all over the front.  ✓

I drove very carefully. I couldn't afford to get stopped. It would have been very embarrassing.

The next day I cleaned the car before anyone saw it. I cleaned the back seat and floorboard with carpet cleaner, scrubbing them with a wire brush. Then I went to a carwash and went over the entire car's outside until I'd spent six dollars.

I drove to another part of town that night and threw the tire tool and the panties in a storm sewer on a practically deserted street. No one saw me. The tire tool and the panties were never found, as far as I know.

The body was found a day later. No one ever connected it to me; there were no clues.

I had gotten away with it in spite of my carelessness. There was a little play in the newspapers for a few days, and then there was nothing more. There were other things for the police to worry about, other things for the reporters to write about.

I had already begun to think about killing again.

# 14

The next day Casey returned the U-Haul, and when she got back to the apartment her books had arrived.

She had decided against hauling them herself, since she hadn't known that someone like Rob would come along and help her unload. It had seemed easier to ship them. That way, someone else would carry them into the apartment.

Now they were here, and she had to do something with them. There was nothing she could do, though. She didn't have any bookshelves. Apartments were not designed for book lovers.

So she had five stacks of boxes of various sizes in her living room. She opened one box and looked inside. A biography of Keats lay beside a biography of Freud. She had no idea what was beneath them. Her packing system was to see which books fit most neatly into which boxes. She knew it was going to be a real job getting everything sorted out, but that would just have to wait until she had bought some bookcases.

Then she worried about space. She supposed that she would have to take up the walls of the bedrooms and the living room with shelves. She sighed. That was the price of being an English major or of simply being someone who liked books.

Margaret was at the table, eating a bowl of Frosted Wheat Squares. She wasn't particularly interested in the books. All she cared about was what was on television. Casey told herself that Margaret would get interested in books later, when she was a little older.

While she was wondering whether to leave the unpacked boxes in the living room or to move them to the bedroom where they would be more or less out of sight, the doorbell rang.

She went to the door, and Rob Hensley was standing there.

"Hi," he said. "I was wondering if I could interest you and Margaret in driving down to Galveston and seeing the Gulf of Mexico."

Casey heard the spoon clatter to the table as Margaret pushed her chair back. "I'd like to go!" Margaret said, running to the door. "I've never seen waves!"

Casey smiled. There was no way she could refuse Rob's offer now, and she wasn't sure she wanted to. It would be good to get away from the apartment and forget about all those boxes.

"Sure," she said. "We'd love to go. When?"

"Take an hour to get ready," Rob said. "Then we can drive down and have lunch before we go to the beach."

"I'll get my suit!" Margaret said, off and running to the bathroom.

Casey had washed the suits out in the sink and hung them on the shower rod the previous evening.

"She's a real bundle of energy," Rob said. "I wish I was that enthusiastic about everything."

"She's been wanting to see the 'ocean' ever since we got here," Casey said. "Thanks for the invitation."

"It'll be fun," Rob said. "I'll be back in an hour."

"See you then," Casey said.

**They drove to** Galveston in Rob's Ford Taurus. It was an easy trip, taking the loop to Interstate 45 and then dropping straight down to the island. Margaret's eyes widened as they crossed the high causeway bridge.

"Why is it so tall?" she said. Her face was pressed to the window as she looked out at the bay, which was dotted with sailboats.

"So the ships can pass under," Casey said.

"There used to be a drawbridge," Rob said. "It's over to the left."

Margaret, who had been looking out the opposite window, walked across the back seat on her knees to look out at the old drawbridge, now permanently raised. She'd never seen a drawbridge before, nor had she ever seen a bridge quite like the one they were driving over. West Texas had nothing to offer to match it.

They came down off the bridge and entered Galveston on Broadway. Margaret marveled at the broad esplanade and the tall palm trees that grew along it.

"We'll drive by the beach so Margaret can see the waves," Rob said. "Then we'll go have some lunch."

They drove to the end of Broadway and then got on Seawall Boulevard.

The waves were a little disappointing. Margaret had seen waves in movies, and the ones coming in from the Gulf were nothing like the movies filmed in California and Hawaii had led her to expect.

"Not exactly a surfer's paradise," Rob admitted. "The waves do get a little bigger at times, but at other times the place is almost as smooth as glass."

"The water's a funny color, too," Margaret said. "It's not blue."

She was right. Casey had been to Galveston only

**83**

once, long ago, and she remembered her own disappointment in both the waves and the water, which was at best somewhat greenish and at worst a muddy brown.

"But it's the beach," Casey said. "Look at the sand."

"The sand's not white," Margaret said.

She was right about that, too. A visitor from Florida might have thought it looked more like mud than sand.

"There's a new park on the bay side," Rob said. "They have white sand there." He didn't add that it had been hauled in from Florida.

"I want to swim in the waves," Margaret said. "Even if they aren't very big."

"Good idea," Casey said.

"It sure is," Rob said. "Any wave is better than no wave. Where would you two like to eat?"

Margaret and Casey had no idea, so Rob suggested seafood. "It's hard to find bad seafood here," he said. "It's just that some is better than the rest."

They didn't want to eat anywhere fancy, since they all had on their bathing suits under their clothes. Rob knew a restaurant that catered to tourists and locals and would meet their requirements.

They had crab balls and fried shrimp and fish with hush puppies and then went to the beach.

The day was partly cloudy, as days usually were at the beach, and not as hot as it had been in Houston. The humidity was just as bad, but the Gulf breeze helped cool things down, as did the tall masses of flat-bottomed clouds.

Rob drove them down off the seawall and to a "pocket park." There was a small admission charge, but the beach wasn't crowded and there were dressing rooms, as well as showers to wash off the salt and sand.

Well covered with sunscreen, Margaret ran into the water, Casey and Rob close behind.

"Are there crabs in the water?" Margaret yelled.

"They'll get out of your way," Rob assured her. He had scanned the water, looking for jellyfish, but there didn't seem to be any. That was the only real danger.

They went out to where the water was waist-deep on Margaret. Casey and Rob could sit and let the waves bobble them up and down. It was very relaxing.

Margaret would jump every time a wave came; she screamed with pleasure when the water splashed her face.

Once there was a wave larger than the others and it came rushing in faster than Margaret expected. She tried to jump, but she timed it wrong and jumped too soon. The crest of the wave crashed down over her, pushing her under the salty water.

Rob was at her side immediately, pulling her up, holding her above the water, laughing as she wiped with her hands at the water that ran out of her hair and eyes. Margaret was choking and coughing from having swallowed a little of the Gulf.

"Got a little wet, did we?" Rob said. "Now you can tell everyone that you've really been in the ocean. And that you tried to drink it."

"Did not," Margaret said between coughs. "It tastes yucky!" Then she laughed too.

It was quite an enjoyable afternoon, all in all, and Casey thanked Rob for inviting them as they were driving back over the causeway.

"I thought you could use a little entertainment," he said. "Moving to a strange city is no fun for a kid. For a grownup, either."

As they drove back up I-45, Casey pointed out to them two of the campuses at which she hoped to be teaching in the fall. One was near Texas City and the other was nearer to Houston.

"You can see them both if you look," she said.

**85**

"The drive won't be so bad," she told Rob. "It all depends on my being able to work out a schedule so that I can teach at both places. Maybe I could teach at one on Tuesdays and Thursdays and at the other on Mondays, Wednesdays, and Fridays. Or in the mornings at one place and in the afternoons at the other."

"Do they offer night classes?"

"Yes," she said. "Those meet one night a week. I'm not sure I'd like night classes, though."

Rob glanced back at Margaret. "If you ever have problems getting a sitter, just let me know. Margaret and I get along fine. Don't we, Margaret?"

"Sure!" Margaret said. "You saved me from getting drownded!"

"I don't think you were in any danger," Rob said. "Your mother was right there, too."

"But you were the one who saved me," Margaret insisted. "Mom might not have known what to do."

Casey smiled, not bothered by her daughter's implied criticism. She knew what a crush was, and she was sure her daughter had one. And Rob wasn't such a bad guy to have a crush on, either. He was very good-looking.

Rob was also smart, Casey thought. He still hadn't put any moves on her, made no demands at all. He had merely taken her and Margaret out, shown them a good time, and now he was taking them home. It was a good feeling to know that there were still some nice guys left. Not everyone was like the Asshole.

She leaned back in the seat and enjoyed the ride.

# 15

Alma Remington had led a completely ordinary life. If anyone had asked her to describe herself, that's the word she would have used —*ordinary.*

She had an ordinary face, sort of round and chubby; ordinary hair that would never take much of a wave; an ordinary body, a little too flat in the chest and a little too round in the hips; and an ordinary job as a secretary at an insurance agency. She had never married, though she had dated two men seriously, and at the age of thirty-eight she was resigned to a life of spinsterhood.

There was simply nothing at all unusual about her.

Not unless you counted the murder.

She lived two doors down from Ellen Forsch, and the night of the murder she had been outside looking for her cat, Stinky. She let him out every evening so that he could take a little ramble around the apartment complex before returning home. He was a neutered male, a gray tabby, and he spent all day and all night inside Alma's apartment with no complaints, but he did like to get out at least once a day and scratch in the grass and scratch a little dirt in one or two of the flower beds.

Stinky had been obstinate that day, refusing to come when Alma called him. That was nothing unusual. He came right away, most of the time, but every now and then she sensed that he was feeling a need to assert his independence and wanted to keep her waiting for a while.

She didn't really mind. She didn't have anything special to do anyway, just watch TV or read the latest Fern Michaels novel, so she always waited patiently, calling Stinky every few minutes until he finally decided to give in and come home.

So she had been outside when the man left Ellen Forsch's apartment.

At least she thought that's where he had come from. She wasn't absolutely sure, but that was because there was nothing unusual about men leaving Ellen's place. Ellen, even though she was skinny, had plenty of men. Alma liked her anyway.

Because there was nothing unusual about a man leaving Ellen's, Alma thought nothing of it. She noticed only that he seemed to have an average build and to be fairly tall. It was dark, and the lights in the parking lot didn't give her a clear look at him.

He got in a car and drove away, and, no, she couldn't identify the car. It just looked like a car to her. It wasn't a big car and it wasn't a small car. That's all she could say. No, she didn't know what color it was. It was hard to tell that under those lights. It was shiny, she knew that, but that was all.

Despite her lack of knowledge, she was the only clue the police had, and for a very short time Alma had achieved a sort of celebrity status among her neighbors and co-workers.

It had been a good feeling, having everyone wanting to know what she had seen, wanting to know what it felt like having a murder take place practically next

**88**

door to her. It was nice having everyone paying so much attention to her, having the investigators asking her all kinds of questions, even though she couldn't answer any of them.

She had been genuinely sorry when it all ended, but new things drew the attention of her neighbors, and the police soon decided that she was not going to be able to help them. She had gone back to being just an ordinary person in an ordinary job, watching TV, feeding Stinky, letting him out for his evening walks, reading books.

Therefore she was almost overjoyed when Howland showed up at the insurance office and told her that he was newly assigned to the Ellen Forsch case and would like to ask her a few questions if she didn't mind.

"Mind?" Alma said in her completely ordinary voice, which served very well to disguise the pleasure she felt. "No, I don't mind at all. If it's all right with my boss."

"I'll clear it with her," Howland said, and he did.

**There was even** a private room at the agency where they could talk. Alma showed it to Howland. It was where she had been questioned before.

The homicide investigator asked the standard questions, and he got the same answers that his colleagues had gotten the first time they went over the ground. Howland didn't mind. It was more or less what he had expected, but it was the proper way to begin.

Then he explained to Alma about the hypnotism.

"Hypnotism?" she was plainly fascinated. "You want to hypnotize me?"

"Well," Howland said, "I won't be the one who does it. We have a police psychologist who does that sort of thing."

"I see," Alma said. She let a little disappointment creep into her voice. She liked this policeman better than the ones who had talked to her earlier, and he was kind of cute in a way. She really wouldn't have minded being hypnotized by him, but a police psychologist was probably just as good. Maybe better.

Alma didn't have too many friends among the residents of the apartment complex, but she knew that everyone would be interested in hearing about how she was hypnotized. She was going to be a celebrity again. It was going to be very nice being the center of attention, even if it was only for a short time.

"So what do you think?" Howland said.

"About what?" Alma said, trying to get her mind back on the topic.

"About letting Dr. Romain hypnotize you. To see if you can recall anything under hypnosis that your conscious mind hasn't been able to come up with."

"I think it's a great idea," Alma Remington said. "When do we start?"

**Howland talked to** Alma's boss, who happened to be a very understanding woman, and arranged for Alma to have the afternoon off.

"I'll pick you up here at the office at one-thirty," he told Alma.

"I have a car," she said. "I can drive to the station."

"That's all right," Howland said. "I'll be glad to pick you up, and I'll bring you back here after the session is over." He didn't tell her that he wanted to make sure she showed up. You could never tell when someone would take advantage of a half-day off by going shopping instead of reporting to the police station.

Alma didn't mind. She was glad of the chance to ride in the police car, something she hadn't done the first time she had been questioned and something that would provide her with even more to tell her neighbors.

She was also glad of the chance to have someone like Howland chauffeur her around.

She ate her lunch quickly—an ordinary lunch that she had brought in a brown bag—and was ready and waiting when Howland came by for her. She had been ready, in fact, for over an hour.

At the station, Howland introduced her to Romain. She did not like the psychologist as much as she liked Howland, who was more of a gentleman. Romain hardly seemed to notice her, and he smoked.

Alma didn't smoke. She had given up the habit years ago when she had read that smoking was not good for pets. She didn't want Stinky getting cancer from breathing secondhand smoke.

Romain explained the process of hypnotism to Alma, and she listened avidly even though the psychologist didn't seem too interested himself. It was almost as if he didn't care if the hypnotism worked or not, or as if he hoped it *wouldn't* work.

Howland wondered about Romain's attitude. After all, he was the one who had suggested hypnotism in the first place. Now it was as if he didn't give a damn one way or the other.

But Howland didn't say anything. This was Romain's baby, and he probably knew what was best.

They took Alma to a dimly lit room and seated her in a comfortable chair. Howland was allowed to remain and take notes, as long as he sat back out of sight and kept quiet, conditions to which he readily agreed.

Alma proved to be a good hypnotic subject. She genuinely *wanted* to be put under and to remember everything about the night of Ellen Forsch's murder, especially the things she hadn't been able to remember before.

**91**

The problem was that Alma really couldn't remember much else.

Romain got her to recall the evening of the murder without any difficulty, and she remembered letting Stinky out of the apartment, even the way that the cat had hesitated at the doorway as if he could sense something unusual in the atmosphere.

"How does he look?" Romain asked.

"His head is down," Alma said, reliving the experience, "and he doesn't seem to want to go out. I give him a little nudge with my toe, though, and he goes on."

She was sitting in the overstuffed leather chair, her head leaning on the soft leather back. Her eyes were half closed as she went back and lived it all again.

"What do you do then?" Romain said.

"I go inside to read and give him a little time out in the yard, like I always do. Then I go back out, but he won't come in. I call him. 'Stinky, Stinky, Stinkeeeeeee.'"

Howland hoped there weren't any cats in the building, but there must not have been. None came running to answer Alma's high-pitched call.

"I don't call very loud," Alma continued, "because I don't want to disturb the other residents. Some of them don't have pets, and they don't like Stinky."

Hell, no wonder, Howland thought, no cat lover himself. He probably pisses in their flower beds.

"Does anything happen while you're outside?" Romain said.

"While I'm waiting," Alma said, "a man comes out of Ellen's apartment. He looks around and sees me."

Howland sat up straighter in his own chair. She hadn't told anyone that part before, the part about being seen. Maybe something was going to come out of this after all.

"What does he look like?" Romain said.

"The light is bad," Alma said. "It's hard to see."

"Try," Romain said. "Try to see him, Alma."

"All Ellen's men are cute," Alma said. "I wish I could get some of them to visit me. I don't know how she gets so many of them. She's too thin, but I guess some men like that type."

"The man in the parking lot," Romain said, bringing her back to the subject. "Describe him."

"It's just a man. He's tall. He's got something in his hand."

Another detail that hadn't come up previously. Howland was almost beginning to get his hopes up.

"What does he have in his hand?" Romain said.

"I can't tell. It's too dark."

*Damn*, Howland thought.

"What does he do with it?" Romain said.

"He puts it in the car."

"What kind of car is it?" Romain said.

"It's just a car. All cars look alike now."

Howland slumped back in his chair. It wasn't going to pay off after all.

"What does he do next?" Romain said.

"He gets in his car and drives away," Alma said.

"I want you to think carefully," Romain said. "Think about him driving away. Does he drive under any of the lights? Does the light ever fall on the car so that you can see him?"

Alma didn't answer for a while. Howland assumed that she was remembering.

Then she said. "He does drive under a light, but I can't see him."

*Shit*, Howland thought. *Double shit.*

"I can see the car, though," Alma said. "It's a shiny blue and there's an oval emblem on it."

Howland sat up again.

"Can you read the name in the emblem?" Romain said.

"Yes," Alma said. "It says *Ford.*"

**That was all** they got.

Stinky had come back and he and Alma had gone back inside the apartment, thinking no more about the man in the car until Ellen Forsch's body was discovered. Alma had come forward and volunteered the information about the man she had seen leaving the apartment, and that was it.

Howland took Alma back to the insurance agency, assuring her again and again that she had been a big help, she really had, even if she couldn't describe the man she had seen or pinpoint the model of the car. Then he returned to Romain's office.

"Not much help, was it?" Romain said, exhaling a thin stream of smoke. He sounded smug, even though hypnosis had been his idea.

"We know what kind of car it was," Howland said. "And what color it was."

Romain laughed. "How many blue Fords do you think there are in Houston?"

"Thousands," Howland admitted.

"We didn't even find out the model," Romain said. "We don't know whether it was new or old."

"It was shiny," Howland said. "I'd bet on new."

"Maybe. Or maybe the owner just takes good care of it. Anyway, it was two years ago. What if it's been traded in?"

"It's just a straw," Howland admitted. "It's all I've got."

"It's nothing," Romain said. "Hell, *I* drive a blue Ford. You don't think I killed her, do you?"

"Of course not," Howland said.

But he had to admit that Romain was a strange bird. Probably all psychologists were.

# 16

When they got back to the apartment house from their trip to the beach, Margaret was asleep. Rob carried her inside and put her on the bed. He looked down at her affectionately and pushed her hair back out of her eyes before leaving the room.

"What are all those boxes?" he asked Casey when he walked back into the living room.

Casey explained about her books. "I was going to move them out of here, but I don't even want to think about them right now," she said, yawning. "I think Margaret has the right idea."

Rob laughed. "It's the salt air and the exercise, I hope, and not the company. Do you think you'll come down to the pool later?"

"Probably," Casey said. "It depends on how I'm feeling." At the moment, she just wanted to wash her hair and lie down for a while.

"I'll see you there," Rob said.

After he left, Casey decided to wash her hair *after* she lay down.

**When she woke** up she was ravenously hungry, and she heard Margaret banging around in the small kitchen. She forced herself out of the bed and into the bathroom.

After she had washed her hair, she wrapped it in a towel and went into the kitchen. The open peanut butter jar was on the table, along with a loaf of bread, a jar of apricot jelly and a knife. The knife had telltale signs of peanut butter and jelly on the blade. Margaret was on the couch in the living area, eating her sandwich and watching the home shopping network, which was offering a CZ sapphire at a real steal.

"You forgot to clean up in here," Casey said.

"I thought you'd want a sandwich, too," Margaret said, her mouth full. "So I left the stuff out for you."

"Good thinking," Casey said, knowing that Margaret had thought no such thing.

Nevertheless, it was a good idea, so Casey made herself a sandwich, slathering on the peanut butter, justifying it by telling herself that she had no doubt burned a lot of calories at the beach. She skipped the jelly, though. Might as well save those calories where she could.

The sandwich was so good that she had another one. Margaret came to the table and had another one, too.

"Are we going swimming?" Margaret asked when they were finished.

"I suppose so," Casey said. "That seems to be what everyone does around here."

"I want to tell Jack and Sandy that I went to the beach," Margaret told her. "They thought it was funny that I'd never been. Is Rob going to be there?"

"Probably," Casey said, smiling.

Casey had washed out their suits, and they were still wet, which made them clammy and uncomfortable.

Casey took them to the laundry room and tossed them in the dryer for a few minutes. Then they changed into the suits and went out to the pool.

Margaret said hello to Rob and immediately headed for the kids' pool, while Casey went to the table where Rob and the others were sitting.

It was the same group as yesterday—Rob, the Warleys, and Dan Romain. Today the topic was murder.

"I think nine tenths of the murders in Houston are drug related," Craig Warley was declaring as Casey walked up. He looked at her as she sat down. "You've moved into the Murder Capital of Texas," he said.

"I thought Dallas had that title now," she said. "Hello, everyone," she added.

The others murmured their greetings.

"No, it's still Houston," Warley said, getting back to the topic at hand. "Statistics will bear me out. Drugs are ruining this city."

"Every city," Rob said. "They're ruining every city."

"It's not always drugs," Tina said. "Surely there are some people who are killed for the old-fashioned reasons. Like love and money. What about it, Dan? You're the psychologist."

"I really don't know much about murder," Romain said, wishing they would change the subject. "But I guess you could be right." He knew they were right, but he didn't want to say so. He didn't want anyone prying into what his job really was.

"Sure, she's right," Rob said. "Craig and I might have overstated the case."

"The hell we did," Warley said, his face reddening. "I'm right, and all of you know it."

"You're always right," Tina said. "Come on, Craig, give us a break."

"You people just don't know what's going on in the

97

world," Warley said. "It's being ruined by dope and by killers that the cops don't ever catch. It makes me sick to think of the things people get away with. I've been reading in the papers about all those young women getting killed. Has anyone done anything about it? Hell no!"

Here it comes, Romain thought. He was hoping it wouldn't be mentioned, but he'd been almost sure it would, sooner or later.

"You think dope is the reason for those killings?" Rob said. "There hasn't been any indication of that in the papers."

Warley looked sly. "They always hold something back. You want my theory on those killings?"

"Spare us," Tina said, looking around the pool area as if hoping for a rescue from somewhere.

No one else was paying them any attention, however, everyone being involved in their own conversation or splashing in the pool. One overweight man bounced on the diving board and cannonballed into the pool, sending a tidal wave of chlorinated water onto the apron.

Craig wasn't going to spare them. "All those women were whores. You can bet on it. They were probably killed by someone who got AIDS from them. It'll all come out eventually."

Romain wondered where people like Warley got their crackpot ideas. "They weren't whores," he said. "They were all respectable, middle-class women. Some of them were even married." It was safe to say that much; anyone could have read it in the newspaper.

"They were whores, you wait and see," Warley said. "Someone's punishing them for their sins. Whores, dope and AIDS. They go together."

"You sound as if you think they *should* be punished," Casey said.

**98**

"Let me ask you something," Warley said. "What do you think the jail sentence is for someone convicted a second time for DWI in El Salvador?"

"What does that have to do with this?" Casey said.

"Just this: there isn't any penalty, because they give the death penalty down there for the *first* conviction. That pretty much takes care of things, wouldn't you agree?"

"Even if they are whores, it seems like a harsh punishment," Rob said. "They weren't hurting anyone."

Warley snorted. "Just the ones they give AIDS to, that's all."

"You don't know any of that," Tina said. "It's just another of your wild ideas."

Warley leaned back in his chair. "You just wait," he said. "If everything ever comes out, you'll see that I'm right."

Romain thought that Warley had a great deal of repressed hostility, but he didn't think this would be a good time to discuss it.

"So what do you think, Casey?" Tina said. "That you've moved into a hotbed of sin and corruption?"

Casey laughed. "There were murders in West Texas, too."

"Not this kind," Warley insisted. "You'll see." No one really thought he knew anything more about the murders than had been published, but they didn't challenge him again.

"Maybe so," Rob said. "But right now, what I need is a beer. How about the rest of you?"

Everyone agreed they could use one, and Rob dug the cans out of his cooler and put them on the table.

Casey took a sip gratefully. It was no fun to be talking about murder when all around them were laughing and shouting and people having a good time. "Let's talk about something else," she said. "You'd think this town didn't even have a major league baseball team."

So the conversation turned to the Astros, and Warley explained why they'd never get to the play-offs this year, or next year either.

It wasn't the most exciting conversation they could have had, Casey thought, but it was better than talking about murder.

# 17

**M**argaret fell into her bed after her bath and went immediately into a deep sleep. She had told her new friends about her trip to the beach and seemed to be adjusting rapidly to her new surroundings.

Sleep did not come so easily for Casey.

She lay awake thinking about the people she had met so far. She still wasn't sure she liked the Warleys. She couldn't quite figure them out. Craig was a real pain in the ass, and she'd never met anyone quite so judgmental.

She still couldn't figure out Romain, either. He didn't seem to have much to say on most topics, though he always looked as if he could have contributed a lot more to the conversation if he had really wanted to.

Rob was the only one she understood. He was really a nice guy, and Margaret liked him, too.

There were probably a lot of other nice people living in the apartment complex, and she intended to try meeting more of them. She knew that it was very easy to get locked into a certain group and never get out of it. She could already see that in the pool area the same people tended to sit at the same tables every afternoon. She didn't want to hurt Rob's feelings, or even the Warleys' or Romain's, but she didn't want to cut herself off from the other residents this soon after moving to town.

After tossing and turning for more than an hour, she dropped off into a troubled sleep, dreaming about waves that gently bobbed her up and down as Margaret floated farther and farther out into the Gulf of Mexico. Casey was trying to swim out to Margaret, but she was making no progress at all. In fact, as she looked around her she could see that she was being pulled closer to the shore by the current at the same time Margaret was being pulled into the open Gulf. It was almost as if the harder she swam, the farther away her daughter was being carried.

She woke up at two o'clock, sweaty and tangled in the sheets. She went to the thermostat and turned it down a notch. The air conditioner rumbled to life.

Then she looked in on Margaret, who was sleeping soundly. She was in the same position she had been in when Casey went to bed and might not even have turned over.

Casey went back to bed, wishing that she could sleep as soundly as her daughter.

## Alma Remington dreamed, too, that night.

She was outside her apartment after dark, calling for Stinky, who was being a bad cat again.

Suddenly, while she was still calling, Stinky came running headlong around the corner of the apartment, his eyes wide, his tail ruffed in fear, the hair standing straight up along the ridge of his back.

Running right behind Stinky was a man whose face Alma could not see. It was obscured by the darkness. The man was waving something above his head, and

Alma could not see what that was, either, though she thought it might have been a knife.

The man was trying to kill Stinky!

Stinky hurled himself into Alma's outstretched arms, sinking his claws into her shoulder. She could feel his heart beating as rapidly as a bird's against her chest.

The man swung the knife, or whatever it was, at them, but he missed. He did not try a second time. Instead, he veered off to the parking lot and jumped into a blue car.

Alma stood there petrified with terror as the car drove away. It was a Ford, and she strained her eyes at the license plate. It was in shadow, but she thought she could make out two of the three numbers on it. There were a 5 and a 3. She was sure of that.

The letters were harder. She didn't need glasses, had always had excellent vision, but it was dark and the car was moving fast. But there was a C, she thought, and maybe a V. Or maybe it was a U. And maybe the C wasn't a C. Maybe it was an O.

Alma woke up shivering. She had never had a dream like that before. All her dreams were ordinary dreams, and she could never even remember most of them for more than a minute after she woke up.

Stinky was on the foot of the bed, undisturbed. She wondered if cats dreamed, and if they did what they dreamed about, and then decided that it didn't matter.

She got up and went to the bathroom. Then she wrote down the numbers and letters she had dreamed about.

Alma didn't really believe that dreams meant anything, but you never could tell. Besides, the dream would give her a wonderful excuse to call the police and maybe even be interviewed by them again. Who knows? Maybe the dream had been triggered by the hypnotic

**103**

session she had gone through. Maybe it was a sort of delayed reaction.

Even if it didn't mean anything, she might get to see that nice policeman named Howland. Maybe they would even put her name in the paper again.

She was so excited that it took her nearly an hour to get back to sleep.

Stinky never woke up at all.

**The Warleys argued** for quite a while before bed.

Tina was tired of Craig's spending so much time working on the computer and so little time with her.

"It's not as if you don't have plenty of time during the day," she told him. "What are you working on in there, anyway? Is there some secret project that you haven't told me about?"

"Don't worry about it," Craig said. He was lying on his back in the bed beside her, not trying to conceal the erection that was pushing up the sheet that covered them.

"I see that," Tina said, swatting at it with her hand. "Is that all you ever think about?"

He pulled her to him. "No, it's not *all* I think about. But don't try to tell me you don't like it."

She didn't try to tell him that. There was no use in lying. She could feel herself getting wet between the legs as he pressed himself against her.

He reached under the covers with one hand and raised her nightgown, running his hand across her soft stomach, moving it down to tangle his fingers in the soft hair below.

"You damned animal," Tina said, spreading her legs.

"You got that right," Warley said, rolling himself on top of her.

**104**

**As usual Romain** had trouble getting to sleep.

He was thinking about the murders, wondering if Howland could possibly come up with anything on the killer. It didn't seem likely. The hypnotism had gone very well, but the woman hadn't revealed anything of value. There was no way Howland could use any of it.

Romain wondered if it might not be time for him to get out of police work. He was nowhere near retirement age, but the job was beginning to get to him. He knew that he really didn't like the work; otherwise he wouldn't be so unwilling to deal with his co-workers and he wouldn't be ashamed to tell the people he associated with after work what he really did for a living.

It probably wasn't too late to go into private practice, or maybe set himself up as a consultant. The trouble with the latter idea was that he didn't want to consult with anyone on his specialty.

He was tired of serial killers. He knew that was the reason he couldn't get to sleep. He was beginning to think too much like the people whom he was supposed to be helping Howland and the others bring to justice. They dominated his waking hours, and now they were beginning to dominate his nights, too.

He was beginning to understand them too well.

That was never a good sign.

**Rob Hensley worked** on an article he was doing about dog racing. The sport had only recently been introduced into the state, and so far only one track was scheduled to open. It was located about halfway between Houston and Galveston, and he had made a couple of trips there, interviewing the people who lived in the town, getting their views, listening to some of their stories. It was going to be a good article, he thought, and he hoped to sell it to one of the better markets. If *Texas Monthly* turned it down, and they probably would, probably had their own writers working on something similar, he thought he might be able to sell it to one of the airline in-flight magazines.

The writing went well, and by the time he went to bed he had most of the article roughed out.

He didn't dream at all, or if he did, he didn't remember.

**Howland stayed up** trying to find some new angle in the cases, but there was nothing.

He was dealing with a killer so careful that he didn't leave fingerprints and who left no tire tracks when he hauled bodies to fields to dump them. A killer so careful that he used a heavy-caliber pistol so that the bullets went through the victim and were then retrieved. So careful that if he killed by strangulation, he used items from the victim's own apartment to do the strangling.

Howland wished that Alma Remington could have come up with something more during the session with Romain, but at least he had a make of car now, and a color. He supposed that was better than nothing.

But not much better.

If only she could have seen something more, like the license plate number. That might have made a big difference.

Howland went to bed late.

He dreamed of blue Fords.

Mustangs, Tauruses, Escorts, Thunderbirds, LTDs.

None of them had license plates.

# 18

I should tell a little about the others. That's what everyone will want to know.

Like I said, I learned a lot from the first one. I learned to be careful. I learned to plan. I made a promise to myself that I would never again simply go in cold, no matter how the noise in my head built up, no matter how urgent it seemed.

The second one was named Susan Martin.

I found that out later, from the newspapers, but I got to know a lot about her before that. I knew everything I needed to know.

I didn't need to know her name. I was going to kill her, after all, not marry her.

She worked at a convenience store where I stopped to buy gas one night. She took my twenty-dollar bill and gave me three dollars in change, looking me right in the eye as if she didn't know I could see them on her.

The blood marks.

They were on her arms, this time. She was wearing some kind of short-sleeved uniform jacket, and the marks were plainly visible on the part of her arms that showed between the elbow and the beginning of the sleeve.

She was about twenty-five and somewhat overweight. Her upper arms were doughy and white, except for the blood marks. They twisted around her arms like snakes crawling up into her sleeves as if they were trying to hide themselves from me.

They couldn't hide, however, not from me.

There were two or three other people in the store, a man buying beer, a teenage boy renting an R-rated video tape, some man picking up a half gallon of milk. I did nothing to draw attention to myself, did nothing to show how the blood marks repulsed me. I paid for my gas and left.

I parked down the block and waited for the woman to get off work. It wasn't late, about ten o'clock, but I was sure she probably worked the four-to-midnight shift. I was going to follow her home.

A man picked her up at about five after twelve. I couldn't tell anything about him except that he was driving an old Chevy with rust spots on the trunk lid. She came out and got in the car, and they drove away.

It was easy to follow them. They didn't suspect anything. Why should they?

They didn't go far, just a mile or so to an apartment house that had probably been filled with happy middle-class families about thirty-five years ago but which was now filled with people who couldn't afford to go anywhere else. Immigrants, legal and illegal, people on welfare, people earning minimum wage. People who couldn't afford anything better.

Some of the apartments were vacant, their windows smashed out. Though it was now getting late, there was still a good deal of activity on the street. Dope deals going down, whores peddling their wares. About what you'd expect.

The car pulled into the lot and parked. I drove slowly by and watched the man and woman get out and go into the apartment house. Then I went home.

It didn't take long to find out that they weren't married, just living together. The man worked days, leaving every morning about seven. The woman took the bus to work every day about three-thirty. That left her alone in the apartment for more than eight hours.

It was going to be easy.

I was going to have to kill her in the apartment, so obviously I couldn't use a gun. I decided on a knife. You can buy a good knife anywhere. I bought one at a Wal-Mart and spent a few days sharpening it. When I was through, I could shave the hairs off my arm with it.

You can buy cheap plastic gloves in any hardware store. I bought a box of those, and I got a cheap raincoat made of clear plastic at another store in another part of town.

I learned as much as I could about the routine in the apartment. The man always left around seven, but the woman never came to the door to see him off. I decided that she liked to sleep late. That was fine with me.

The only problem I could see was getting into the apartment. There were a lot of people there who didn't work at all, and they would be at home most of the day, hanging out in doorways, sitting around their entrances in dilapidated lawn chairs, visiting and gossiping.

Most of those people wouldn't be up at seven o'clock, however. That was when I was going in.

I did it like this: I walked right in. It was easy. I bought some pants at one store and a shirt at another, making an outfit that looked a little like a uniform. Then I bought some patches and sewed them on the sleeves and over the shirt pocket.

It didn't matter what kind of uniform it was supposed to be; that was the point. It wasn't supposed to be

**109**

any particular kind at all. The patches didn't matter, either. I didn't think anyone who saw me in the uniform would be too curious, and they probably wouldn't be able to read the patches anyway.

I went one morning about a month after I first spotted her. I waited until the man had left. Then I parked a couple of blocks away from the apartment and walked right to it. I didn't look shifty or guilty. I just marched through the parking lot like I belonged there, and in a way, of course, I did. I was carrying a clipboard and a small briefcase, and it was obvious to anyone that I had a job to do.

No one took any notice of me. I don't think anyone really saw me. The people in the parking lot, and there were only one or two of them, were getting in their cars, getting ready to go off to work. They didn't care about me.

I went right up to the apartment door and rang the bell. I had to ring several times before the woman came.

She opened the door a slight crack. There was one of those chains that anyone could break, but I didn't break it.

"What do you want?" she said sleepily. I could tell I'd waked her up.

"City health inspection," I said. "There's been a report that this building has roaches in it. I've been sent around to check."

"Well, there's plenty of 'em here, that's for sure," she said, and she pushed the door up, took off the chain, and let me in.

Just like that. I could hardly believe it. Any women reading this could learn a good lesson right there, but I wouldn't want any of them to read it until I won't be using this method anymore.

You see, I knew all along she'd let me in eventually. I had created a lengthy spiel, and on the clipboard there was a pretty genuine-looking checklist that I'd created on my computer. I'd even dummied up a letter from the Health Inspector's office, with a fake seal on it in case she demanded to see some identification.

But people are really pretty trusting. She had no reason to believe that I was going to do anything to her. She was tousled and sleepy and, let's face it, not very attractive at all. She probably couldn't imagine, not in her wildest dreams, that anyone would want to rape her, which of course I didn't, and she probably didn't have any enemies who'd want to kill her.

Except for me, of course. And she didn't know about me. Not yet, she didn't.

I can see that I'm getting off the subject, as usual. I'm sure no one wants to read about my theories of why she opened the door, so let's get back to it.

She was wearing a chenille robe that was worn smooth in spots. It was probably ten years old. She had on a pair of house shoes that flopped up and down in back, and her hair looked like a rat's nest. She didn't have on any makeup, and she was a bit older than I had thought at first, but not too much. There were red indentations on one cheek where the pillow had been wrinkled and pressed into her face while she slept. Her skin was a sort of pasty white. I guess she didn't get out in the sun much.

She didn't give a damn how she looked, though. I was just some man who'd come in to look for roaches. What did she care?

The robe had long sleeves, so I couldn't see the blood marks. I'd have to get the robe off. I had to see the marks before I killed her.

The sound in my head was there, getting louder and louder, but I ignored it.

She followed me into the kitchen.

**111**

"You'll see traces of the little bastards all around. This is the roach capital of the world."

"Actually it's not," I said. "Miami is. Houston is the flea capital."

"We got fleas, too. Don't even have a goddamn dog, but we got fleas." She sighed. "Open up one o' the cabinets, though, you'll see roaches. What're you gonna do about 'em?"

"We'll see," I said. I didn't really care about the damn roaches. I reached inside the waistband of my pants and pulled out the knife, then wheeled around to face her, the knife in my hand.

"Don't make a sound," I said.

Her eyes were wide. I have to admit that the knife was an impressive sight. Nearly a foot long.

"I ain't got no money," she said.

"Turn around," I said.

"I ain't got no money. I don't know what you want, but I—"

I stepped right up to her and clubbed her in the temple with the pommel of the knife. She hit the floor like a bag of dirty clothes, which in a way is all she really was.

When she came to, she was already trussed up. I had used the belt from her robe to tie her hands, and I had torn the robe into strips to tie her ankles. She was wearing an old sleeveless polyester gown, and I could see the blood marks plainly.

I had taken off my uniform and put on the raincoat and gloves, which I'd been carrying in the briefcase. I suppose that she knew what was going to happen to her, or at least she had a pretty good idea. I certainly must have looked bizarre, and, of course, I was holding the knife.

I had stuffed part of the robe into her mouth so that she wouldn't yell when she came to. She simply lay

**112**

there on the floor and looked at me. There wasn't much else she could do.

The floor wasn't very well cared for. It was green linoleum of some sort, cracked and broken. There was dirt in the cracks. Clearly she wasn't much of a house-keeper. Neatness is important in a home, I've always thought, but she hadn't been taught about that. Or if she'd been taught, she'd long since forgotten. The whole apartment was a mess, to tell the truth. There were dirty clothes in the broken-down chairs, empty potato chip sacks on the couch in front of the TV, old newspapers lying on the stained rug, dirty dishes stacked in the sink. I've never understood how people can live like that, but there are apparently a lot of them who don't seem to mind.

But none of that matters. I'm wandering off the subject.

She was looking at me, her eyes almost begging for me not to do what she knew I was going to do. Her eyes had no effect on me, however. I hardly noticed them. What I noticed was the blood marks on her bare arms.

They were getting redder and redder as I looked, bulging like a tangle of thick worms. I knew I had to do something about them soon, so I didn't even bother to take the gag out of her mouth.

Sometimes I've regretted that. I would have liked to hear her beg. I would have liked to make her say "please."

But I knew I couldn't do that. If I did, the blood marks might get away, might crawl right off her arms and onto the floor and slither across that worn-out rug and hide under the furniture where I'd never find them.

They were feeding off her fear. Her fear was making them strong.

I had to do something about that.

**113**

I plunged the knife into her throat and pulled it hard to the side. It was very sharp, as I'm sure I've said.

Her eyes bulged out and she sucked in on the piece of robe in her mouth. It was almost comical. If the knife hadn't killed her, she might have strangled.

Blood spurted out and spattered like raindrops on my arm and chest, but it didn't matter. I had on the raincoat.

It was very exciting, but I didn't lose control. I almost did, but I didn't.

I had told myself to be strong. I had hit the first one a lot of times, not even counting, not even watching the blood marks die.

I wasn't going to do that again.

So I stood and watched her for a second or two. I have to admit that my breath was coming fast, and, of course, there was that sound in my head, like music that wasn't really music.

The blood marks had already started to fade, but they were still too strong.

I stuck the knife in her stomach.

Twice.

The second time I ripped straight up to her breastbone.

There really wasn't much blood this time. I think she must have been dead by then. Her heart had probably already stopped.

Just to be sure, I stabbed her twice more, in the general area of the heart. I'm not a student of biology, so I didn't know the exact location, but I did my best.

It must have been good enough, because the marks faded almost as white as her pasty arms.

That didn't satisfy me, naturally. As long as there was any sign of the marks, I wouldn't be satisfied.

And that's why I cut her arms off.

# 19

The call got through to Howland as soon as he walked into his office the next morning.

"Says her name's Remington," the switchboard operator said. "Says you know her."

"I know her," Howland said. "Put her on."

Alma was thrilled to be put through so quickly, and she explained to Howland about her dream.

Jesus Christ, he thought. Now I'm having to listen to dreams. He fleetingly remembered his own dream about the blue Fords, but it passed through his mind and out as if it had never occurred. Howland had never put much stock in dreams.

When Alma got to the part about the license plate, however, he perked up.

"I think it might be important," she said. "I think it might have been caused by the hypnosis. I didn't remember then, but my whaddyacallit, my subconscious mind, remembered and brought it to me in the dream."

It was just crazy enough to be possible. "All right," Howland said. "Give me the numbers."

"The letters were first," she said.

That meant the plate had been issued in the last few years. "All right," Howland said. "Give me the letters."

"There were a C and a V," Alma said hesitantly. "Or maybe they were an O and a U."

Trouble already, Howland thought.

"Or an O and a V," Alma said. "Or maybe even a C and a U."

Howland could see that this was going to be more fun than he had thought at first. "What about the numbers?"

"I saw those better," Alma said. "I'm positive that there were a five and a three."

"In that order?"

"Well . . ." Alma said. Then there was silence.

Howland waited patiently.

Finally she said. "I'm just not sure. I think the five came first, but there might have been another number between it and the three." There was another pause. "Or there might not have."

"If there wasn't, do you have any idea what the last number might have been?"

"Well . . ." Alma said. "I guess I don't."

And it was all just a dream any way. "Thanks, Ms. Remington," Howland said. "You've been a big help."

"Do you really mean that? Do you think this will help catch the man who killed Ellen?"

"I'm sure it will," Howland said. What else could he say?

"Do you need to talk to me again?" Alma said. "Try the hypnosis again? I might remember more this time."

"I'll let you know," Howland said, hanging up the phone.

"'Don't call us, we'll call you,'" Alma said into the dead phone in her hand. "Damn." She hung up.

Howland was no mathematician, but he could see

**116**

that the possible combinations of letters and numbers would mount up quickly. And then there was the missing letter and the missing number. All Texas plates had three letters, except vanity plates, of course, and most of them had three numbers. So if he carried this out he had to check out the plates having any combination of C's and V's, C's and U's, O's and V's, and O's and U's. Followed by some combination of 5 and 3.

Fortunately there were computers these days. It could be done.

Then he had to see which of those plates went with blue Fords.

That could be done, too.

Even though the Forsch murder had been two years ago, the plates might not have changed. Texas plates were not replaced annually, as had once been the case. Now you simply affixed a new sticker to the old plates each year. You could get new plates if you requested them, but most people preferred not to have to go to the trouble of taking off the old ones and putting the new ones on.

Even if the car had been sold, a possibility that Romain had brought up, there would still be a record of who had been the original owner of the plates.

Howland realized that he was taking the dream seriously. He couldn't believe it. He had been handed this case only a couple of days ago, and already he was ready to move on a flighty woman's dream.

He decided he wouldn't put the computers to work just yet. He wanted to talk it over with Romain first.

**Romain never smoked** outside the office. The cigarettes were a part of his office personality, and though he smoked at least two packs a day on the job, no one at the apartment complex had ever seen him light up. It

**117**

was just one more way he had of compartmentalizing his separate roles.

Howland did not know that, naturally, and when he entered Romain's office, the psychologist was grinding out a butt in an ashtray that already had three other butts in it.

Romain lit another Camel and smoked it thoughtfully while Howland told him about Alma Remington's call.

"What I want to know," Howland said when he had finished his recitation, "is could this be a real lead? Or is it just some lonely woman's dream that doesn't mean a damn thing except that she wants someone to pay a little attention to her?"

Romain looked sharply at Howland. "You're a pretty good psychologist yourself," he said.

"Bullshit. Anybody can see that Alma Remington's starved for attention. What about the fucking dream?"

"I believe in the significance of dreams," Romain said. "I certainly can't vouch for their prophetic value, but I wouldn't say that this one is meaningless."

"What the hell does that mean?" Howland said. "Talk English, all right?"

"I mean it might be a genuine memory. Or it might not."

"That's what I was afraid you were going to say. I can't afford to take the chance, though, can I?"

"I don't see how you can. After all, what else have you got?"

"Not a damn thing."

"Then you can't afford to take the chance that the dream is meaningless. You have to check it out."

"Damn," Howland said. He gave Romain a hard look. "I'm going to look like a fool if anybody ever hears about this."

"Surely you don't think I'd tell anyone."

"You never know," Howland said. "I've got to admit, though, you don't look any happier about this than I am."

Romain wasn't happy at all. The more leads that Howland came up with, the more he would be coming around, asking for advice, asking for help. Romain didn't want that.

There wasn't anything he could do about it, however.

Howland left to give instructions to the computer guys. Romain sat and smoked thoughtfully.

What sort of personality was it that would leave the crime scenes so perfectly clean? Obviously their killer was obsessive as well as careful, but did that mean the killer was obsessive in his daily life?

Romain looked around his own office, at the rapidly filling ashtray, at the papers piled all over his desk, at the books stuck haphazardly in the shelves, at the ashes on his clothes and on the computer keyboard.

How different it all was from his apartment. His apartment was almost like a military barracks. The bed was made with hospital corners, and you could bounce a quarter on the bedspread. His kitchen was spotless, though he liked to cook his own meals and often did. He vacuumed the rug at least twice a week and cleaned the bathroom every other night.

He wondered what someone would make of that if they ever discovered the way he lived his separate lives. But he didn't much care. The more he thought about it, the more he thought he would give up his job soon.

Private practice was looking better all the time.

**Howland got complaints,** but he was going to get what he asked for. It would just take a while. He wondered about Romain, though. There was one strange guy.

119

He didn't seem enthusiastic about Alma Remington's dream, but then what should Howland have expected? It was a fucking dream, after all.

Still, he had hoped that Romain would jump one way or the other, either giving him an enthusiastic "yes" or a firm "no" about whether to proceed with it. Hell, for all Romain had said, Howland might as well not have gone to him in the first place.

There wasn't anything to do but go on with it. Howland had never felt quite so useless in his entire life. Maybe he should talk to Alma Remington again. It would give him something to do besides sit around with his thumb up his ass feeling sorry for himself. It wouldn't be so bad to spend a little time with her. Maybe she would even remember something else from the dream. It was worth a try.

He picked up the phone and called her back.

# 20

**A**lma hung up the phone.

She couldn't believe it. Mr. Howland was going to pick her up after work and then they were going to have a drink and dinner and talk about the murder. It was official police business, of course, he'd made that clear, but still—dinner!

She went into her boss's office and asked for the afternoon off. She wanted to go have her hair done. Maybe she could get some kind of wave in it so it wouldn't be so plain, so ordinary. She had to do *something*.

Alma was a good worker, never sick, never late, willing to work overtime if necessary. She never took days off for frivolous reasons.

Her boss was glad to give her a few hours. Business had been slow lately, anyway.

**Howland couldn't believe** it, either. What had he done? He must be getting old and sentimental, that had to be it. Otherwise, why on earth was he taking Alma Remington to dinner?

Howland wasn't old, but he wasn't young anymore. He was getting on toward that gray area called "middle age," however, and maybe that explained things.

He shook his head. It had been a while since he'd been out with a woman. A long while. He couldn't even remember how long it had been. Maybe it had been too long, and maybe that was another reason why he'd found himself asking Alma to dinner.

Howland had been married once, a long time ago, and it hadn't worked out for the same reasons that a lot of police/civilian marriages don't work. He worked bad hours, he took the job home with him, he let some of its frustrations affect his relationship with his wife, he tended to pal around with other cops and tended to confide in them (because they could understand) rather than his wife.

He had never blamed her for walking out on him, and he had never quite gotten over the feeling that it was all his fault.

Another thing he had never quite gotten over was the slight but nevertheless very real feeling of relief he had experienced.

Now he could work whatever hours his job demanded and not have anyone waiting up for him or worrying about whether he would be coming home at all. If he wanted to go out for a drink with the guys, he could do it; there was no one to answer to except himself. He was alone a lot of the time, and that didn't seem to bother him particularly.

He and his wife had never had children, which was a good thing, Howland thought, and there was really no sense of intimacy left between them by the time his wife left. He realized after a week or two that he didn't really even miss her. And of course he felt guilty about that, too, for a short time anyway.

But all that had been years ago, and now he had to

admit that he was beginning to feel lonely some of the time, like when he would get to his apartment late at night and there would be no one to talk to, no one to tell what had happened to him, no one to smile at him, or even to frown at him and complain about his coming in so late.

It wasn't that he wanted to share his life with anyone like Alma Remington, though. If he had ever concocted a fantasy about the next woman he would let into his life, she would never have been the one he thought about. She was too ordinary.

He saw himself with some gorgeous blonde, mid-twenties, a college degree, probably a good job with an accounting firm, or maybe an executive in one of the banks. Someone like that. Not an ordinary secretary for an insurance agency.

Well, he'd asked her to dinner now and he'd have to go through with it this time, but never again. Probably he'd just done it because he felt sorry for her.

Sure, that was it.

**They went to** a seafood restaurant near the Astrodome. It was a well-known place, famous for its buffet. Nothing fancy. Howland had been there several times, though Alma never had.

He noticed that she'd done something to her hair, and he had to admit that it made her look better, not that she'd looked all that bad in the first place. So she didn't have the figure of Raquel Welch. What difference did that make?

She talked animatedly all through dinner, telling him about her work in the office and about her cat, Stinky, as they worked their way through dishes of crab casserole, bowls of shrimp gumbo, platters of baked fish.

Howland didn't mind listening. He didn't much like cats, and he'd never owned one. Cats didn't require

**123**

much care, but they required more than he was willing to give. It was fine with him if other people wanted to have cats, though.

He even found himself telling Alma a little about his own life, how he had never thought he'd be a cop, how he'd planned to be a teacher but somehow found himself drawn to police work because it seemed like just as good a way to help other people as teaching, and you probably got to use your reasoning ability even more. It wasn't the kind of thing he usually talked about to anyone, but since he hadn't talked to anyone except cops, victims and perpetrators for the last few years, he didn't really have the chance to engage in small talk.

After they had gone back to the buffet for dessert, Alma brought up the subject that they were supposed to have been talking about all along.

"I don't really think you put much stock in my dream," she said, taking a bite of pecan pie.

"I didn't at first," Howland said. He had gotten a slice of chocolate cake. "But after I thought about it awhile I decided it might be something we needed to discuss. There's always the chance that you might have come up with something here."

Alma smiled, obviously pleased. "Do you really think so?"

"It's possible," Howland said. "But there's a problem." Then he explained to her about the possible combinations of license numbers.

"And there are all the colors of blue we have to consider," he said. "Not to mention black and gray, which can look like blue at night or under the lights of a parking lot."

"So what does that leave you with, in round numbers?" she said.

"Four or five hundred," he said. "I haven't counted."

"Oh," she said. "I didn't realize there would be so many."

"There are," he said. "Trust me."

The printouts were on his desk at the station. He hated to think about going through them, but it was something he would have to tackle, beginning in the morning.

"I just wish there was something more I could do," Alma said. "I just wish I had been more observant that night."

That was Howland's cue to try to find out if there was anything left in her memory for him to use.

"You said that he was carrying something in his hand," he said.

"Yes, but I didn't see it."

The waiter came to their table to clear away the plates and refill their coffee cups, and they sat in silence until he was gone.

"You might have noticed something else, though," Howland said. "Like how he was holding it."

Alma thought about it. "He was holding it down by his leg like he was trying to hide it."

That fit, Howland thought. Ellen Forsch had been beaten severely with something, something like a piece of pipe or a tire tool, something that could be partially concealed by a man's leg.

"And he looked at you."

"Yes. I'm sure he did." Alma shuddered, and Howland knew why. She was lucky the man hadn't stopped to take care of her or that he hadn't come back and dealt with her later.

"And he put whatever it was he was holding in the back seat of his car, is that right?" he said.

"Yes. He opened the car door and—"

"Wait a minute. If he opened the door, couldn't you see his face then?"

"No. It was still in the dark, outside the car."

"All right. I'm sorry I interrupted. What were you going to say?"

Alma concentrated and a wrinkle formed between her eyebrows. "He opened the car door and pulled the seat forward and put something in the back."

"He pulled the seat forward?"

"That's right."

"So it was a two-door car," Howland said. "That's good. That's a help."

Alma smiled, happy that she had remembered something new.

"Then he got in the car?" Howland said.

"That's right. Then he got in the car."

"You should have seen his face then. The light should have been on until he closed the door."

"I . . . I didn't see him. His face was in shadow, I think. The shadow of the roof."

Howland was disappointed, but he didn't show it. "I can't expect you to have an instant ID for me," he said, and smiled.

"I really want to help you," Alma said. "I just wish I could remember more, but I can't." She drank the last of her coffee. "There's one thing I was wondering, though."

"What's that?"

"Why are you suddenly interested in Ellen's murder again? It's been two years. I thought everyone had forgotten about it."

Howland found himself wanting to tell her the truth, but he couldn't do that. "I've just been assigned to the case," he said. "We don't like unsolved crimes. We don't ever give up, not even after two years."

"That's good to know, I guess," Alma said. "I always wondered if it was one of Ellen's men friends that killed her."

"We don't think so," Howland said. Everyone with even the remotest connection to Ellen Forsch had been thoroughly and painstakingly checked out from the beginning. Now he would check out the ones with blue Fords, but he didn't expect to find anything.

He just hoped he could find something before whoever had killed struck again and killed someone else, but he was not optimistic, not at all. For all he knew the killer could be sitting at the table next to them, planning his next crime.

It was not a comforting thought.

He took Alma to her apartment and even walked her to her door. Chivalry was not dead.

She looked up at him shyly and asked if he wanted to come in for a drink. "I have a little white zinfandel," she said.

Howland hated to admit it, but he had actually enjoyed himself at dinner. Before they had started discussing Ellen Forsch, he had talked to someone about things entirely unrelated to his job and he had realized that it was nice to do that. It was a good feeling just to have someone to talk to about trivialities.

"If you don't like cats, I understand," Alma said.

"No, no. I don't exactly *dislike* cats," Howland said. "Sure, I'll come in for a minute."

He had no idea what he was letting himself in for, but he suddenly decided that there were times when it might be a good idea to do something a little bit different, even if it meant nothing more than spending a few minutes in the company of a completely ordinary-looking woman like Alma Remington.

So when she unlocked the door, he followed her inside.

**127**

# 21

Casey Buckner spent the day moving the boxes of books into her bedroom. She didn't unpack any of them, but she wanted them out of the way. Margaret helped, but her heart wasn't in the work. She was beginning to miss her father for the first time.

Margaret didn't think of the Asshole in the same way her mother did. To Margaret he was "Daddy," and though she knew that he had done something wrong, she wasn't quite sure exactly what it was. Casey had kept most of the details of the divorce from her daughter, and she had made it a point never to discuss the custody arrangements.

It hadn't seemed so bad to Margaret when they were in Lubbock and she had known that she could call her father on the telephone any time she wanted to. And although he had not asked for custody or even visiting privileges, he dropped by to see her now and then. Casey never tried to stop him.

Now, in a new town, surrounded by strangers, Margaret was beginning to worry.

It had been all right at first. Moving, meeting new

people, getting to go to the beach, swimming in the apartment house pool every day, all those things had been novel and interesting. They had kept her attention off the fact that her father wasn't around. But now the realization was hitting home, and Margaret didn't like it.

As Casey stacked one of the last boxes on a pile, Margaret said, "Is Daddy ever going to come here for a visit?"

Casey had been half expecting a question like that, but she wasn't really prepared for it. Expecting it and being able to answer it when it came were two different things. Things had been going along well, and she had been halfway hoping that the question wouldn't be coming after all.

"I don't think so," she said. Might as well tell the truth and get it over with.

Margaret looked puzzled. "Why? Doesn't he like me anymore?"

Now how do you answer something like that? Casey thought. The real answer, judging from the Asshole's behavior, was "No, he doesn't like you. He doesn't like me, either." But Casey wasn't about to say that.

She decided on a half truth this time. The truth would carry you only so far. "I think it's me he doesn't like," she said.

Margaret reached out and traced her finger over the letters on one of the boxes Casey had packed her books in. It was a Jack Daniel's box.

"Why doesn't he like you?" she said.

That was another good question, and Casey knew that she had been guilty of oversimplifying the situation. She thought that the Asshole probably did like her, that he was just trying to prove to himself that he was still attractive to coeds, but how were you going to ex-

**130**

plain an aging male's midlife crisis to a kid Margaret's age?

"Maybe he does like me," Casey said. "Sometimes grown-ups don't really know *what* they like."

"Why not? Did you do something to him?"

"No," Casey said, hoping that she was right. As far as she knew, she had never given the Asshole any cause not to like her. God knows, she had been faithful to him, and she had never gotten tired of hearing him read Byron. Well, not until right at the end, not until after she found out about his bimbo.

She'd gotten pretty tired of everything by that time.

"I want to see him," Margaret said.

They had talked about this before, in Lubbock, before they had made the move. Casey had tried to explain that they were moving a long way from home and that they would not be seeing the Asshole (though of course she hadn't called him that) again for a long time.

She had thought Margaret understood, but when you're nine years old, a week can be a long time. Casey knew she should have thought of that, but she'd been trying to make things easy on both of them and had glossed over things as much as she could.

Now she was beginning to be sorry that she had.

Margaret was still tracing the outline of the words on the boxes, but her face was getting sadder and sadder.

Casey remembered a time a couple of years back when Margaret had lost her favorite Barbie doll. She'd been playing at someone's house, and when it came time to leave, the doll had somehow been left behind. That night, Margaret thought of it and asked where it was. Casey and the Asshole had no idea, and they had searched the entire house. When they had been unable to find it, Margaret had looked much like she did right now, the corners of her mouth turning slowly but inex-

**131**

orably down, her eyes focused on something in the distance that only she could see.

In just a few minutes, Casey knew, Margaret would close her eyes, her chin would begin to tremble, and big tears would squeeze themselves from beneath her lowered eyelids.

Casey tried to distract her. "Wouldn't you like to go in and see what's on TV?"

Margaret didn't answer. She just shook her head.

"Maybe we could go shopping. I think we could both use some new clothes for when school starts."

"Don't want any new clothes," Margaret said.

That was a good sign, Casey thought. At least she was talking. It was time for the ultimate bribe.

"I've been thinking," Casey said. "Maybe it would be nice if we had some kind of new game to play. Something like Nintendo."

She had never really wanted to buy a video game because she had hoped that Margaret would begin to take an interest in reading. Casey thought her daughter watched too much television as it was and that a video game would only add to the time spent in front of the set. But desperate situations required desperate remedies, and Margaret had often expressed her wish to have a Nintendo like the one her friend Jon had owned in Lubbock.

It was too late for the bribe to be successful, however. Margaret's eyes had clamped themselves shut and the tears had begun to squeeze out, big round drops that hung for a second or two at the corners of her eyes and then slid slowly down her cheeks.

Margaret made no attempt to brush away the tears, and she made no sound as she cried. She stood by the boxes and her shoulders shook.

Casey knelt beside her and put her arms around her, holding her tightly. "Don't worry, baby, everything will be fine," Casey said, wondering if she was telling the truth. "We'll be fine."

"I want my daddy," Margaret sobbed.

Casey didn't know what to do. She couldn't think of anything to say, at least anything that would be a comfort.

She was saved from saying anything, however, by the ringing of the doorbell.

She stood up. "I'll go see who that is," she said. "I'll be right back."

Margaret didn't say anything. She just stood there, the tears still coming.

Rob Hensley was at the door. He was holding a large stuffed toy that looked something like an alligator.

"Hi," he said. "Is Margaret at home?"

"She's in the bedroom," Casey said. "What on earth is that?"

"It's an alligator, as anyone can plainly see." Rob held it up and turned it slowly. "Someone gave it to me as a gag gift last year, and I thought Margaret might like to have it."

"Come in," Casey said. She and Rob went to the couch and Rob put the alligator on the coffee table.

"Margaret's not having a good day," Casey said. "She's missing her father."

"You mean she's sort of down in the dumps?"

"You might say that. She's not at her best."

"Then this is just what she needs," Rob said. He flicked a switch in the alligator's belly and it began to waddle its way across the table, twitching its tail from side to side, opening and closing its mouth and making what Casey assumed was supposed to be an alligator noise of some kind. It sounded a little more like the barking of a dog than an alligator, however. Casey couldn't help laughing.

Rob laughed too. "We have real alligators here,

**133**

too, you know," he said. "If you'd like to see some that is."

Margaret stuck her head out of the bedroom. "I'd like to see some alligators!" she said. She came into the living room, rubbing her eyes with her fists. She stood by the couch and watched the toy on the coffee table as it waddled along, its mouth snapping. "Where are the real ones?"

"Not far from here," Rob assured her. "We can go one day soon if you'd like to."

"I would!" Margaret said. Her father was forgotten, at least for the moment.

"You can keep this one with you for now," Rob said. "He'll remind you of what the real ones are like until we can see them." He showed her how to turn the toy off by flicking the switch.

"Thanks!" Margaret said. "Can I keep him in my room?"

"That sounds like a good idea," Casey said, but Margaret was already gone, the alligator tucked under her arm.

Casey watched her go, then turned to Rob. "Thanks," she said. "You came at just the right time. Do you have ESP?"

"I don't think so," Rob said. "I just happened to see that alligator and think of Margaret." He thought for a minute. "That might make a good article. Stories of co-incidences like that."

He took an index card and pen out of his pocket and made a note on the card. "This'll remind me. I'm likely to forget things if I don't write them down."

"Have you had lunch yet?" Casey said.

"Nope. What did you have in mind?"

"How about a peanut butter sandwich?"

Rob laughed. Casey found herself liking the sound

**134**

of his laughter. "Best offer I've had today," he said. "What kind of jelly do you have?"

"Apricot."

"Sold," Rob said.

**Margaret and Casey** went swimming again that afternoon. Casey still had not gotten used to the humidity, but she liked getting out of the apartment for a while every day.

Margaret wanted to tell her friends about the alligator, which she had named Rob, for obvious reasons.

"Can they come to the apartment tomorrow and look at him?" Margaret said before they left.

"Sure," Casey said. "They might like to see a few of your other toys, too." She hoped that if the friends came over, Margaret would get interested in playing with them and not think so much about the Asshole.

"What about the Nintendo?" Margaret said.

"You never forget anything, do you?" Casey said, regretting already that she had been tempted to offer the bribe.

"Nope," Margaret said with a grin. "I've got a good memory."

"Well, we'll see about the Nintendo for your birthday. That's coming along next month, you know."

"All right," Margaret said. She was apparently willing to wait, for which Casey was grateful.

At the pool, Margaret stopped at the grown-ups' table for a minute or two, telling them all about the alligator. Tina seemed interested, but Craig didn't even try to fake curiosity. He seemed preoccupied. Dan Romain was unusually dour, his thin face solemn, but he at least expressed enthusiasm when told of the gator's wagging tail.

When Margaret had gone to the smaller pool,

**135**

Rob said, "It must be great to be young and impressionable."

"Not so great," Romain said. "Lots of terrible things happen to children. Things that change them forever."

"Trust a psychologist to say something like that," Craig Warley said. "You guys are always telling us that our personalities are formed when we're kids and that there's nothing we can do about it. That's a pretty damned lousy way to look at life, if you ask me."

"Nobody asked you," Tina reminded him.

"Who cares? It's still lousy. If you listened to enough of that, you'd think a man could never overcome his past. Hell, if I'd believed that, I'd never have amounted to anything."

"Had an unhappy childhood, did you?" Rob said. He was leaning forward, his elbows resting on the table, and Casey glanced at the one which had been broken.

"I sure as hell did," Warley said. "My old man was about as worthless as they come, never held a job for long, never provided for us the way he should've. It was really tough on me and my mother."

"Maybe we ought to have you talk to Dan about that," Tina said. "It might explain why you work so hard all the time, day and night."

"You got any complaints about what I provide?"

"No," Tina said. "I'd just like a little more of your time to be devoted to me."

Dan didn't want any part of that. He tried to divert their attention. "I didn't have such a great childhood, either," he said.

"Do you vant to diz-cuss it, doc-tor?" Craig said, trying for a German accent and missing by a mile. At least his attempt had the virtue of giving everyone a laugh.

"Unhappy childhoods aren't all that uncommon,"

Romain said when they stopped. "My story isn't that different from Craig's. My parents might have been a bit more abusive than his, that's all."

"I doubt that," Warley said darkly. He pointed to his head. "You see this scar?"

They had all noticed it at one time or another.

"Sure," Rob said. "What about it?"

"My father gave me that. About the only thing he ever *did* give me."

"You win," Romain said.

"You sure do," Rob said. "I guess I'm not like most people. I remember my childhood as really wonderful. The sun shone all the time and it was summer all year 'round. And my parents"—he smiled broadly "—they were just wonderful. I don't think I ever even got a spanking."

Casey was listening carefully to Rob's voice. There was something in it, a strange tone of evasiveness, and she had the feeling that he was concealing something. She ignored her feeling, however. She was probably mistaken. She herself had certainly had a happy childhood, and she didn't mind telling about it.

Although both her mother and father had died in an automobile accident when Margaret was only one year old, she remembered them both with the greatest affection. There was something else that worried her, however.

"What about the effect of a divorce on children?" she said.

"Ah," Warley said, putting on his accent again, "so now ve haff anozzer client for ze doc-tor. Alvays it is the free advize that ze people are vantink."

They all laughed again, but somehow Casey didn't think it was funny this time. She was genuinely concerned about Margaret.

"Don't worry about your daughter," Romain said.

**137**

"She seems to be making a remarkable adjustment. Some children are that way, very resilient. I'd say your daughter was one of those."

"Good," Casey said. "I certainly hope you're right."

"He's right," Rob said. "I can tell."

It was nice to hear them say so, but Casey was still worried. She supposed that was what parents were for.

# 22

**D**ealing with Casey Buckner is going to be even more difficult than I thought at first.

I've never been in almost daily contact with one of the carriers of the blood marks before. I thought it would be a help because it would give me a chance to study her, get to know her habits, help me to make a sound plan for eliminating her. And all without any risk to myself.

But it hasn't turned out exactly that way. Being around her makes me nervous. I'm afraid the marks will touch me somehow, infect me. I can't let that happen.

On the other hand, I can't let her know how she affects me. I don't want anyone getting suspicious, not now. They might remember something after she's killed.

And there's another problem. A big one. The daughter.

I don't know why I didn't notice the first time I saw her, but it wasn't until last night at the pool that I saw them.

She has the blood marks, too.

I don't suppose that I'm surprised. I should have known that the marks might be hereditary, and I should have suspected that they would be much harder to see on a child.

That's why I missed them. They aren't like the marks on her mother or on any of the women I've dealt with. They're very faint, not even red yet. Just little lines of pink on the skin of her cheeks, that's all they are now.

But I know what they are. There's not any question about that. I suppose that as she grows older, they'll get redder, thicker.

Now I have to kill them both.

That could be difficult. I've proved to my own satisfaction that it's not always hard to catch a woman off guard, even to get one to let you into a locked apartment without much argument, but I'm not too sure what might happen when there are two people involved.

Having the daughter around might make the mother more alert, and the girl, by virtue of being younger, might be more attuned to danger. It's a troublesome proposition.

Not that there's any question about what I have to do.

They both have to die, and I won't shirk my duty.

Which is all a little off the main subject here, the fact that I cut the arms off the woman named Susan Martin.

It was a messy job, but the apartment was already in a mess, so I didn't really mind adding to it.

I'd never cut off anyone's arms before, however. That was what made it tricky. I'd done things in biology class when I was in school, that's all. You know the

**140**

kind of thing I mean, dissecting a fetal pig, cutting up frogs. That kind of stuff.

It's different with a human being, believe me. I don't mean that I felt any different about it. It didn't bother me any more than cutting up the pig or the cat.

It's just a lot more work, that's all, and it takes forever.

Her arms were thick, and not as soft as they seemed. Or rather, they were soft, but they were tough. There's a lot of muscle and gristle in even the softest person. My knife was very sharp, as I believe I've said, but it was still pretty heavy going.

And then there was the bone. I couldn't saw through it with the knife, and I realized I should have brought a hatchet of some kind, but I didn't have one and there was no time to look for one. She probably didn't have one in the apartment, anyway.

So after I cut through all the skin and fat and muscle and exposed the bone, which as I said took a long time, I stood up, took her hand, put my foot on her shoulder, and yanked the bone right out of the shoulder socket.

There was a loud noise, sort of a cross between a grinding and a cracking sound, and then the arm separated from the shoulder.

Drops of blood spattered up the walls and across the ceiling. I threw the arm on the floor. The blood marks had withered and died.

Getting the arm off the body wasn't as hard as it sounds, once everything had been cut away. It was just tedious.

I did the same thing for the other arm, and then it was time to go.

I wiped my knife with a small towel I'd brought, first. The blade was bloody and there were tiny bits of

**141**

skin and fat clinging to it. I admit that I licked it, just to see what it was like. It wasn't as bad as you might think it was if you're the squeamish sort.

Licking the knife is probably the kind of thing that not everyone would openly admit, but I want to be completely honest here. I wouldn't be writing this if I wanted to conceal anything.

I wiped my face with the towel, too. I had a few spots of blood on me, but not much. I've read that some people who commit a messy murder actually take showers at the scene, but that's just stupid. God knows what you might leave in the shower—hairs, blood, things like that.

Things the cops can use against you.

I had no intention of leaving anything behind.

I folded the towel, took off the raincoat, folded it and stuck everything in my briefcase. There was absolutely nothing in the apartment to reveal that I'd ever been there.

I was still wearing the gloves, but as soon as I opened the door a crack, I took them off and put them in the briefcase, too.

Then I left. If anyone saw me walking across the parking lot, no one mentioned it to the newspapers later. I was just some guy in some kind of uniform, and no one paid any attention to me at all.

It was as easy as that.

Of course the newspapers thought some kind of maniac was at work when they learned about it. They always want to sensationalize things. They make the most of any opportunity to sell a few more papers, and to do that they'll appeal to any kind of perverted reader that they can.

I don't really know why anyone would want to read stories like that. I've always avoided them myself. Obviously those kinds of readers have a real problem, one they naturally wouldn't admit to anyone.

At least I have an excuse for what I do: I have to get rid of any women with the blood marks. Those women are dangerous—to everyone, not just to me.

I'm doing the world a favor, but what reason is there for reading about it in the newspapers? Prurient interest, that's all.

It was the arms that made them write that kind of story, I suppose. They should have talked about the cleverness of the person who had committed the crime, about how there were absolutely no clues, but no, they couldn't do that. They had to write about the severed arms, which at least one writer called an "atrocity," and talk about the "twisted mind" of the killer.

That's one reason I'm writing this material.

I want people to know that there was a perfectly valid reason for my severing the arms of that woman. I certainly didn't do it for fun. If you've ever worn one of those plastic raincoats, you can imagine how I was sweating after cutting those arms off. It was extremely uncomfortable, but the job was something that had to be done.

I would never have cut her arms off if the blood marks hadn't been on them. It was an act I took no pleasure in, and one that I had no desire to repeat.

It was just something that had to be done, nothing more, nothing less.

For the same kind of reason, I shot the third woman in the face. I'd gotten a gun by then. It's really very easy to get a gun in Texas, though I have no idea what it's like in other states. You can buy them at flea markets here, even, which is where I got my first one.

The man who sold it to me was an unsavory-looking character, a man with a three-day beard and a shirt that was stained with sweat under the arms. He smelled as if he hadn't bathed recently, and he was probably selling the pistol so that he could afford to buy liquor.

I assumed that the gun was stolen.

It didn't matter to me. I needed a gun, and he had one for sale. It was a .357 magnum, and he even sold me some ammunition for it. I never even fired it until the night I killed Madeline Verver. I wasn't exactly concerned with marksmanship. All my work was going to be close-up stuff.

Verver is the one I picked up after she got off work at the restaurant where she worked as a waitress.

I went there as a customer only once because after I saw the blood marks on her I knew that I was going to have to kill her, and I didn't want to be seen there again. Instead, I watched the restaurant and learned her routine, which didn't take long.

Every night after closing, she would walk to her car, which was parked at the back of the lot, and drive away. There were several other employees who parked nearby, but they were going to be no problem.

I parked my car several blocks away in another lot and walked to the restaurant.

I had a coat hanger, and I used it to unlock her car, a simple procedure, really. I bent it up into a tight little ball and put it in my pocket once I was in her car.

Then I waited in the back seat for her. I had my pistol and several other items with me, and I put them on the floor. I was wearing a pair of the plastic gloves, of course. No fingerprints this time, either.

When she came out and got in her car, I lay on the back floorboard and let her drive off the lot. Then I sat up and stuck the pistol in the back of her neck and told her where to go.

She didn't put up any fight. What could she do? She

knew that I would shoot her if she didn't follow my directions. I made that painfully clear to her.

The noise in my head was not as loud this time, probably because we were in the darkened car. I couldn't see the marks very well, and besides, she was facing away from me.

The marks were on her forehead.

We drove down I-45 until we came to an exit that led to a road that went through a sparsely populated area. I had her exit and take the road.

We soon came to a field where there was an open gate. I had opened it earlier that night.

I had her drive through.

She knew that something was terribly wrong by then, but she thought she was still going to get out of it all right.

She kept saying, "I'll do whatever you say. Just take the pistol away. You don't need it. I'll be really nice to you, you know what I mean?"

I knew what she meant, all right, and the idea sickened me. My stomach churned, and it was all I could do to keep from puking in the back seat.

Can you imagine what it would be like, fucking someone with those hideous marks on her forehead? Like fucking an animal, that's what.

She didn't feel that way, of course. She kept on talking.

"I'm really good," she said. "Lots of guys tell me that. I really enjoy it, you know what I mean?"

She said that a lot, that part about knowing what she meant.

"I'll do anything you want me to, honey, French you, doggie-style, anything. You can even get a little bit rough if you want to, you know what I mean? I don't mind. I even kinda like it."

I was going to get rough, all right.

**145**

But she wasn't going to like it.

I told her to stop the car when we were well into the field. Then I told her to get out.

"It'd be better in here, honey. If we get out, there's gonna be mosquitoes and all kinda bugs. And that grass is itchy, you know what I mean? It'd be a whole lot better for both of us if we did it in the car."

"Get out," I said again. Maybe there was something in the way I said it, but she didn't argue anymore. She got out.

I followed her out, keeping the gun trained on her.

I looked up at the sky. There was just a little piece of crescent moon that night, and you can't see very many stars that close to Houston. Too many lights. And then it's nearly always cloudy, too.

She stood there in the dark. She didn't try to run. She knew it wouldn't do any good.

"Take off your clothes," I said. She'd changed out of her waitress uniform at the restaurant. She was wearing faded jeans and a shirt.

"Honey, I'm telling you, this grass—"

"Take off your clothes. Now."

She took them off, the underwear too. It was kind of pathetic, the way she did it, trying to be seductive, letting me know that I could have such a good time with her.

I was going to have a good time, all right, but it wasn't the kind of good time she was thinking about.

"Lie down," I said when she was finished.

She didn't even argue about the grass. She lay down on her back, reaching up with her arms.

"Put that big old gun down," she said. "I bet you've got something bigger to show me."

"No, I don't," I said. I bent down and put the pistol to her forehead where the blood marks were beginning to shine redly in the dark. They were pumping with

**146**

blood, pulsing up and down. She didn't even seem aware of them. She was confident that everything was going to be all right, that all I wanted was a piece of ass.

I decided to change that.

"I'm going to kill you now," I said.

"Jesus, no!" She tried to back away, tucking her head and scooting on her ass. "No, honey! I can be real nice to you! Put that thing down!"

I was in control again, just like the first time. It was a wonderful feeling, let me tell you, but I knew better than to prolong it. That's how people get caught. You've got to do what you came to do and get out. Forget drawing out the pleasure. Deny yourself.

I had to say one thing, however. "Say please."

"Jesus, please, please, Jesus, put it down. Jesus, please."

The noise in my head was rising in pitch, like it always does.

"I'm not Jesus," I said.

I shot her in the forehead, pulling the trigger three times.

The gun jumped hard in my hand, jerking it up, and I had to re-aim the pistol after each shot.

The shots were very loud, but there was no one but me there to hear.

There wasn't much left of her face after that, and nothing at all was left of the blood marks.

I got in the car and drove out of the field. At one point the road crossed a bridge near what had once been a toxic waste dump. Now the dump was one of the so-called supersites, scheduled for cleanup at some future date at tremendous cost to the taxpayers.

There was a little stream there, and maybe some of the toxic materials had seeped through the ground and into the water. I didn't know. But I did know that the water was thick and black and greasy and that every single tree along the stream bank was gray and dry and dead.

I didn't think that anyone was going to be searching in that stream for anything, so that's where I threw the gun. As far as I know, it was never found.

When I got back to the restaurant parking lot, the other cars were all gone. I got the Dustbuster I'd stashed in the back seat and vacuumed the car carefully.

Then I walked to my own car and went home.

# 23

**H**owland wondered what had happened to him.

He woke up feeling better than he had in weeks, months probably. Surely it couldn't be the result of having spent five or six hours in the company of Alma Remington. Could it?

Maybe it could. He had found himself relaxing in her apartment even more than he had in the restaurant, found himself talking about things he hadn't talked to anyone about in years—the kind of movies he liked (he liked cop movies with lots of violence), the kind of music he listened to (country and western), the kind of TV shows he watched (he watched "Cops" and thought it was by turn realistic and fakey).

It turned out that Alma shared only one of his enthusiasms, country music, but it also turned out that it didn't matter. She listened to him tell about the movies he had seen, and he listened to her tell about Woody Allen pictures.

"I think he's very funny," she said. "Just looking at him makes me want to smile."

Howland didn't especially agree, but he had to ad-

**149**

mit that some of Allen's movies were pretty funny. He liked *Radio Days* a lot.

Both of them usually rented their films instead of watching them in the theater.

"I never really have time to go to a theater," Howland admitted. "I have pretty strange hours, and I'm always on call."

Alma rented for a different reason, but she didn't explain it. She had plenty of time on her hands, most every evening, in fact. The only company she ever entertained was Stinky, and he would not have minded if she left him there while she went to a movie.

But she never went. She didn't like the idea of going alone. There was something about being the only person in the theater who wasn't with someone else that bothered her. Seeing all the couples laughing and talking, sharing cold drinks and popcorn, holding hands, all those things made her feel out of place and even more lonely than she felt while sitting in front of her TV set at home. So she rented movies.

All she said was, "I like to rent because it's so convenient. You don't have to dress up or anything."

Howland even found that he didn't dislike Stinky. He didn't exactly *like* him, either, but he didn't hate him.

As for Stinky, he couldn't have cared less whether Howland was there or not. He ignored Howland completely, being satisfied to get a good head rub from Alma and then going out for his evening look at the flower beds.

Howland wasn't much of a wine drinker, being partial to beer, but he thought the zinfandel wasn't bad. It wasn't really a white wine, or at least it didn't look white. It definitely had a tinge of red in it, and Howland guessed that was why he liked it. He thought drinking white wine was a little bit effete for a cop, especially a homicide cop.

The evening had gone fast, and before he left he had discovered that Alma Remington wasn't as ordinary as he had thought.

What happened was that he got to know her. He found out that she was unique, as any human being is unique, with her own feelings, thoughts, ideas, attitudes.

As a policeman, Howland had gotten into the habit of placing the people he met into one of five classes: perpetrators, suspects, victims, informers and witnesses.

He had no desire to get friendly with any one of those classes.

Somehow, however, Alma Remington had gotten past his defenses and had become something different. She had become a person. It wasn't the way she looked, and it wasn't even her desire to be lifted out of the crowd because she had helped the police. Howland wasn't sure what it was.

Howland had planned to question her further about what she had seen that night, hoping that the combination of the wine, the relaxing influence of the familiar surroundings of her own apartment, the soothing knowledge that she was being questioned in a friendly and open manner, would all lead her to remember still more about the night of Ellen Forsch's death.

Now, however, Howland found himself concerned with more than learning the killer's identity. He had suddenly developed a different kind of interest altogether.

"What kind of woman was Ellen Forsch?" he asked. "I mean, you said something about her having a lot of men around, and I know from reading the file that she

**151**

apparently had an active social life. What was there about her that attracted men to her?"

They were sitting on Alma's floral-covered couch, not touching, but not that far apart, either. Stinky was lying in the rocking chair across the room. Alma was scared that Howland was going to move over closer, and she was also scared that he wasn't.

She sat there, leaning back on the cushions, twirling the stem of the empty wineglass between the fingers of her right hand.

"I used to wonder about that," she said. "Why she had so many dates, that is. *I* certainly never—"

Alma decided not to pursue whatever it was that she had never. "I mean, she never even seemed to have to try with men. They just flocked around her all the time."

Howland wasn't as surprised at that as Alma seemed to have been. He had known a couple of women like that. They attracted men like sugar attracted flies, though there was really no discernible reason why.

"It wasn't her looks," Alma went on. She set her wineglass on the table. It made a clinking noise, and Stinky looked up. When he saw that nothing was amiss, he put his head back down and closed his eyes.

"I thought at first that's what it was," Alma went on. "Her looks, I mean. But she wasn't really that attractive."

She looked at Howland out of the corners of her eyes. "I know that I'm not very attractive to men," she said. "But I always thought that I was at least as pretty as Ellen."

"It's not always looks," Howland said. "There's more to it than that. I can't explain it either. Not that you're unattractive, by the way. You shouldn't sell yourself short."

Alma blushed. She hadn't been fishing for a compliment, and she couldn't meet Howland's gaze. "Anyway," she said, "I always thought Ellen was too skinny. Her legs were too thin, and she didn't have any . . . bosom, either."

She blushed again, and rushed on. "She did have very pretty hair and nice eyes, though. Maybe that was it."

"Probably," Howland said, knowing that it was not. It was pure old sex appeal. Some had it, some didn't. It was that simple. There was no reason for it that he had ever been able to determine.

"What about her face?" he said.

Alma thought for a minute, as if she wanted to be absolutely fair. "She wasn't really pretty," she said at last. "Not really. Striking, maybe. I don't think anyone would have called her pretty. That might just be jealousy talking, though."

Howland didn't think so. He didn't think beauty was the answer, either. He had seen shockingly beautiful women ignored by every man present when women with more sex appeal walked into the room.

"Did she have any especially interesting features?"

Alma thought again. "Well, she did have a small birthmark on her cheek, one of those little oblong brown marks, you know? It didn't detract from her looks at all. It just made her look interesting."

Howland thought he remembered reading that in the file, but he hadn't really thought about it before. He wondered if it was possible that something like that connected the victims.

Then he realized that there could be no connection like that. Someone would surely have noticed if every woman had had a birthmark of some kind. Nevertheless, it might be worth checking.

"So she dated a lot of different men?" he said.

**153**

"A lot." Alma laughed. "I used to think she needed a personal computer to keep up with all of them."

Then she thought of something else. "She did dress beautifully, I have to admit that. She loved to shop. In fact, she'd been shopping the night she was killed."

Howland made a mental note to check on where the other victims had been, though he didn't think it would do any good. He could remember several of them who hadn't been anywhere for hours before the murders except at home or at work. He would check it out anyway.

After that, they had talked about other things, and when he left he found himself asking Alma if he could see her again.

She said she'd be delighted.

So the next day, Howland felt like a new man. He also felt as if there might be something in the reports on the murders that everyone had overlooked, and he spent the day going over them for what seemed like the ten thousandth time in the past few days.

The idea about shopping was a complete washout. Only two of the women had been shopping before they were killed, and they had been shopping in completely different parts of the city.

The birthmark idea didn't pan out, either, or so Howland thought at first.

Ellen Forsch had a birthmark on her cheek, but the second victim, Susan Martin, had no birthmark at all. Neither did the third victim, Madeline Verver. Howland threw the folders on his desk and leaned back in his chair. He didn't think there was any need to look any further.

But then something occurred to him. The Martin woman had always especially bothered him because her arms had been removed. There didn't seem to be any reason for it. The killer hadn't taken the arms with him,

**154**

after all. They were still lying right there on the kitchen floor when the police arrived on the scene.

He got out the Martin file again and read the physical description of Susan Martin.

She had been tattooed on both arms, a result of having spent her younger days as the old lady of a member of one of Texas's toughter cycle gangs. On the right arm there had been a dragon, and on the left had been a snake coiled around the biceps.

It wasn't a birthmark, but Forsch's head had been beaten to a pulp and Martin's arms had been removed.

What about the third victim?

He looked into the folder and discovered that Madeline Verver had had a small scar on her forehead, not that there was anything left of her head for the medical examiner to describe the scar. There was a picture of Verver in the file, however, and the scar was plainly visible. It couldn't have been more than a quarter of an inch long, but it was there.

Howland was beginning to think he was onto something. He started going through the other files.

Victim number four, Janet Peters. Small scar on chin as a result of childhood fall.

Victim number five, Fran Landon. Small brown birthmark near right ear.

Victim number six, Lucille Hamm. Round puckered scar on left cheek where her brother accidentally shot her with his archery set when they were children.

Victim number seven, Joan Pollet. Small strawberry birthmark below right earlobe.

Victim number eight, Marnie Manten. Large mole over right eyebrow.

Victim number nine, Laura Roberts. Birthmark on neck.

Howland was sure he had the link among the victims.

**155**

The marks were so small as not to be noticeable in some cases, more obvious in others. The medical examiner would never have noticed them because the killer had destroyed them, but they had to be the link.

Had to be.

No one had noticed it before now because the marks seemed so insignificant, but it might be the very thing that explained why Martin's arms had been removed.

In every other case, the victim's head had been destroyed, except for Laura Roberts, the one with the birthmark on her neck.

She had been garroted.

# 24

After the swim, Rob Hensley had asked Casey and Margaret if they would like to come by his apartment for dinner.

"Pizza," he said. "I'll have it delivered."

Casey wasn't particularly in the mood for pizza, but Margaret was enthusiastic.

"Do you have any more alligators?" she said. "I like alligators!"

"No," Rob laughed. "No more alligators. But I do have a lot of books around the place."

Margaret made a face to show that she wasn't impressed. "Books aren't as much fun as alligators," she said.

"What if I have a book about alligators," Rob said. "How would that be?"

"Well," Margaret said, "that might be all right." Her expression plainly said that she didn't really think so.

"I take it that you're accepting the invitation anyway," Rob said.

"Sure," Margaret said, she knew where her priorities were. "I like pizza."

"I guess that settles it," Casey said. "Give us time to go change and we'll be there."

"Great," Rob said. "I'll call in the order."

**Less than an** hour later, Casey and Margaret rang the bell at Rob's apartment.

He opened the door and bowed. "Welcome to my humble abode," he said, ushering them in. He was wearing white tennis shorts, Reebok tennis shoes and a blue polo shirt.

"What's an abode?" Margaret said.

"That's a place where people live," Casey said. "Like an apartment or a house."

"Absolutely right," Rob said. "Some abodes are fancier than others, but I bet mine has more books."

"Mom's books are all in boxes," Margaret said. "But I bet she has as many as you do."

Casey wasn't so sure. There were makeshift bookshelves everywhere in Rob's apartment, most of them made from bricks and boards. Casey hadn't seen shelves like that since she had been in grad school.

Rob saw her looking at them. "Crude, but effective," he said.

"I was thinking in terms of having to buy expensive ones," Casey said. "But this is just as good. Maybe better. I can do this myself."

She walked over to the shelves to see what kind of books Rob had. Like anyone else who loved books and reading, she always had to see what other people liked to read.

Rob had a wide selection. There was William Goldman, of course, whom they had discussed before, with *The Princess Bride* prominently displayed beside *The Silent Gondoliers*.

"I was going to let you borrow that one," Rob said. "Here, take it before I forget."

He pulled the slim volume from the shelf and handed it to Casey.

"Thanks," she said absently, looking along the shelves.

There were more Goldman books, including *The Color of Light* and *Marathon Man*. There were quite a few mysteries, with Robert B. Parker, John D. Mac-Donald and Rex Stout well represented. There were westerns by Justin Ladd and Louis L'Amour, horror novels by Stephen King, Robert McCammon and Peter Straub, and a couple of strange-looking fantasies about a drive-in movie by someone named Joe Lansdale. There were a number of other fantasy novels in the sword-and-sorcery vein, as well, by people like Robert E. Howard and Michael Moorcock.

On other shelves there were numerous reference books, including an encyclopedia, *Bartlett's Quotations*, dictionaries, books on Hollywood and movies, books about music, a thesaurus and quite a few books about the Old West.

There was one shelf devoted exclusively to true crime, with titles like *The Stranger Beside Me*, *The Cop Who Wouldn't Quit* and *Daddy's Girl*.

Margaret wasn't interested in any of this. "Where's the book about the alligators?" she said.

Rob looked around the reference shelf and came up with a thin book called *All About Alligators and Crocodiles*.

"Here you are," he said. "Everything you ever wanted to know but were afraid to ask."

"I'm not afraid to ask," Margaret informed him.

"I should have known," he said.

Margaret started flipping through the book, looking for the pictures.

**159**

"You really do have a lot of books," Casey said. "Maybe more than I have. And yours are certainly more varied."

"You never know what you'll need to know," Rob said. "I don't like to have to go out to the library unless it's absolutely necessary. I could call, I guess, but I like to have things at hand when I'm working."

Just then the doorbell rang. The pizza had arrived. Rob paid the delivery man and they went into the kitchen area to eat. There were even books in the kitchen.

"Cookbooks," Rob said. "I have to admit, I use them less than any other books I have."

The table was already set, and Rob got some ice from the freezer and dropped it in their glasses. Then he poured them some Coke from a two-liter bottle.

The pizza was hot, with double pepperoni and double cheese. They devoted themselves to eating it without much conversation. Margaret finished first and asked if she could go back in the other room and look at her book.

"I'm trying to figure out the difference between an alligator and a crocodile," she explained.

Casey told her that she could go, and when she was out of earshot, Casey decided to ask Rob about something that had been bothering her.

She looked at him across the table. The pizza box was between them, its top slightly open. She reached out a hand and pushed the top down.

"I wanted to ask something," she said. "I hope you won't think I'm prying. At least not *too* much."

Rob chewed on a piece of crust. Then he said, "It all depends on what you want to ask."

"It's about something that was said earlier, at the pool," Casey said. She really didn't know where to begin, and she wasn't sure that she should be asking in the first place.

Finally, however, her curiosity got the better of her. "It's about your childhood," she said.

Rob put the last piece of crust down on his plate. "What about it?" he said. He wasn't smiling.

"You said something about how happy it was, but I got the feeling you were holding something back."

"Maybe I was," Rob said. "But maybe I had a reason."

Casey felt awkward. She didn't know why she had brought it up in the first place.

"I'm sorry," she said. "It's really not any of my business."

Rob stood up and carried his plate to the sink. He came back and took Margaret's and Casey's plates. When he had run water on them, he sat back down and looked at Casey.

"You're right, of course," he said. "I was holding back."

"It's all right," Casey said. "I didn't mean to pry."

"Sure you did," Rob said. This time he smiled a little.

"OK, I guess I did. But, well, I just thought you might like to talk about it to someone."

"There's not really too much to say." Rob took the last swallow of Coke from his glass. The ice had nearly melted, and thin slivers slid down the side of the glass when he set it back down.

"Let's talk about something else," Casey said. The conversation was making her uncomfortable.

"No," Rob said. "You're the only person who's ever caught me in a lie before. I suppose you deserve to know the truth."

"I didn't think you were lying," Casey said, wishing

**161**

she hadn't brought it up. "I just thought there was more to the story than you were telling."

"You were right. My childhood wasn't as wonderful as I tried to make it sound. The truth is, I don't remember much about it."

Casey didn't say anything. She didn't know whether Rob was talking about amnesia or something else.

It turned out to be something else.

"I've talked to professionals about it," he said. "In the course of my work as a writer, not formally. They tell me it might be because I moved around so much. I don't really remember my real parents. I lived in a lot of foster homes."

"There's nothing wrong with that," Casey said.

"No, of course not. I just don't like to talk about it much."

Casey told him about the deaths of her own parents. "What happened to yours?" she said.

"I'm not sure. That's part of what I don't remember. I think I was taken from them when I was pretty young."

Rob held up his arm, the one with the broken elbow. "I do know that this is a souvenir from the early days. My foster parents always treated me just as I said they did this afternoon. I don't think I was ever spanked by any of them. But somewhere back in the time I don't remember, with my real parents, something must have happened."

"You told me you fell out of a tree," Casey remembered.

"That's my standard story," Rob said. "For all I know, it might be true. But, then again, it might not."

"I did fall out of a window once," Casey said. "I've got a scar to prove it." She put her hand to her left eyebrow. "It's not much of one, not many people notice it."

162

She ran her finger slowly along her eyebrow. The scar was about an inch long, but it was very faint.

She winced at the memory. "It wasn't a high window, but it was about four feet to the ground. There was a rock there, and I landed right on it. I was lucky in a way, I guess. I could have landed on my eye and maybe even lost my vision. But it was really nothing serious. I bled a little and cried a lot, but that was about all."

"Margaret has one, too," Casey went on. "Even less noticeable than mine. It's on her right cheek, high up, just under the eye."

"I did notice that," Rob said.

"You're very observant, aren't you?" Casey said.

"I'm a writer. I'm supposed to be observant. Actually, it's a habit. You never know what you might want to use."

Casey put out her right hand and touched the pizza box, moving it slightly on the table.

"It's not much of a story," she said.

"I told you my story, whether it was much of one or not."

"All right," Casey said. "I've always blamed myself for that scar, which is probably why I don't like to talk about it. I was driving to the store when Margaret was a baby, and I was in a hurry. I hadn't strapped her in her safety seat, since the store was only a few blocks away. I was sure nothing would happen."

"That's always the way it is," Rob said. "A lot of the worst accidents happen pretty near home. I wrote an article about that once."

"It wasn't an accident," Casey said. "A cat ran out in front of me, and I braked too hard. I didn't hit the cat, but Margaret was thrown into the dash. She hit the tuning knob on the radio and it opened a little cut under her eye. It didn't even need stitches, and I never

**163**

dreamed it would leave a scar. It's not very noticeable, really. Makeup will cover it when she gets older."

Rob smiled. "That's a good story, and I'm sure it's true. But what if you couldn't remember what happened? What if you had a suspicion that you or someone else, your husband maybe, had abused Margaret, but you were ashamed to say so. Wouldn't you make up a story like mine?"

Casey didn't know how to respond to that. She was saved from having to do so by Margaret, who came in with the book she had been reading.

"I still don't understand," she said. "What's the difference between an alligator and a crocodile?"

Rob took the book from her and flipped through it. He found a couple of pictures and began explaining the differences.

Casey watched him as he smiled and talked to her daughter. One thing was for sure. If he had been an abused child, there was no sign of it now, and she was glad of that.

# 25

**H**owland went immediately down to Romain's office. The door was closed, but Howland didn't bother to knock. When he opened it, he automatically stepped back, being greeted by a haze of gray smoke.

He fanned the smoke away and peered inside. Romain was sitting at the desk, his feet propped up on the writing arm that slid out on the right side. He was not, at the moment, smoking. He was simply staring up at the ceiling, as if the answer to some question might be written there.

"I've got something," Howland said.

"Did it come to you in a dream?" Romain said, swinging his feet to the floor and turning to face the doorway.

"It's nothing like that," Howland said. "It's a supposition, but it's based on facts."

Romain frowned. "In that case, you might as well come on in. The door's open, anyway."

Howland entered the office and took a seat. "Doesn't all this smoke ever bother you?" he said.

"No," Romain said. He wasn't going to explain to anyone that the cigarettes provided him with a smoke screen that kept most people away. Howland was just more persistent than most people. "And you forgot to close the door."

"I didn't forget," Howland said. "I thought it might be nice to be able to breathe while we talked."

"Hmph," Romain said. "All right, we'll leave it open, though I prefer the confidentiality of having it closed. You never know who's walking down the hallway listening for gossip."

Howland knew that Romain was right, but it was really stuffy in the office today. The air conditioner couldn't deal with the smoke. If there had been a smoke alarm in the place, it would have been beeping.

"Go ahead," Romain said. "Tell me what it is that you've got."

Howland told him.

Romain was less than enthusiastic. "Even if what you're saying is true, what good does it do you?"

That was something Howland hadn't thought about. He had been so excited about finding a common feature among the murdered women that he hadn't really considered the practical aspects of it.

When he thought about it, he realized that there weren't any.

"I guess we can't warn every woman in Houston with a mole or a birthmark or a scar on her face to be on the lookout for a killer," he said. "Damn. I thought I was onto something."

"You probably are," Romain said. "It may be that the killer is repelled by women with a facial disfigurement, no matter how small. It tells us something about him, but it doesn't really help us warn any of his future victims."

"What does it tell us about him?" Howland said. With the door open, the air was getting better in the office already. Much of the smoke was being sucked out into the hall.

**166**

"Well, there again we have a little problem," Romain said. "It's hard to say exactly what it tells us, beyond what we already know."

"Wait a minute," Howland said. "What did we already know?"

"That he's hostile toward women," Romain said. "I thought that went without saying."

"I wish you'd said it anyway," Howland told him. "I suppose I assumed it, though. So what else do we know? Besides the bit about facial disfigurement."

Romain couldn't resist getting out a cigarette and lighting up. He held it between his thumb and forefinger and took a puff.

"We don't *know* anything. But we might go on the assumption that something was done to him at some point in his life by a woman with some sort of facial disfigurement."

"What sort?" Howland wanted to know.

Romain of course disappointed him. "It's impossible to say. It could be anything. He hasn't exactly restricted himself to women with one kind of mark, has he? It would've been easier if he had."

"Yeah," Howland said. "And we would've spotted it a lot quicker."

"You might consider this, too," Romain said. "Since he's done everything else right, he might very well be varying his victims to throw us off the track. If so, he's been successful."

"Goddammit," Howland said. "I thought I had something, but there's nothing here even to go to the Chief with. Much less the newspapers."

"I wouldn't even think about the newspapers," Romain said. "The Chief's another matter."

"Why?"

"I think he might be interested in the fact that

**167**

you're making progress. It's more solid than hypnosis and dreams."

Howland hadn't told the Chief about that, either, but he had been thinking that he would. He owed the Chief a report.

"You're probably right," he said. "I'll give him what I've got. If we went to the newspapers, every woman in Houston would panic."

"Probably," Romain said. "But it would do wonders for the sale of cosmetics."

Howland went back to something Romain had said earlier. "What might have been done to this guy by a woman?"

"Anything," Romain said. "It's really useless to speculate in a case like this. However . . ." His voice trailed off.

"What?" Howland said. "Come on, Romain. Let's have it."

Romain mashed out his cigarette. The ashtry was overflowing, and Howland wondered if it had been emptied the previous evening or if Romain was just smoking more.

"In a number of cases of serial killers," Romain said, "there's been a history of child abuse. Not in all of them, not by any means, but in a significant number."

"So what does that tell us?"

"Nothing, really, except that I was just thinking. What if the killer's mother had a birthmark, a scar, something like that—a prominent one? And what if he had been severely abused? That might explain the pattern that you've discovered."

Howland thought about it. "But even if you're right, we're still not any closer to the killer, are we?"

"Not a bit," Romain said. "If you were to round up every man in Houston who'd been abused as a child, you'd probably have quite a crowd."

"And then I'd have to ask them about their mothers," Howland said.

"And of course they wouldn't tell you," Romain said.

"Great. Just great. Well, at least it's something to tell the Chief, even if it's nothing to go on."

"There are always those license numbers," Romain reminded him.

"Right. And I got those from a dream."

Romain almost smiled. "Hey, it's better than nothing."

"Yeah, right," Howland said. "Sure it is."

**The Chief received** the news stoically. There hadn't been another murder of a young woman recently, so he was willing to be patient.

Up to a point.

"You know what this place is like," he told Howland. "If you and Romain know these facts you've given me, sooner or later someone else is going to know. And not long after that, the newspapers are going to find out. It's inevitable."

The Chief didn't have to spell out for Howland what he was really saying. He was really saying that if Howland didn't get on the ball and do something before there was another murder and before the reporters found out what was going on, the newspapers would come down on the department like a lead boot. They would come down on the Chief especially heavily because he'd concealed information from them.

The Chief wouldn't like that.

There was a mayoral election coming up, and one of the biggest issues was police salaries. Naturally, the Chief was lobbying for higher pay, and it wasn't going to look good at all if there was a series of unsolved murders on the books, particularly a series of unsolved murders that the Chief had been withholding information about.

169

The Chief put a hand to his forehead as if he had a headache. Maybe he did. "And all you've really got is part of a license number."

"I don't exactly have that, either," Howland said. He hadn't mentioned the dream yet. "You might say that information is pretty iffy."

"You don't have a damn thing."

"That's about right," Howland admitted. "But I'm going to start going through the license numbers today. If I can come up with anything, I'll let you know."

"You do that," the Chief said by way of dismissal.

**Howland returned to** his own office to begin going over the license numbers. He didn't know exactly what he was looking for, but he supposed that any car registered to a known sex offender would be immediately under suspicion. Might as well throw in all convicted felons, too. He was going to need the help of the computer guys again.

He began to go down the list, eliminating all the cars owned by women. He thought he could safely do that, but nothing was certain. The killer might be married, and the car might be registered in his wife's name.

But you had to start somewhere.

Howland decided to skim the list first to see if any of the names were familiar to him from past cases. It would be quite a coincidence if one of them was, but stranger things had happened.

The printout was pages and pages long. It would take days to track down every male owner, probably weeks.

He hoped he would get a break. It would have been nice if the killer had been the proud owner of a vanity plate reading something like MAD DOG, but things like that just never happened.

He got a cup of coffee and tried to get comfortable in his desk chair. It was going to be a long day.

# 26

Tina Warley was getting worried about Craig.

Not only was he spending a lot of time away from home, he was becoming more and more obsessive about the secrecy of his work. Even when they were both in the office, as they were today, he kept referring to "his" clients and "her" clients.

She was getting tired of it. "I thought this business was a partnership," she told him.

They were sitting at their separate desks, each one equipped with its own personal computer. The office was in a small strip shopping center, and their window looked out on the parking lot, which was sparsely populated at eight o'clock in the morning, the hour that Craig insisted on being at work. It didn't matter how late he stayed up at night; he was always out of bed by six-thirty the next day.

"It is a partnership," Craig said. He was dressed the way he thought an accountant should be dressed, in a conservative gray suit with a dark tie. "It's just that you work better with certain clients, and I work better with

171

some of the others. We need to keep things separate that way."

"What about the times you're out of the office?" Tina said.

Craig had told her that he liked to go out and meet with his clients at their own places of business when he could. "Lets me get to know them better," he said.

"There are lots of times when 'your' clients call and ask questions, and I can't answer them," Tina said. "I need access to your records."

"We've gone over this before," Craig said. "You keep your records, and I'll keep mine."

He clearly wasn't going to discuss it further, and Tina decided it wasn't worth the effort to pursue it. She and Craig had been growing further and further apart lately, though he didn't seem to recognize the symptoms. Like a lot of men, he thought that everything was fine, just as long as he could still arouse her in bed. He didn't seem to realize that sexual arousal had nothing to do with love, and that relationships were built on something more.

She knew that she was contributing to the distance between them by her constant nitpicking. She had noticed herself questioning him each afternoon as they tried to relax at the pool, but his know-it-all attitude was so obnoxious that she just couldn't help herself.

She had never questioned him about his comings and goings before, but now she found herself wondering whether there might be someone else in his life, some other woman.

Craig, for his part, didn't seem worried about a thing. The business was going well, and that was all he cared about. They had a solid base of clients, and the base was gradually growing. Their financial situation was sound, and getting better. He was already looking

**172**

around for investments that would take away a little of their tax burden.

He didn't even know that Tina was worried about anything. He had become so absorbed in his work and his own projects that she was just someone who was there, more like someone who worked in the office with him than a wife.

Tina recognized these signs and wondered what was going on. She knew that Craig had not had a good childhood, though he seldom talked about it, and she had heard that people who came from backgrounds where money was tight often became obsessed with making and keeping money in their adult lives. Maybe that was what was wrong with Craig. Maybe that was why he was so possessive of 'his' clients. He wanted to have something of his own to hold onto in case the rest of the business went down the tubes.

She hoped that was it. She didn't like to think of what else it might be, but that had been all she could think about for the last few days.

She couldn't come up with any answers, however, and she wasn't ready for a confrontation. She would wait a bit longer, see how things developed. If they didn't get better, then it would be time for a showdown.

She wasn't looking forward to it. Craig had quite a temper when he was angry, and she thought that might be why she was putting things off. She had seen him really angry only twice, and one of those times he had gotten into a fight with a man at a nightclub.

He had beaten the man up, breaking his nose and opening cuts on his face, and only the fact that everyone there agreed that the other man had started things had kept Craig out of jail.

So she would just let things slide a little longer. Their life together wasn't unbearable yet.

**173**

She would talk to Craig before it became unbearable. She would have to.

It was always possible things would get better, she told herself, but it didn't do any good. She was hard to fool.

**Casey spent the** day working on her bookshelves. She had bought some unfinished mahogany boards and some bricks and started in her bedroom.

The shelves wouldn't be very high. She didn't want to take a chance on their becoming overbalanced and toppling to the floor. But if she built enough of them, they would hold most of her books. It was a cheap way to get the books out of the cartons and onto shelves, and she was glad she had visited Rob's apartment and gotten the idea.

Margaret helped take the books out of the boxes when the first shelves were ready.

"What books are these, Mom?" she said. "School books?"

Most of them were. Volumes of Romantic poetry, all of which reminded her of the Asshole; a lot of critical commentaries on various authors and genres; and assorted novels and collections of stories. Casey hadn't packed them in any special order. Most of her paperbacks of popular fiction, however, were in other boxes.

"Don't you have any good books?" Margaret asked as they shelved them. "Like books about alligators?"

"Nope," Casey said. "I don't have books like that. But you have some books in here somewhere, you know."

She and the Asshole had bought Margaret books for years, and they had read them to her faithfully, but she had never showed any particular interest in them before. She had always preferred to watch TV or to play with her toys.

**174**

"Let's find them," Margaret said, opening a couple of boxes and looking inside. "I remember the one about the tan tomcat."

It was nice to know that Margaret actually recalled one of the books which had been read to her. Maybe she had absorbed more during the reading sessions than Casey thought she had.

"Why this sudden interest in books?" Casey said. "Not that I'm complaining, you understand."

"I like books," Margaret said. "I want to have a lot of books like you and Rob."

"Aha," Casey said. Rob certainly did have a way with women, or at least young girls. He still hadn't tried anything with Casey. After they had talked about his childhood the night before, he had spent a lot of time going over the book about alligators with Margaret.

But when Margaret got sleepy, he didn't try to persuade them to stay any longer. He walked them the short distance back to their apartment and said a polite good night. That was all.

Casey wondered if there was something wrong with her. She wasn't manhunting, not by any means, but she would at least like to think that she was still attractive.

It was probably the fact that Margaret was always with her. Rob was too much of a gentleman to try anything with her as long as Margaret was around.

That had to be it. He was a gentleman, and he could also sense that she wasn't quite ready for another man in her life. As nice as he was, she didn't think it was a good idea to start thinking of him in a romantic way. There were probably lots of other single men at the apartment house, and she remembered that she had promised herself to start meeting some other people.

It was time to begin doing that, and she would. That afternoon, she promised herself. That's when she would start.

175

She and Margaret had emptied four boxes of books, and they stepped back to admire the shelves. Casey thought they looked pretty good. She liked to see her books lined up and available in case she wanted one of them.

"I wish I had shelves in my room," Margaret said. "And I wish we could find *my* books."

"We'll make you some shelves, too, then," Casey said. "You can put your dolls on them, along with the books. And don't worry; we'll find them sooner or later."

"That's good," Margaret said. "I like books more than dolls, though."

Casey smiled. Things were certainly changing, and it looked as if they were changing for the better.

# 27

Reading over what I've written so far, I see that I've been a bit more reticent than I had intended. Some people will be wondering about the sexual aspects of the deaths of Verver and Martin.

It's not that I'm trying to avoid or deny anything here. I want to tell the absolute truth. It was pretty much the same every time that it happened, actually. The entire time I was with the women, any of the women, there was a feeling of tremendous arousal, building higher and higher as the sound built louder and louder in my head.

When the women died, the sound died with them, but the sense of arousal continued. It was so intense that it was almost painful, as if my erection were swollen so much that it was going to burst. I could hardly walk, it was so big.

I knew that all I had to do was touch it, just touch it, and I would be relieved, but I hated to do that.

It was almost as if the pain was pleasurable, too, if you can understand that.

It hurt, all right, but it felt good to hurt.

So I let it hurt as long as I could stand it, letting the feeling grow for as long as I could. Then I touched it, and it was like the first time all over again, streaming out in hot, ropy streams, endlessly.

I hope no one reading this thinks that I'm not normal sexually because of my reactions to the killings. That would be a big mistake. I'm perfectly normal, a heterosexual, and I've always been able to satisfy any women I choose. I could give you references.

But the feeling I get when the blood marks are destroyed is something else entirely. It's not like real sex, although I suppose it's related to that, and I know it at the time.

It's a feeling that comes from something else, from the power, from the control that I have.

I don't believe that a man is ever really in control with a woman in so-called normal sex. Women like to let men think they're calling the shots, but you never know whether they're really feeling what they seem to be or whether they're faking it.

It's probably easy to fake. That's the way women are, natural fakers. But they can't fake it when they see death in your eyes, when they know that you have the power to destroy them, to obliterate the blood marks, and that you intend to use that power.

When they beg you then, there's no faking. You can hear the emotion in their voices, and it's absolutely real.

And when you see the blood marks disappear, you know that they can't control *you* anymore, that they'll never have control again.

It's no wonder that you can just keep on coming.

I know that there will be people who think I'm some kind of freak who hates women, who doesn't trust them.

That's just not true. I love women. I really do. Women have never done anything to harm me.

There will be some who say it goes back to my home life when I was a child, but that's wrong, too. My mother was wonderful. She really was. She cared about me. She wanted me to be good and do the right things.

But I've said before that all this has nothing to do with my mother, so I suppose I'm getting off the subject again.

I just wanted to stress that point about my mother, though. She's not to blame. She did her best. I'm sure she did her best. None of the women has been in the least like her. Not in the least, and that's important, I think. It's just another reason why I'm sure that what I've done has nothing to do with her. It's me, that's all.

I don't know why I do it. That's what everyone will want to know, but I can't answer it.

Of course, there are the blood marks, and I have to destroy them; I've explained that.

But why am I the one who sees them, out of all the men in this city? Why am I the one chosen to eliminate them?

I just don't know.

Sometimes that bothers me. I'd like to know, to have a reason. I don't mind doing the job, nothing like that. It has to be done, but one day I'd like to know *why*. It may be that someone reading this will be able to answer that for me. I hope so.

I had never noticed the marks before I saw them on the Forsch woman, but the instant I glimpsed them, I knew what I had to do.

And I did it. I don't mind admitting that. I want everyone to know that, when the time comes. It was as if I'd been waiting, just waiting, for something to happen, and when I saw the marks, it did.

It's not that I hadn't been successful in life up until that point, I don't mean that, and I wouldn't want you to get the wrong idea. I'm not like a lot of the serial

**179**

killers I've studied who have been real losers in every facet of their lives.

Henry Lee Lucas, for one. What a loser he was. He was clever, I'll give him that, but he would never have made a go of it in life. No education, certainly no looks. Can you imagine him in a business suit?

But I'm not like him. I look fine in a suit, I make good money, most people would regard me as a success.

So I wasn't looking for a way to express my frustrations at being shut out by society or something like that. Not at all.

I was just chosen, for whatever reason, by whatever power, to eliminate the women with the blood marks. Sort of like some biblical prophet.

And I'm the only one.

That's why this record will be valuable. Those who read it will wonder about the blood marks, but they may never be able to see them.

To see them, you have to be chosen, and few people have that privilege.

Even I almost missed them on Janet Peters. She was number four.

I came so close to missing them that it scares me. I don't know what might happen if I miss one of them.

She was working at a little gift shop that I just happened to stop in one day. I can't even remember what I was looking for or what I bought, but she waited on me and sold it to me.

She had long hair, and that's what threw me off. Her hair was dark brown and it swung loose and hid a lot of her face. She was very attractive, with high cheekbones and a wide, sensuous mouth, the kind of woman that interests me under normal circumstances.

I was looking at her hair and her mouth, and I never noticed her chin, not until she had taken my money and was giving me change. Then she smiled and brushed back her hair and sort of tilted her head back, looking at me and telling me to have a nice day.

That's when I saw the marks. They were just under the front part of her chin. If you were looking at her other features, as I was, and if her head was down, you would never have seen them.

But I saw them. They can't hide from me, no matter how they try.

I didn't reveal myself. I took my purchase, thanked her politely and left.

I came back later to see where she went when she got off work.

She got in a red Toyota that was parked at the back of the store and drove out to Loop 610 and followed it to I-45 South, then headed in the direction of Galveston. I followed her, which wasn't hard in the rush-hour traffic. She couldn't go very fast, and she would certainly never notice another car that was going her way. There were thousands of them.

She got off the interstate at Monroe and drove to a Mexican restaurant, where she met a man. They had a few margaritas, then ate a fajita dinner for two. I was watching all the time.

They didn't go home together, so I followed her from the restaurant. She lived in an apartment not far away.

I'm good at getting in apartments.

Three nights later, I was at her door, in a uniform. This one looked a little like a police uniform, and I told her I was from Security, that we'd been having complaints about noise from her apartment. I was even wearing a kind of badge.

She watched me from that little peephole that doors have in them and told me that there was no one there except for her and that she had been watching TV, but that it wasn't turned up loud.

I said that if that was the case, she wouldn't mind letting me check.

She let me in.

I still can't believe how easy it is, but people really are too trusting. They'll believe almost any story you tell them and then open their doors for you. I don't know why. I do know that I would never open my own door for anyone. It's just a stupid thing to do.

This time, I'd waited until after dark to go to the apartment, and I don't believe anyone saw me. I simply drove into the parking lot, parked in an inconspicuous spot between two cars and waited until there was no one around. Then I got out and walked to her door.

When I was inside the apartment, I pretended to look around, just to make things look good, and then I got ready to leave, telling her that I was sorry to have bothered her but that she probably understood how people were when they thought there was unnecessary noise in the apartments.

She was walking me to the door, and she started to tell me that, yes, she understood, when I hit her.

I pivoted on my foot and punched her in the stomach as hard as I could. I really put everything into it, since I couldn't afford to make a mistake. She was young and firm and had a hard stomach, but still my fist almost touched her backbone.

Her breath whooshed out and she went down. She lay there gagging and trying to get her breath, her face extremely red, and for a minute I was afraid I'd killed her already.

I certainly hoped not.

There were things I wanted to do before she died.

I got my gloves out of my pocket and slipped them on. I had avoided touching anything until then.

Then I tore her shirt—she was wearing a shirt and shorts—and tied her and made a gag. By the time I got the gag on her, she was almost able to breathe, and she was taking in huge gulps of air. She got even redder when I put the gag on, and maybe some of that was fear, but she did have a bit of trouble getting enough air in through her nose.

She did all right, though.

I stood there and watched her until I was sure that she was going to be able to breathe. I was smiling pleasantly at her, or at least *I* thought it was a pleasant smile. By the look on her face, I could tell she didn't share my opinion, but I didn't really care.

Then I could smell something foul. I looked at her, and her shorts were wet.

It was disgusting, and I almost killed her then, but I wasn't going to let her off so easily. She had to be taught a lesson.

"Can you hear me?" I said.

She nodded frantically. It was too bad about the gag, but I really couldn't afford to take it off. She was obviously not in a fit state to be trusted, even if she promised to be quiet.

"You know that you're in serious trouble, don't you?" I said.

She nodded again, her head wagging up and down. It was gratifying to see how cooperative she was being.

"Good. Now I want you to know something." I smiled even more pleasantly. "I'm going to kill you."

It was the first time I'd ever really warned one of them. I wanted to see her reaction.

It was not disappointing.

Her eyes got huge and round, she shook her head from side to side, and big tears boiled out of her eyes.

The noise in my head responded by getting louder than it had ever been before. It was almost as if her eyes were speaking to me, begging me not to do whatever it was I had in mind.

**183**

I took my knife from inside the jacket and let her see it, holding it so the light reflected off the blade. It was a pretty impressive sight, if I do say so myself, and I knew what it could do, even if she didn't.

"You have the blood marks," I said.

She looked puzzled then, as if she had absolutely no idea what I was talking about.

Maybe she didn't.

I looked at her chin, however, and the marks were there. There was no mistaking them now, as they pulsed up and down like slimy leeches that had attached themselves to her.

I cut them off.

She almost inhaled the gag, and then she screamed.

Even with the gag on, with the blood running down her chin and making red streaks on her neck, she screamed.

It wasn't loud, but it was a scream, nevertheless. I couldn't have that. Someone might hear. I had to stop her, so I cut her throat.

Blood fountained out, hard; I must have sliced one of those arteries in there, and I was sorry I hadn't worn the raincoat again. I should have, because blood got all over me, making dark stains on the uniform. But that was all right. I didn't intend to be seen, and it was dark outside by that time anyway.

I had to cut her face some more, just to be certain that the blood marks were gone. She was wearing a mask of blood now, and I couldn't really tell.

You can understand that I had to be sure. I didn't do it for the enjoyment. It *is* enjoyable, I'm sure I've mentioned that, but that's not why I do it. I *have* to destroy the marks, and the fact that it provides a certain amount of enjoyment is just a fortunate side effect.

Anyway, what I mean is that I didn't enjoy cutting her face up. It was enough to kill her.

But I have to make sure the marks are gone.

I didn't do a very good job of it, I'm sorry to say. I made a slit up both sides of the face and then peeled the skin back toward the ears, but it's not as easy to do something like that as you'd think. I kept tearing the skin, and it just wouldn't come smoothly, so I settled for ripping it back as best I could and leaving it at that.

There was no way the blood marks could survive something like that, or at least I didn't think so.

When I was finished, I looked out the peephole in the door. There was no one around, and I opened the door a bit.

I didn't see a soul, so I walked out, closed the door, removed my gloves, and went to my car.

I'm sure there was blood on the doorknob and the facing, but no fingerprints. The gloves took care of that.

I passed no one, and no one saw me from a window as far as I know. I drove away and parked on a dark street and touched myself.

I couldn't wait any longer.

# PART TWO

# A CHILD'S

# GARDEN OF

# PERVERSITY

## THE KILLER'S STORY

# 28

When he was small, his father was the one who took up for him.

"What you wanta pick on the kid for, Edna? Jesus, he ain't even big enough to understand what you're sayin' to him."

His father was a little man, not over five feet three inches tall, and about as thin as a razor blade. He looked like he could slither under a door like a lizard if he wanted to.

His mother was not little.

People who saw her and his father together always smiled behind their backs, or laughed outright, wondering how on earth such a couple ever got together. There were lots of jokes made about Jack Sprat, who could eat no fat, and his wife, who could eat no lean.

His parents never heard the jokes, however. No one would dare say anything like that in front of his mother.

She was closer to six feet tall than to five, and she weighed in at around two fifty. Even she didn't know for sure.

That was as high as the bathroom scale went.

His father never had a very good job, and he was never able to hold any job for very long.

Whenever he got fired, there was always a good reason, however.

"The boss didn't like the way I talked up to him. He thinks ever'body oughta kiss his ass, but I don't do that for nobody. He can get himself another boy, that's all. Bastard."

Or: "They said I was late ever' day last week. Shit. I wasn't late, not one damn time. And if I was, it was because the damn buses ran late. Jesus. Is it my fault if the fucking public transportation in this town can't keep to a schedule? If they want to fire me because of that, then they can take their job and stick it."

Or: "Said I didn't take any pride in my work, didn't have what it takes to 'advance.' What the hell do they want? I give 'em a full day's work for the little bit they pay me and don't bitch about nothin'. Fuckers want a robot in a dress suit, let 'em hire one."

Or: "Said I was dippin' in the till! Goddamn! What do they think I am, some kind of two-bit thief? Hell, if they paid a decent wage, then they wouldn't be thinking any such thing."

Nevertheless, he always seemed to work. It might be as a used-car salesman, it might be as a telephone solicitor, it might be as a swamper at one of the bars, it might be as a short-order cook, it might be nearly anything at all. He had a way of presenting himself and making himself seem like a good risk.

He wasn't, but it usually took the employers quite a while to find out that he was chronically late, habitually absent, lazy as a cat and completely unable to resist taking money that wasn't very carefully watched.

For however long it took to be found out, he would bring home his pay and be a good provider. In a way, he wasn't even a bad head of the family. He didn't go out

**190**

and get drunk and waste what little money they had, nor did he spend what he earned on things that they didn't really need.

Still, he had not the least trace of ambition. He was content to live in the cheapest housing he could find, eat the cheapest brands of food, wear the oldest, most worn clothes.

His wife didn't care.

They had met at some bar or another one evening and recognized somehow that they were kindred spirits. As long as they could exist at a certain minimal level, they would both be happy. Neither would make any demands on the other.

All she cared about was being allowed to stay at home, have a few beers whenever she wanted them, watch TV and do whatever work absolutely had to be done—that and no more.

She didn't like to do housework, she didn't like to cook, she didn't like to be bothered.

It all worked fairly well for a good long time, and then the baby boy was born, more or less by accident.

She hadn't wanted him, not at all.

"Kids don't do anything but make a mess and cause trouble," she informed her husband when she was sure she was pregnant. She was sitting on the couch watching a game show on TV, eating potato chips out of a plastic bowl that she held in her lap. "I think we oughta do something about it."

He knew what she meant, but he wasn't in favor of it.

"Sure, the little brat'll be a lot of trouble, but kids are kinda nice, you know?" he said. "It might be kinda nice to have one around the house, somebody to carry on the old family name."

"What the hell," she said. "What family name is

**191**

that? You think you got a name to be proud of? You been fired off more jobs than a dog's got fleas."

He was an amiable sort, not given much to argument. When he got fired, he left the job without a word or a backward glance. If they didn't want him, then who cared?

He was the same way at home. He didn't like conflicts.

"If that's the way you feel about it, then," he said, reaching for some of the potato chips.

It was the way she felt, but she was about as much of a self-starter as her husband. She wanted to terminate the pregnancy, but she didn't seem to have the energy to do so. She just lay around the house and got bigger and bigger.

The house wasn't much to brag about, but it was almost paid for. The husband had inherited it from an uncle who had paid on it for twenty years and had only five more years to go. The payments were low, even if the location was bad.

It was in a decaying neighborhood of similar houses, all wood, which did not stand up well to the Gulf Coast climate unless taken good care of. The roof sagged, the yard was overgrown, some of the boards were rotten. But it was livable, and that was all they cared about.

The baby was born at a charity hospital, and they brought him home in the middle of the winter. The house was warmed by space heaters, but it was never too hot. There were too many drafts.

The baby was trouble from the start, crying and demanding a lot of time and care that no one wanted to give. Neither husband nor wife wanted to get up in the middle of the night, walk across the cold floor and take care of the feeding or changing or whatever needed to be done.

So they didn't.

The baby got used to being deprived, to being hungry and eating voraciously whenever something was offered to him, to having a terrible case of diaper rash.

He got used to it, but he didn't stop his crying.

Edna didn't like it, and she would often swat him, trying to make him stop. The father took up for him, but that didn't do much good. Edna didn't pay much attention.

"Shut up, kid, for God's sake," she would say, slapping him lightly or not so lightly across the face. "I'm trying to watch TV."

He got used to the slapping, too, or at least managed to ignore it.

At first, it naturally caused him to cry that much harder, to express his dissatisfaction more loudly, but after a while, he seemed to withdraw more into himself.

Edna was pleased. "Just goes to show you got to let the little fucker know who's the boss," she said.

She changed him when she thought about it, fed him when she got around to it. That was all she intended to do.

He survived. Children are much stronger than most people think, and they can get by under circumstances that would seem to some to be quite impossible.

So he grew up. He eventually learned to crawl, not that he ever got any encouragement, and then he got into even more trouble.

Edna didn't want him in the way, and she didn't want him messing things up. It wasn't that she kept things especially clean. In fact, it was probably the other way around. She didn't keep things clean, and she didn't keep them neat, but she did keep them in a kind of order.

"Don't touch that, you little sonofabitch," she would say as he reached out for the potato chip bowl or the TV section of the newspaper. "Leave it where it is."

**193**

He didn't understand a word, naturally enough, so he kept on reaching and touching.

Edna would belt him, or kick him or push him away so hard that he might crack his head against the wall.

"I told you not to touch it, didn't I?" she would say.

He wasn't stupid. He soon learned from her tone of voice what she was demanding. But he was stubborn. He kept on reaching and touching and getting belted.

There were other signs besides the tone of voice that he learned to watch for as well.

His mother loomed above him, big as a mountain, but when he looked up at her, he always seemed to notice her face. She had legs like tree trunks, and a kick from one of them could send him halfway across the room, but the legs didn't claim his attention. Even the pillow-like stomach that pushed out the front of her polyester pants didn't distract from the face. She was never well groomed, and her hair was always hanging loose and wild, but the hair was not what he noticed, either.

It was always the face, probably because of the livid scar that ran from the corner of the left eye in a jagged line down the cheek to about the point of the mouth.

It was a scar that she never explained to anyone, not even her husband, who didn't care where she got it. It wasn't any of his business.

It was a thin scar and looked as if it might have been caused by a razor blade or a very sharp knife, but it might have been the result of some kind of automobile accident. It didn't really matter.

What mattered was the way the scar behaved.

It was just there, ashen and gray, most of the time.

But not when Edna got angry.

Then it was another story entirely.

When she got angry, the scar would begin to

**194**

change, to redden, only slightly at first, and then more and more.

Oddly enough, her face never really changed its color. Only the scar changed.

And as it got redder and redder, it seemed almost to develop a life of its own, to writhe on her face like some creature that was drawing its strength from her, feeding on her anger, growing as her rage grew. It would actually enlarge, becoming more of a welt than a simple line of scar tissue.

Even when her open hand was coming at him, even when her foot was aimed at him, the scar was the only thing he could see.

He never tried to escape her, never tried to move away.

He always stared in fascination at the scar.

Watching it grow.

Watching it redden until it became the color of blood.

# 29

It was raining.

It rained a lot in Houston, sullen thunderstorms that came in from the Gulf, covering the sky with thick gray clouds and sending down the rain in steady, depressing streams.

The roof of the house leaked, but not much. It was nothing that the husband, whose name was Carl, couldn't live with, and Edna didn't give a damn as long as she didn't have to clean up any water.

Carl just set a bucket under the leak and let it go. Every few hours he would empty the bucket in the sink, and that took care of things.

The boy didn't know much about the rain, and he knew less about the purpose of the bucket. He wasn't even old enough to know what the bucket was or what it was for.

All he knew was that something was on the floor.

The bucket was bright red plastic. Carl had found it somewhere, maybe even in his own yard. He didn't know what it had held originally, but he thought it might be useful sometime, so he took it in the house. It turned out to be just right to put under the leak.

The color of the bucket was probably what attracted the boy to it, and he crawled over to it.

No one was paying any attention to him at that moment. Edna was watching something on TV, a soap opera, and Carl wasn't even in the room.

When he got over to the bucket, he sat up. He could hear the steady plop, plop, plop of the raindrops falling into the water, and he looked up at the ceiling to see where the drops were coming from.

The ceiling was stained brown, with a small, darker brown circle near the source of the leak and lighter circles around it. The leak had been there for a long time.

He stuck his hand out and one of the raindrops hit it. It felt wet and cold, and he licked his hand. There wasn't much taste, except for the dirt that he had picked up in crawling around for several days. He didn't get many baths.

He reached for the bucket, grabbing the rim. It was about half full, and there was some resistance. He gave it a jerk, wanting to pull it closer to him, but naturally he pulled it over instead. The water spilled out on the floor, running across the worn linoleum and under his legs and bottom.

The water was cold, but he didn't cry out. He knew better than to do that. He knew what would happen.

It happened anyway.

Edna heard the bucket topple and the splash of the water.

"What the hell is that?" she yelled, knowing very well what the hell it was.

He started to crawl away as fast as he could, his small hands slapping the floor, his knees making little thudding sounds as they hit.

He didn't get far.

Edna saw the bucket and the water, and her suspicions were confirmed.

"The little fucker's knocked over the bucket," she yelled, trying to get Carl's attention. He was taking a nap in the other room. He was between jobs, and he liked to sleep on rainy days. The sound of the rain pounding the room was soothing to him.

Edna's yelling woke him up and he got out of the bed.

"Guess it was time I was emptying that bucket anyhow," he said, rubbing his face. He was wearing his socks, no shoes, and when he stepped in the water, his socks absorbed it quickly. He didn't seem to mind.

"You're no better than he is," Edna said, pointing at the boy, who was trying to hide behind a broken-down rocker. "Don't go tracking that all over the room. I know damn good and well who's going to have to clean it up."

Carl knew damn good and well who was going to have to clean it up, too.

He was.

Edna would gripe about it for hours, but she would never break down and get the mop and soak up the water. He would be the one to do it, if it got done at all.

Hell, it was only water. It wasn't as if it would do anything to the floor. Probably be good for it, if the truth were told. The fucking floor probably hadn't been mopped in a month. Or more.

But she was going to take it out on the kid again.

She always did.

She was walking over to the rocker, and the kid was sitting up behind it, watching her with big eyes.

"I'll clean it up," Carl said. "Don't bother the boy. He didn't mean to do it."

She wheeled around on him, her weight shifting ponderously. "What difference does it make if he meant

**199**

to do it or not? He did it, didn't he? He's gotta learn not to cause a mess like that."

"He didn't mean to," Carl said again. He couldn't think of anything else to say.

"Bullshit," Edna said. She jerked the rocker out of the way, shoved it across the room.

The boy looked up at her. He didn't try to get away. He knew better than that even at his age. If he tried to get away, he would just make her that much madder.

Carl figured it wasn't worth arguing about anymore. He'd seen her in action enough times to know that she didn't want any argument from him. It was easier just to go get the mop and clean up the water and let her get her mad out.

It was too bad she had to take it out on the kid, though, he thought. He left the room, looking for the mop.

"Thought you could get away with it, didn't you?" Edna said. She had small black eyes that looked out of her pasty face like raisins stuck in pie dough.

The boy looked up at her. He wasn't old enough to talk, but if he could have he might have said something about the scar, which was already beginning to redden.

"What're you lookin' at?" Edna said. She put a hand briefly to the scar. She knew it was there, though she probably did not know how it behaved when she was angry. She had always been overly conscious of it, and she often put her hand to her face, partially covering it when she talked.

"You don't see a damn thing," she said. "I don't know what you think you see, but there ain't nothing on my face. You hear me?"

The boy didn't answer, of course.

She didn't expect an answer, but the fact that he just sat there looking up at her made her angrier, and as a consequence the scar got still redder.

**200**

"You little fucker. You look the other way, you hear me?"

"Come on, Edna," Carl said, coming back into the room with the mop. "Give the kid a break. He don't understand what you're sayin'."

"I'm gonna give him a break, all right," she said. "I'm gonna break his fuckin' neck."

"Jesus, Edna," Carl said.

She turned to face him, and he saw the scar like a thick vein, red and pumping. He didn't say anything else. He just started mopping up the water. There really wasn't all that much.

The boy sat on the floor, his back to the wall, looking solemnly up at Edna. His eyes were black like hers.

He watched the scar.

Edna leaned down and slapped him across the face. Her hand popped against his skin, and his head bounced off the wall, but he didn't cry out. He blinked and then he just kept looking at her.

She became even angrier, slapping him repeatedly. It was clear that her anger was aroused by something much more than the mere turning over of the bucket of rainwater, but it wasn't clear to any of them what it was that caused her to go into such a rage.

Carl threw down the mop and tried to stop her, grabbing one of her arms. His hands were so small that he could hardly even get a grip on her, and she shook him off like a horse might shake off a bothersome fly. Then she swatted him across the chest and he sailed across the room, slamming into the rocker. The rocker collapsed under him, just before he hit the wall.

She hit the boy several more times.

She never made him cry out, but she did make him stop looking at her.

When she had finished with him, he lay still on the floor, his eyes closed, swollen shut, and he wasn't looking at anything at all.

**201**

# 30

The boy developed slowly, which would not have surprised a pediatrician, but which Carl and Edna couldn't quite figure out.

"Wonder why he can't seem to learn to walk?" Carl said one day when the boy was past two years old and showing no signs of wanting to leave off crawling and take a step or two.

"Little bastard hasn't got any sense, that's why," Edna said. "He can't say a word, either."

Actually, the boy was much smarter than either of them knew. He had learned now not to touch things in the house, and he crawled here and there with an exaggerated care that was lost on his parents, who never noticed him much in the first place.

If Carl was not at work, he was usually taking a nap or watching TV with Edna, who never tired of her game shows and soap operas, day or evening. She was also quite fond of professional wrestling and firmly believed that it was entirely on the up-and-up, a true sport of champions.

So as long as he didn't disturb them, the boy was

able to go where he pleased. If he chose to crawl to get there, it didn't seem awkward to him. There was no danger of falling if you crawled, and he wanted to avoid danger if he could.

As for talking, he had no reason to make any sound at all. Another thing he had finally learned was that making the sounds did him absolutely no good at all and was in fact likely to cause him harm.

So he made no demands. He crept silently through the house, watching, absorbing.

He ate when he was offered anything, but if nothing was offered, he kept quiet about it. Surprisingly enough, he was fairly healthy. He rarely even had a cold, which was a good thing. Had he ever gotten seriously ill, it is unlikely that he would have received any medical care.

Edna, for her part, had gotten to the point where she could pretty well ignore him.

There was still one big problem, however.

The dirty diapers.

She was tired of changing them, not that she did so with any regularity. She tried to put the job off on Carl whenever he was there, but if he wasn't around someone had to do it sooner or later. She didn't care about the boy, but if she let the boy go without changing for too long, the smell got unbearable.

"Time to teach him to use the toilet," Carl said one day as he was carrying a particularly odoriferous disposable diaper to the trash.

"Don't put that goddamn thing in the trash," Edna said. "You take it outside."

Carl obeyed and took the thing to the galvanized can outside. It was still going to stink like hell, but at least it wouldn't be fouling the air in the house.

As he walked back inside, Carl wondered why Edna even cared. It wasn't as if the house smelled like a rose garden. The dirty dishes in the sink smelled pretty bad after a few days, and she hardly ever took out the garbage. If it got done, he was the one who had to do it.

"You're gonna have to be the one to teach him," Edna said when Carl came back into the room.

Carl wondered for a minute what she meant. Then he thought back to what he'd said about teaching the boy to use the toilet.

"Can't," he said. "I start down at the Dairy Queen tomorrow. Pretty good hours, too."

"Shit," Edna said.

Carl smiled to himself. "Shit" was right.

"I can't do it," Edna said. "The nasty little fucker."

"He's probably old enough to try using the toilet," Carl said. "He might pick it right up."

"Shit," Edna said.

It was a day or two before she could get up the energy to try it.

She changed his diaper, then took the soiled one and dumped its load in the toilet with a dirty splash. She went out and got the boy and brought him into the bathroom.

The linoleum floor was cracked, and the toilet sat at a slight angle. The porcelain bowl was chipped at the bottom.

Edna grabbed the boy's shoulders and stood him up. "Look in there," she said, forcing his head so that he was staring into the toilet bowl.

The infrequently cleaned toilet bowl was stained and brown. The contents of the diaper floated in the brown-stained water.

"That's where shit belongs," she said. She reached for the handle and pressed it down. The toilet flushed with a sucking rumble as the water swirled down the toilet, carrying the fecal matter with it.

The boy watched it disappear with fascination. He wondered where it went.

205

As the bowl began to refill, she caught the boy up and put him on the toilet seat. He was so small he nearly fell in. He felt a terrible empty sensation as his stomach seemed to drop down in his body, and he grabbed the edge of the toilet seat and hung on hard. His face turned red, and he opened his mouth to scream, but at the look on Edna's face he bit off the wail that was forming and tried to steady himself.

When Edna saw the problem, she laughed.

"Goddamn, it wouldn't be a bad idea," she said. "Flush your skinny ass right down the tubes, right down there into the sewer pipe. That's where you belong, all right."

She pressed the handle, and the sucking, swirling rumble started again, this time right beneath the boy as he held tight to the seat, his fingers red with the effort, his body rigid.

"You cause me any more trouble, that's right where you're goin'," she said. "Right down there with all the shit of the world." She stared into his eyes. "You know what I mean?"

The boy, as usual, said absolutely nothing.

But he got the message. Edna could see that. His usually blank black eyes were filled with terror.

"You just sit there for awhile and think about it," Edna said with satisfaction. She turned her back and started out of the bathroom.

The boy didn't know what to do. He knew that if he let go of the seat, he was going to fall in that brown water. Then, if someone pushed down that handle, he was going to be sucked down into whatever darkness there was where the water went.

He didn't know how long he could hold on.

He also didn't think he could get down. To him the toilet seemed frighteningly high above the floor. He

**206**

could not walk, and if he tried to turn himself around and slide off the seat, he would probably fall.

If he fell, Edna would hear him.

He didn't want that. He didn't want her to come back in there and put him in the toilet and push down that handle. He didn't want to go where the water went.

He started crying. Silently. Tears ran down his face into the corners of his mouth and underneath his chin, where they hung for a moment and then dropped off.

He had worked himself as far to the back of the seat as he could, and he had to lean slightly forward to balance himself. When the tears dropped off his chin, they dropped into the water below.

He didn't look down to see where they went. He concentrated everything into hanging onto that seat. He looked around the bathroom without really seeing the bathtub, its black ring almost a permanent part of its surface, without seeing the peeling paint on the walls or the grimy window above the bathtub. There was a thin ray of sun that had forced its way through the window, but the boy didn't notice that, either.

He didn't know how long he had been sitting there before he realized that he needed to urinate. Before, he had never thought about it. He had simply done it.

But now, he could feel a peculiar sensation in his body, a kind of burning that wasn't entirely unpleasant.

After quite a while, his curiosity got the better of him and he looked down at himself, trying not to see the water below.

He had never taken any interest in his body parts before now, but he could not help noticing that his small penis was almost erect, since that was where the sensation was coming from.

He wanted to touch it, but he didn't dare let go of the seat.

**207**

There had to be some way to get down from there. He knew that there was. In fact, he knew that he could stand alone if he wanted to. No one had seen him do it, but he could do it. He had pulled himself up on a chair several times in the kitchen when no one but himself was in there.

Maybe if he could slide off the seat, he could hold onto the toilet and stand up. Then he could touch himself.

He never thought of the fact that it was not his fear of being flushed that finally drove him off the toilet. It was, instead, the thought of his possible pleasure.

His was not a life that had known much pleasure. His was not a life that had known pleasure at all, or at least pleasure in any normal sense. Edna would not even let him watch TV. She didn't want him distracting her from her programs. Every time he tried to watch, she swatted him in the head and drove him away. It didn't take long for him to lose interest in the moving pictures on the screen.

He squirmed forward on the toilet seat until he got close to the front of it. Holding his breath, and keeping a firm grip with one hand, he turned himself around, looking only at the commode tank, never looking down into the water.

He still didn't have the courage to look into the water again.

As he slid off the seat, he scraped his penis on the wood, but the feeling was not unpleasant. It felt almost good.

Then he was sliding down, and his feet suddenly touched the floor. He kept his grip on the toilet seat, steadied himself and looked toward the door of the bathroom.

There was no one in sight. He could hear the TV set

in the other room, and he knew that Edna would be in there.

He looked down at himself. His penis jutted out now, and he reached for it with his free hand. The pleasant burning sensation increased, and he could feel the pressure building up in his bladder.

He strained, his face growing red, but nothing happened.

Then he relaxed, touched himself gently, and the yellow urine began spraying out in a powerful stream, hosing the walls, the floor, the toilet, the bathtub.

That was when Edna came into the room.

He turned in both fear and surprise, losing his grip on the toilet and falling backward.

As he fell, the hot urine sprayed up into Edna's glaring face, and just before his head hit the toilet bowl he heard her loud scream of fury and disgust.

# 31

He was only momentarily stunned by the blow on the head, and when he looked up again he saw Edna standing over him, gawking at him with urine dripping from her face onto his body.

He tried to crawl away, but she reached down for him and grabbed him by both arms, hauling him up into the air to dangle in front of her face.

"You worthless little turd," she said. "You stinking little piece of garbage."

She raised him above her head and seemed about to hurl him to the floor, but she changed her mind and put him down almost gently instead. She walked over to the sink, ran some water, and splashed it on her face.

The boy tried to crawl past her and make his escape out the door while she was rinsing her face, but her huge leg lashed out almost casually, with surprising speed, and kicked him back against the tub, where his head hit with a clonging noise.

When Edna had finished rinsing to her satisfaction, which did not take long, she dried her face and then looked at the boy.

The scar was horribly red, which was surprising in a way, since Edna was otherwise icily calm.

"Fucking piece of garbage," she said. She walked out the bathroom door and slammed it behind her.

There was nothing the boy could do. He sat there, his naked back against the cold side of the tub, waiting for her to return.

He should have been afraid, but for some reason he was not. He felt instead a kind of powerful satisfaction, something he had never felt before. For the first time, he had succeeded in getting back at Edna for all the things she had done to him.

He remembered the good feeling, the feeling of release, that had come over him as the urine spurted out.

He remembered Edna's look of horror as it struck her in the face.

Then he did something that was rare in his experience. It was something that Edna and Carl had hardly ever seen him do.

He smiled.

He stopped smiling, however, when he heard Edna at the door. He knew that she was not going to let him off lightly this time.

As if she ever did.

The door opened, and the boy's eyes went directly to the scar, which was why he did not see the knife in Edna's right hand or the piece of bread in her other hand.

The scar was redder than he had ever seen it. If the room had been dark, the scar might have glowed.

Edna saw where he was looking and waggled the knife around. "Look here, you piece of filth," she said. "You see what I got here in my hand? You know what this is?"

He didn't exactly know. He wasn't familiar with knives, so he just looked at her.

"It's a goddamn butcher knife," she said, holding it close to his face. "I guess you don't know what that means, either. Well, I'm gonna show you what it means."

She put the piece of bread down on the floor by his feet. "Look at that," she said.

It was hard for him to take his eyes off her face, but he did. He looked at the piece of bread.

The knife flashed through the air, the thin ray of sunlight glinting on its blade, and whacked into the floor, slicing the bread in two.

The boy jumped. Now he knew what the knife was. He tried to drop down and crawl away, but Edna grabbed him by the shoulder and sat him up, pushing him against the tub.

She held him there with the pressure from her forearm, and at the same time she took hold of his penis.

"I'm gonna cut it off," she said, bringing the knife to rest at its base and putting a light pressure on it.

The boy could feel his scrotum tightening.

"Then," Edna said, "I'm gonna throw it in the toilet and flush it down the sewer."

The boy started crying silently again. He believed her. Through his tears he could see the scar burning ferociously on her face, a blood-red streak, thick and wormy.

Edna pulled his penis out as far as she could and sawed on it lightly with the knife. A thin line of blood broke through the skin.

"Jesus Christ," Carl said from the doorway. He had just come in from his new job. "What in the hell are you doin' to the kid, Edna?"

"Cuttin' his dick off," Edna said. "He pissed all over me. All over the room, too."

Carl walked over and grabbed her arm, pulling it up and away from the boy's penis. "Holy shit, Edna. You

**213**

can't do that." There was real fear in his voice. "If anybody found out about it, they'd put us both so far back in the jail, they'd have to pipe in the daylight."

"He pissed on me," Edna said, but she was getting control of herself. She knew that Carl was right. The scar began to lose a bit of its color, and she relaxed the pressure on the boy.

As soon as she did, he crawled away, moving faster than anyone would have thought he could. He crawled into their bedroom and under the bed, where he lay in the darkness for hours.

No one made any effort to find him.

He could hear his parents talking in the living room, though he didn't understand what they were talking about.

"You got to watch that temper of yours, Edna," Carl said. "It's gonna get you in trouble. Me, too, since it's my kid you're messin' with."

"He pissed on me. Goddamn it, he pissed on me."

"Maybe it was an accident," Carl said. "It coulda been an accident."

"I don't care if it was. He looked like he enjoyed it."

Carl could understand that, though he would never have admitted it to Edna. Hell, there were times when *he* would've liked to piss on her. And the way she treated the kid, it was no wonder the little guy had taken a shot. It was about the only way he had of getting back at her. Carl had tried to stop her when she abused him, but she would never listen to him. It seemed like she thought the kid was indestructible.

Or maybe she just didn't care.

"I don't know," Carl said, "but it seems like you just got a mad on about the kid. Like you wanted to hurt him or something."

"Why don't you shut up?" Edna said. "You got to show the little fuckers who's the boss."

**214**

"Yeah, but you don't have to try to *kill* him."

"I wasn't gonna kill him. I was just gonna teach him a lesson."

"Teach him a lesson?" Even Carl was horrified. "You were gonna cut his *dick* off, for God's sake."

"We'd be better off if you didn't have one, that's for sure," Edna said. "Then we wouldn't have that little turd on our hands."

"He ain't a turd," Carl said. "He's just a kid. You can't expect a kid to know how to behave. You gotta teach him."

"That's what I was tryin' to do."

Carl could hardly believe what he was hearing. He was not especially sensitive, but at least he was human.

"Come on, Edna," he said. "There's a difference in teachin' somebody and in cuttin' his dick off. It's gettin' so I'm scared to leave you here with the kid."

"Maybe you want to stay here and take care of him, then, if you think it's so easy."

"I've gotta do my job," Carl said. "We gotta have money from somewhere."

"Yeah. You do your job. And I'll be the one taking care of the little turd. The way *I* want to do it."

That was enough for Carl. He had argued with Edna more than he usually did, and any more would just be asking for trouble. Carl sure as hell didn't want *his* dick cut off.

And Edna was just the one to do it.

**215**

# 32

About a year later the boy started walking.

No one saw him take his first shaky steps; no one ever saw him fall. One day he was crawling, the next he was walking. He had practiced, of course, but not where anyone could see him. He didn't want any help. He didn't want Edna to put her hands on him.

She had not threatened him with the knife again, but she had put him on the toilet and threatened him with the sewer.

He had become toilet trained very quickly. The pleasure he found in simple bodily processes, he concealed from everyone. All of the pleasures were somehow associated with the sight of Edna's surprised and disgusted face, but he concealed that even from himself.

Soon after he started walking, he began to talk.

As with the walking, no one heard his first stammering attempts. No one heard him lisp childish distortions of words. When he started, he started talking in complete sentences.

But he talked only when he felt it was absolutely necessary. He was not interested in trivial conversation, and since the only one he had to converse with was Edna, he was generally not interested in conversation at all.

That was another of his problems—the lack of contact with other children. He was kept in the house all day, summer and winter, spring and fall. His range of experience was extremely limited.

Edna never really thought about that part of his life. If she had, she would no doubt have let him roam the neighborhood unattended; but she simply never considered him as needing any kind of play or social contact beyond his own living room.

He had a lot of time to himself, a lot of time to think.

He thought mostly about Edna. She was his god and his devil, and there was not much difference between the two.

As a god, her business was punishment and vengeance.

As a devil, it was just about the same.

He did not look for a deliverer to come. Carl was as close as he had, and Carl was mostly ineffectual. At only a little more than the age of three, the boy had made his decision.

He would be his own deliverer.

He didn't want to kill Edna. He knew about killing now. He had smashed enough roaches, which were plentiful in the house, to know about death. But death was not what he had in mind. In some way, one that even he probably did not recognize, he still thought of her as his mother. There was still some kind of inexplicable attachment between them, an attachment so deep that neither one of them might have known it existed.

But it was there, just the same. So he didn't want to kill her.

He just wanted to get rid of the mark.

The mark, the mark the color of blood, had come to represent to him all her anger, all her violence, all the threats.

He watched it all the time.

When she was sitting on the couch, eating potato chips out of the bowl, watching TV as she did all day, he would sit silently in a corner of the room, his eyes fixed on the mark.

From a distance it was almost invisible. He sometimes even imagined that it was gone. Those were happy times, for if the mark were gone, then he would be safe. No more screaming, no more hitting.

Then she would catch him watching her. Her eyes would glare at him from her doughy face and she would rise off the couch like a land leviathan, coming toward him slowly and with deadly intent.

The mark would be glowing like hot coals.

He no longer tried to run from her. In some terrible way, he had actually begun to look forward to the punishment, almost to enjoy his suffering at her hands.

"What're you lookin' at, you little shit? What're you starin' at, sittin' there in the corner, you bastard?"

Then the hitting would begin.

Sometimes Carl would notice the bruises, but more often than not he didn't even see them. It was getting harder and harder for Carl to get work now, and he had more problems to worry about than what Edna was doing to the kid. Edna was constantly complaining that he was no longer a good provider.

Even if Carl saw the bruises, he didn't say much. Edna would just tell him that the kid had fallen off a chair or had been running through the room and hit the wall. Her lies were not very convincing, but that didn't matter. Carl didn't require much convincing.

There was no help from Carl.

**219**

Sometimes the boy would even look at the mark late at night, when Edna was asleep.

He slept in a bed in his own room. The mattress was old and lumpy and the springs were nothing to speak of, but he liked it. He liked being alone in the night.

He went to bed when he felt like it, often sleeping in his clothes. Edna didn't care.

Then, after the others were long in bed, he would come creeping out and go into their room. They slept in an old double bed that was in as bad shape as his own, except that the mattress sagged even more, especially down toward Edna.

Edna snored, so the boy always knew when it was safe for him to go in. She snored like a hog snuffling around in its sty, more of a snort than a snore, and the boy wondered why. He didn't think he could sleep if he made a noise like that, and he wondered how Carl could sleep with it in the same room.

The boy would stand by the bed and look at her, her face distorted in sleep, her mouth open and closing as she snorted and snored.

He was not interested in her mouth or in most of her face, of course. He was interested in the mark.

Sometimes he thought he could see it glowing, red and hot. Once he started to touch it, but he drew back his hand. He had burned his hand on the stove once, and he thought that this might be a very similar experience. He didn't want to be burned again.

So he only looked, thinking of other things he would like to do.

One of those things was closely connected with the butcher knife. He had never forgotten the lesson Edna had taught him in the bathroom, the way the knife had flashed through the air, catching the ray of sun on its way down, and separated the slice of bread so cleanly.

**220**

He had wondered even then, though he had not consciously realized it, whether the blade would separate the scar from Edna's face.

And he wondered what would happen if it did.

That was the part that scared him.

He imagined himself holding the knife in his hand, and he imagined making the cut—swiftly, silently, without remorse.

But then he imagined the scar falling from Edna's face. He could see it hitting the bed and wriggling there like some eyeless worm, blindly looking for whoever had struck it off.

He imagined it flopping to the floor and humping itself toward him like a sightless snake as he fled the room, still clutching the knife.

If it caught him, it would get on him. It would become a part of him, sticking to him forever, taking its life from his own.

He didn't think any of that was really possible, but nevertheless it scared him.

That was why it was quite a long time before he actually did anything and he might never have done anything at all if Edna had not driven him to it.

It was another trivial incident that started things, nothing at all really, at least as far as the boy was concerned, but still magnified by Edna to the proportions of a world war.

She was watching TV, as always, and he was in his own room. Now that he was older, he spent most of his time there. No one ever bothered him, and he could do whatever he wanted to do.

What he was doing this time was playing with his penis.

He had liked to do that ever since his experience with spraying Edna in the face, and though he knew that

221

Edna, and even Carl, would not have liked his doing it, he did it anyway.

He liked to stroke it, make it come erect, which it did easily. He had never gotten to urinate on Edna again, but he liked to think about it as he stroked himself. It made him feel warm inside.

This time, however, Edna caught him.

He hadn't heard her get up from the couch, though she usually made enough noise for anyone to hear, as much noise as an elephant getting up from a roll in the dirt, with a lot of grunting and sighing.

She had probably made that much noise this time, too. He had just been too involved with himself to hear her.

"You filthy little shit," Edna said.

He looked up to see her standing in his doorway, taking up the entire space, her wide bulk stretching from one side to the other. If she got any bigger, she would have to turn sideways to get through.

"You stinking pervert," Edna said.

He didn't know what a pervert was, but he knew it couldn't be good, not if he was one.

"Look at you," she said, her scar growing red. "Can't even let it go when somebody's caught you at it."

He looked down and saw that he was still gripping his penis in his hand. He gave it one last squeeze and let go of it. It was getting limp, anyway.

Edna shouldered her way into the room, looking down at him disdainfully. She reached out her fat hand and grabbed him by the shoulder.

"I'm gonna show you what we do to perverts," she said, slamming him against the wall.

The shock went through his body. She had hit him plenty of times, but this time she really seemed to mean it. She slammed him against the wall again.

Then she grabbed his penis.

"You like to handle it?" she said. "Well, how does this feel?"

She almost ripped it off his body. He tried never to let her hear a response from him, but this time he could not help himself.

He screamed.

"That's right," she said. "Hurts, don't it?" She jerked it again, even harder.

He screamed again.

"Don't worry," she said. "I can't pull it off. But I'm gonna make it so you can't ever use it again." She laughed. "That'll serve you right, you little turd. You'll never use this thing on a woman to let another little turd into the world."

She was squeezing him intolerably, getting ready to give a really tremendous pull. He did the only thing he thought might save him. He sank his teeth into her hand, trying to bite through and make them meet.

He did not quite succeed, but he did well enough to get Edna's hand off him. She yelled, jerked back and put her hand to her mouth.

"Bastard!" she said, to no one there. The boy had already scooted around her and out the door. He was in pain, but he could still run.

He rarely went into the yard, but he did now, running across the street and into a stand of bushes on a vacant lot. He hid there, not making a movement or a sound.

Edna sucked on her hand, cursed the boy and then searched the house for him. When she couldn't find him, she went outside and stood on the porch. She didn't bother to get off the porch, however. She knew that if he was out there anywhere, he could easily outrun her. She wasn't much good at running.

**223**

The boy watched her from the bushes, his black eyes not missing a movement.

She put her hand to her mouth and sucked it. He hoped the bite was painful, but it was not nearly painful enough to make up for what she had done to him.

This time, she was going to pay. After all, what had he been doing? Nothing to hurt her. If she had left him alone, everything would have been fine. If she had left him alone, how would she have been bothered by what he was doing?

After a minute or two, Edna went back into the house. If the little filth had run away, it was good riddance. She was for damn sure not going to look for him. Maybe he would get hit by a car. As far as she was concerned, that was the best thing that could possibly happen. Then she wouldn't be bothered by him again.

She thought about what she had caught him doing. Pulling his pud, for God's sake. He was just a kid. She didn't know kids that age were interested in that sort of thing, and it just went to show that she was right. He was some kind of pervert. If he got killed in the street, she was well rid of him. He wouldn't be pulling on his dick in *her* house anymore.

It was hard to make Carl see it that way when he came home. He had been out all day looking for work and hadn't found any. He was tired and depressed.

"Jesus, he was just curious about himself," he said. "You didn't hurt him, did you?" He was afraid that he already knew the answer.

"No," Edna lied. "I didn't. But I told him he better not do it anymore. I guess he didn't like that. He ran right out of the house and down the street."

"Did you go look for him?"

"Of course I did. What do you think I am? I couldn't find him, though. You know how kids are. If they don't want you to find 'em, you can't, and that's that." Edna was secretly disappointed. She had listened carefully to the five o'clock news on TV, hoping to hear of a child killed in an accident, but there had been no such report.

"Anyway," Edna said, "he'll be back. Soon as he gets hungry, you can bet he'll beat a path right back here. He knows where the food is."

Carl thought about that. The usual supper was frozen dinners heated up in the stove for him and Edna and a peanut butter sandwich for the kid. He could get something that good nearly anywhere.

"What if he don't come back?" Carl said.

"If he don't, he don't." Edna, of course, hoped that was exactly what would happen.

"If he's not back by tomorrow, I'm gonna call the police," Carl said.

"You do that," Edna said. She wasn't worried about that. She didn't think the cops could find Godzilla if he was walking through downtown. Not unless he was smoking a joint. *Then* they'd probably bust him.

The boy had no intention of going far enough away for the police to be called, however. He never left the bushes across the street, not until that night.

Then he went back home.

# 33

He waited until well after dark. It was uncomfortable sitting on the hard ground, and the bushes were full of insects that kept crawling on him and stinging him, but he ignored all that. He wasn't going back until he was sure that Carl and Edna were asleep.

It was easy for Edna. She just popped in the frozen dinners and watched TV, then went to bed and slept the sleep of the righteous. As far as she was concerned, if the kid was gone, he was gone. She didn't even think about him again.

Carl was different. He knew that the boy had been a lot of trouble to them, especially to Edna, but Carl still worried about him. He was just a little guy, and there were lots of different things that could happen to him out there.

Unlike Edna, Carl wasn't worried about accidents so much as about the kind of people who preyed on children. He'd heard about the chicken hawks who sold kids to horny old men who couldn't get it up for grown women, or for grown men, depending on their tastes. He hoped no one like that got hold of the boy.

227

He didn't go out and look for him, however. Edna wouldn't have that.

"He's big enough to take care of himself," she said. "If he's big enough to play with himself, he's big enough to look out for himself. You stay here where you belong."

"He might be in trouble," Carl said.

"Not as much trouble as he's gonna be in with me when he comes back here."

Carl was offended. "You ought not to talk like that, Edna. The boy ought to feel like he can come back to his home anytime he wants to."

"I didn't say he couldn't come back. I just said he was gonna be in trouble. What's the matter with you, Carl? You think we oughta let him pull on his pud all the time?"

"It wasn't all the time. It was just the once."

Edna snorted. "Just the once that we know about. I bet he does it all the time, hanging out in that room of his. Never even watches TV."

Carl didn't say that the boy didn't watch TV because Edna wouldn't let him. He didn't see any need in getting into a different argument from the one they were already having.

He decided that he would just let it go until morning. But if the boy wasn't back by then, Carl was going to do something about it.

**The boy waited** until long after the lights had all been turned off in the house. Then he stood up and stretched, scratching the places the insects had bitten.

It was quite dark. There was a streetlight on the corner, but it had either burned out or been broken long ago and never replaced. The moon was out, but it was obscured by clouds.

The boy was not afraid of the darkness. He thought

of it as his friend. He heard a dog bark somewhere and wished for a minute that he had been allowed to have a pet. Edna didn't like animals, however, so there was no dog or cat or anything else.

He walked cautiously across the street and stood in front of his house. There was no one moving around inside, and he stepped up on the porch and opened the door. Carl never bothered to lock it. Everyone knew that there was nothing worth stealing in a house like that.

The boy walked silently through the front room and into the kitchen. He had no trouble avoiding the few pieces of furniture.

He had a bit more trouble in the kitchen. He wasn't familiar with the drawers in the cabinet, though he thought he knew where to find what he was looking for.

He could hear Edna snoring in the bedroom. He hoped he wouldn't wake her up.

The silverware jingled under his hand as he searched one of the drawers. It was not much of a noise, but he stood frozen for a moment, waiting for Edna to come charging through the door and squash him like a roach.

The snoring was interrupted by a brief grunt, but then it resumed. The boy, even more carefully now, ran his hand over the cutlery.

Moving aside a pair of heavy scissors, his fingers closed on the wooden handle of the butcher knife. The wooden handle was smooth, and it seemed to fit his hand as if he had been holding it forever.

He pulled the knife out of the drawer and held it in front of his face. Even in the darkness the blade seemed to glitter with a light of its own.

The boy smiled.

Without bothering to close the drawer, he started toward the bedroom.

**229**

**Edna was having** a dream. She was young (as she had once been) and svelte (as she had never been), walking down the street and attracting admiring glances from all the men she passed. None of the men looked like Carl. Most of them looked like Tom Selleck, though a few looked like Paul Newman, only taller.

One of the men whistled at her, and she turned her head to look in his direction. The man smiled knowingly, arching one eyebrow.

Edna smiled back, letting him know that she was ready if he was.

He started following her down the street.

**The moon had** come out from behind the clouds, and the boy saw Edna turn over. There was a smile on her face, and he realized that he had hardly ever seen her smile. He could not remember the last time.

In the faint light, the mark on her face was easy to see. It was not as vivid as it usually was, but the boy knew why.

It knew about the knife in his hand.

It was trying not to call attention to itself.

But it was there. There was no way it could hide from the boy. It was there and it was red, suffused with blood. It might not look red, but it was. He knew it was.

He was standing very close to the bed, almost holding his breath as he watched Edna and Carl sleep. He had stood there before, but he had never felt quite so good as he did now, with the knife in his hand. The knife gave him confidence. He was about to attack his problems at the source.

There was only one thing wrong with the scene, as far as he was concerned. He wanted Edna to know what he was about to do.

It would be stupid to warn her, and the boy was not

stupid. He was not going to say anything, but it would have been nice to have her know, to have her see him there, see the knife as it flashed down toward her face.

It would have been even more pleasant to hear her beg him not to do what he was about to do. He knew that she should be grateful to him, but he also knew that she would not be.

He was going to do her a favor by removing the mark from her face, but she wouldn't see it that way. She would think he was trying to hurt her.

Well, he was. At least, he hoped he was. But at the same time, he was definitely doing her a favor. She would look a lot better without the terrible mark on her face.

He was doing himself a favor, too, of course. In some way, he had come to connect the scar with her feelings toward him, and he even believed that if the scar were gone she might change. Things would be better if she changed. He knew that.

But she wouldn't understand his point of view. She would want the mark to stay, and he would have liked to hear her beg him to leave it.

He would have liked to hear her say, "Please."

She had never said that to him. It would have been nice to hear it once, at least.

After the mark was gone, then he would hear it. She would be nicer to him then, and everything would be different.

If the mark didn't get him first.

He had thought about that, though, and if the thing came for him after he cut it off her face, he would just stand his ground and use the knife on it, chop it into two pieces the way Edna had chopped the bread.

He knew he could do it, if he just didn't run.

But first he had to cut the thing off her face.

He raised the knife.

**231**

**Edna looked back** over her shoulder in her dream. Sure enough, the man was following her, just as she had thought he would.

How could he resist, after all? She had the best ass in town.

The man caught up with her before she got to the corner. He put his hand under her elbow to stop her.

"Hey, babe, where you goin' in such a hurry?" he said.

Not only did he look like Tom Selleck, he sounded like him. Edna was so happy that she could hardly stand it.

"I'm not in a hurry," she said. In the dream she did not sound like herself. She sounded a little like Meryl Streep sounded in *Kramer vs. Kramer*. In fact, she looked a little like Meryl—classy, poised. Svelte. Very svelte.

"Got some time for me?" the man said.

"Depends on what you have in mind," she said, looking at him from under lowered eyelids.

"Why don't you come with me and find out, babe?"

Edna didn't want to be too eager, but she knew she was going with him. She knew what he had in mind, and she wanted it just as much as he did.

She was so happy that she started to laugh.

Then the laugh turned into a scream.

**The boy didn't** hesitate, not after he made up his mind.

The knife went up, then came down as hard and as fast as he could bring it, right toward the mark.

Things did not work out as he had hoped, however.

The mark was not sliced cleanly from Edna's face as he had thought it would be. There was blood, a little, but not enough.

232

The mark was still there.

He remembered the time Edna had pulled out his penis and started sawing on it. Maybe that would work. He leaned all his weight on the knife and started sawing at the scar.

There was more blood, but Edna was screaming and making a commotion. She was thrashing around in the bed like a hippo in heat, her arms flailing and her big legs kicking the mattress.

The boy jumped back from the bed, but he did not run. He wasn't going anywhere until he saw what happened to the mark.

Carl came awake, sitting up and looking wildly around the room.

"What is it?" he yelled. "What's happening?"

He looked at Edna, who was also sitting up, her hand pressed to her face. Blood was oozing between her fingers.

"Somebody cut me!" she said. "Somebody cut me!"

Carl scrambled out of the bed and turned on the light. The boy was still there, still clutching the knife. Blood dripped off the blade and onto the floor.

"He tried to kill me!" Edna shrieked. "The little fucker tried to kill me."

"Did not," the boy said, but he said it so quietly that no one heard him.

Carl, who had never lost control of himself with the boy before, lost control at that moment. He swung a small fist hard at the boy's head.

The boy did not move. He could see the fist coming almost as if it were in slow motion, but he did not try to dodge it. In some strange way, he welcomed it.

He knew he deserved it. He had tried to do something good, for both himself and for Edna, and he had messed it up. Now he was going to get hit. That seemed only fair.

**233**

Carl's fist connected, his knuckle opening a big cut on the boy's head over his eye. The boy went reeling backward, but he didn't lose his hold on the knife.

Carl followed the boy and hit him again, practically in the same place. It was as if all Carl's frustrations were being released on the boy, all his frustrations with Edna, all his frustrations with job hunting—everything. It felt good to hit the boy. It felt right.

He hit him again.

Edna was out of the bed by then. She was waddling across the room with her hand still pressed to her face.

She wasn't going to let Carl have all the fun. After all, she was the one the boy had tried to kill.

"Get outta the way," she told Carl.

Carl didn't appear to hear her. He drew back his fist to hit the boy one more time.

"I said to get outta the way," Edna told him, grabbing his arm and jerking him back.

Carl watched her move by him. He shook his head to clear it of whatever it was that had come over him.

"Wait," he said.

Edna wasn't waiting for anything. She was going to take care of the little turd this time for good and all.

The boy watched her coming. He felt strangely calm, despite what he saw on her face.

The mark seemed to grow as she came at him, feeding on the blood that still trickled from it. It was redder than ever, filling itself with the blood as it dropped down to cover Edna's chin, as it grew from side to side to cover her cheeks. As it climbed above her eyes to mask them. As it grew over her forehead and into her hair.

She was going to kill him. He knew that, even if Edna didn't.

He couldn't let that happen.

Just as she got to him, he extended his arm, plunging the knife into her huge belly.

Edna stopped for a moment, puzzled. There was a strange burning in her stomach.

Then she looked down. The boy had let go of the knife handle this time, and Edna could see the smooth wood extending from her stomach. She reached for it with both hands.

The boy watched. The mark had covered her face completely now and had run down her neck and into her nightgown. He was sure it was going to take over her entire body. He had tried to save her, but it was too late.

She got her hands on the knife and pulled it out. Her mouth opened in a silent scream, and then she fell at the boy's feet.

Maybe, he thought, he hadn't been too late after all.

# 34

Edna didn't die.

She had plenty of padding in front of her vitals, and the boy really didn't have the strength to force the blade in to its hilt. Carl called 911 from a pay phone, and the paramedics got to the house within five minutes. Edna didn't even lose very much blood.

In the five minutes that it took for the paramedics to arrive, Carl cooked up a story. It wasn't a particularly good story, but the paramedics didn't care. They had dealt with a lot of things weirder than a woman with a butcher knife in her belly that she supposedly put there herself.

That was, in fact, Carl's story. He told them that he and Edna had heard a noise in the house and that he had gotten out of bed to investigate, thinking that it might be a prowler.

"You never know when one of them dopeheads will come after whatever you got," Carl said.

One of the paramedics, a skinny woman with glasses that made her look like an owl, glanced around the room where Edna was lying. There was nothing there that anyone could sell for more than a dollar. The woman didn't say anything. It wasn't any of her business.

Edna had gotten out of bed, too, Carl said, and realizing that there were no weapons in the house, she had gone into the kitchen for the knife.

There had been no prowler, of course.

"It was just the boy, gettin' up to use the bathroom. He musta tripped over a chair or somethin'," Carl said. "Cut his head open."

The boy nodded in agreement. He knew when to go along with a story. He had to have five stitches in his forehead, but that didn't bother him. He hardly even felt them.

He was still stunned at what had happened to him. Carl had hit him, and his head still rang with the blows. Edna's mark was still where it had always been.

Edna didn't say anything. She was still in shock, though she would recover quickly. She was taken to the hospital merely as a precaution. She came back the next day.

By then, the boy was gone.

**Edna didn't ask** where he was for several days. She just sat in her usual place on the couch and ate chips, one bag after the other. She didn't even talk to Carl.

Finally, one evening during a commercial, she said, "You can't keep the little turd hid out from me forever. I'm gonna get him. Sooner or later he's gonna have to come out."

"He ain't hidin'," Carl told her. "You won't have to worry about him anymore."

Edna perked up, showing more of a spark than she had since returning from the hospital.

"You mean you got rid of him yourself?" she said. "I got to admit, I didn't think you had it in you."

"That's right," Carl said. "I got rid of him myself."

"I won't let on to anybody," Edna said, thinking that Carl had no doubt killed the kid and buried him in the backyard. "You can trust me, honey."

"I know it," Carl said, thinking that he could trust her like a bird with a broken wing could trust a hungry cat. That was why he hadn't told her the whole truth, which was that he hadn't done anything to the boy at all, or at least he hadn't done anything physically harmful. There were other ways to get rid of someone.

He had talked it over with the boy. "You can see why I got to do it, can't you?" he said.

The boy nodded. It sounded fine to him. He didn't want to stay there any longer than he had to. He didn't want to be there when Edna got back from the hospital. She would still have the mark, and the mark was going to get him if he was still there. He was sure of that.

"You can live with my sister up in Marshall," Carl said. "I talked to her on the phone, and she said she'd like that. She don't have any kids of her own, and she's always wanted one."

Carl was telling the truth to the boy, though he'd been forced to lie a little bit to his sister. He'd told her that he had been in an accident and was going to be out of work for a long time. He had no insurance, and the accident had been entirely his own fault. So he had to do something about his son, and he'd thought of his sister at once.

"He's a real good boy," Carl told her. "Quiet. But real smart. He won't be a bit of trouble to you."

His sister was easily persuaded, and Carl took the boy to the bus station. It took just about every penny Carl had to pay for the call on the pay phone and to buy the boy's ticket out of town at the bus station that night.

"You know you won't be hearin' from me again," Carl told the boy. "You can see why it has to be that way."

**239**

The boy could see. It didn't bother him much. He was glad to be getting away from Edna, from the horrible mark on her face. He didn't want to be with Carl anymore, either. Carl had hit him just the way Edna did.

When he got on the bus, the boy didn't even look back.

Carl knew that he wouldn't be hearing from his sister about the boy. They had never been very close, and she had always been possessive. She would be thinking the boy was hers within a week or two. She might consider writing Carl, but she never would get around to it. And since Carl didn't have a phone, she wouldn't be calling.

He hoped the boy would be all right.

**The boy was** fine.

He didn't miss Edna, and he didn't miss Carl. He didn't particularly like his aunt, but she had a much nicer house than the one he was used to, she fed him well, and she let him go outside whenever he wanted to.

For her part, the aunt was delighted with him. He never bothered her, was unfailingly polite and never asked for anything. It was almost like having a pet, only better. It was a little expensive, but nothing that she couldn't handle. Her husband had died suddenly of cancer a few years earlier, and he had been a big believer in life insurance. Money was no problem.

So the boy grew older, went to school, worked hard and did well. He even came out of his shell a bit, made friends, played with the other children and seemed to be perfectly adjusted to his world.

To look at him, no one would have known that he was anything but normal, and in most ways he was.

His past, most of it, was forgotten by his conscious mind, and he got along fine, just fine.

Until that night many years later when he saw Ellen Forsch, saw the blood marks on her face.

After that, he was never just fine again.

# PART THREE

# TROPICAL

# DEPRESSION

# 35

It was almost the end of August and no one had called Casey Buckner about a teaching job. She understood that for financial reasons it was impossible to offer a job to a part-time teacher until after the students had registered and the classes had been filled, but that understanding did nothing to make her feel better about her chances.

She told the group around the pool her problem, but they dismissed her worries.

"You won't have any trouble at all," Rob Hensley said. "You're just the kind of person these community colleges are looking for. You have all the qualifications, you have the right degrees, and most of all, you're desperate for a job."

"Not desperate," Casey said. "If I were desperate, I could always get a job delivering pizza."

"Hell, if you were desperate, I could give you a job at my place," Craig Warley said. "I can always use a woman."

The way he said the last sentence implied that he could use a woman for lots of things, many of them not

**243**

connected with business, and Tina jabbed him playfully in the ribs with her elbow. At least it was supposed to look like a playful jab. It seemed to jar Craig, and his eyes flared briefly.

Dan Romain leaned back in his chair. "I don't know why anyone would want a job," he said. "I wish someone else had mine." He was more tired than ever of dealing with the psychology of killers, and he was beginning to worry about himself even more than previously. He had even gone so far as to inquire about the price of office space in a couple of the better areas of the city. Private practice was looking better and better to him.

Casey wiped her face with a towel. It was blazingly hot and unbearably humid, so humid that you could get almost as wet sitting beside the pool as by getting in the water. She didn't feel like explaining that she needed the job as much as she wanted it. Or them. She was still hoping to get more than one.

"I just like to keep busy," she said. "I don't like the idea of being one of the idle rich."

"Maybe I can do something to help you," Rob Hensley said. "I might know one of the department chairmen. Which campuses did you say you were particularly interested in?"

She told him again.

"Well," he said, "I don't know anyone at any of those places, but I do know someone at the University of Houston. I'll call around, see what I can do."

"Thanks," Casey said. She would have preferred to get work on her own merits, but she realized the value of knowing people. It nearly always paid off; in fact, it was often better than a good résumé.

"Glad to do it," Rob said, smiling.

Casey smiled back. For just a second it was as if they were the only two people at the little table. She and Rob had gotten to know each other better and better in the last few weeks, and she was becoming convinced that he was just what he appeared to be—a very nice man, solid, the kind she might not mind getting involved with.

He also seemed to be quite sensitive, never pushing her but making her aware that he was as interested in her as she was in him. Maybe more interested.

It gave Casey a good feeling, and she had abandoned her idea of getting to know a lot of the other people in the apartment complex. She had met quite a few of them, but none of them seemed as attractive as Rob, and none of them proved on short acquaintance to be any more interesting then the Warleys or Dan Romain.

Maybe it was simply inertia, but the days had slid by and she had come to look forward to the afternoons at the pool, the light conversation, maybe a late meal cooked on the portable grill at Rob's apartment. It was an easy life.

At the same time, she didn't want to get used to it. She wanted to get a job, do something, feel useful. And of course to earn some money.

Margaret was getting ready for school to start, too. She told Casey that she was tired of watching TV all the time. She had even been reading some of Rob's books, and Casey was beginning to believe that there might be another English major in the house. Not that that was necessarily a good thing.

Margaret wanted to go to school for other reasons, too. She had made a couple of friends in the other apartments, but there was no one she really liked. She was hoping that she would find someone to be really close to in her school.

Casey hoped so as well. It would be nice for Margaret to have a real friend.

Casey would have liked to have one herself. She counted Rob and Dan and Craig as friends now, but

Tina was really the only woman she had met, and Tina didn't really seem to like her.

Casey thought that she knew why. Craig and Tina were always arguing, and Tina probably did not like the looks that Craig sometimes gave Casey.

The looks that bothered Casey were not Craig's, however. She was more disturbed by Dan Romain.

She couldn't quite figure him out. Lately she had more than once caught him looking at her covertly as they sat at the table near the pool. When he noticed her glance in his direction, he would quickly look away. There was nothing lustful in his look, as there probably would have been in Craig's if Casey had caught him staring at her. Romain was looking more thoughtful than anything. Casey didn't quite know what to make of it. He had seemed distracted for several days, maybe for a week or more.

The reason Romain was distracted was simple, though, of course, he still hadn't told anyone what his job really was, so no one knew how he spent his days. Howland was coming by his office more and more often, trying to get his opinions about the killer Howland was hunting. There wasn't much more that Romain could say that he hadn't already said, but Howland was getting more tenacious as his leads failed to turn up anything.

It had seemed like a real breakthrough to Howland when he had discovered the common link among the killings, and Romain had hated to disappoint him by pointing out that there was no way to do anything with that particular link. And according to Howland, the Chief hadn't received the news with any great enthusiasm. He'd just put the pressure on Howland to come up with something better.

That had left Howland with the license numbers, and the method of obtaining them was a little short of scientific. Romain was a firm believer in the power of

**246**

the unconscious mind, but even he had to admit that trusting in a dream for a license number was pushing the limits of psychological credibility.

But it was all Howland had, so he'd been painstakingly investigating every single person on the printout he'd gotten.

It was a slow and frustrating job. Sometimes the owners of the cars had sold them or traded them in on newer models by the time Howland got to them. The updated information had not yet reached the computer.

Most of the time, the owners Howland was able to meet were either able to provide airtight alibis for most, if not all, of the murder times or were patently not the type of person Howland was looking for.

Or so Howland thought. That was one of the things that Romain had discussed with him only recently.

"There *is* no type," was what Romain had told him when Howland used the word.

"Damn it, I know that," Howland said, waving his hand in front of his face. Romain didn't take the hint and kept on smoking. "But this guy was just a real wimp. Not over fifty-five. Probably less. Wore glasses. Scared of his fucking shadow. Had a house full of books, and a lot of them were poetry, for God's sake. Keats. Byron. People like you have to read in high school."

"Do you think a poet can't be a killer?" Romain said. "What about Jack the Ripper?"

Howland smiled. "I wouldn't call those notes to the police poetry, exactly."

"Maybe not," Romain said. "But the man you described may be just exactly the 'type' you're looking for."

"Impossible," Howland said. "Fucking impossible."

"Think about it. Small, ineffectual. Frightened. The kind of man that's been dominated all his life by people who are bigger, stronger, faster than he is."

247

"The world's not like that anymore," Howland said.

Romain laughed and almost choked on the smoke he had just inhaled.

"Those things are gonna kill you," Howland told him.

Romain stopped coughing and stubbed out the cigarette. "Maybe. But you shouldn't make me laugh like that. You might kill me first."

"I don't see what's so damn funny."

"You are, if you think the world's still not run by the strong. The weak can get by if they're intelligent. So can the rich. But the strong can always dominate them in a face-to-face confrontation."

"Not if the weak man has a gun."

"Or a knife. Or a club. Any weapon would do. That's what I've been trying to tell you."

Howland thought about it. "I think I get it. When he was young, he didn't have a weapon. He could have been dominated by anyone. And now that he's got a weapon, or a lot of them, he's not being dominated anymore."

"That's a possibility," Romain said. "Now he's taking it out on everyone who hurt him before."

"So you think it's some little guy with a complex?"

"I didn't say that. I said it *could* be someone like that. You can't rule anyone out. Not anyone."

"Damn," Howland said. "I guess I better talk to that little guy again. I didn't even press him very hard. I just knew he couldn't be the one I was looking for."

"He's probably not," Romain said. "But he very well could be. There just isn't a 'type' in something like this. It could be a poetry reader or an illiterate. It could be a dock worker or a hairdresser. If you let your preconceived notions about what kind of man could be your killer cloud your thinking, you're going to be in big trouble. You might talk to him for hours and never know that he's the right one."

"You think he could fool me like that?"

"You, or anyone. We've already determined that he's very clever. And that he may not even be aware of what he's doing. If that's the case, we could say he's fooling even himself."

"Damn," Howland said again. "You're not making this any easier."

"That's not my job," Romain said, feeling a slight headache coming on. Talking to Howland was beginning to affect him that way.

"I wish the Chief would give me a few more men," Howland said. "I'm never gonna get through that printout by myself."

"You'll get through it," Romain said. "You don't have any choice."

"Damn," Howland said.

# 36

As far as Howland was concerned the only good thing that had happened to him in a long time was Alma Remington. She wasn't the kind of woman he would ever have envisioned himself falling for, but he was pretty sure he was falling.

If he'd thought about it, which he didn't very much, he would have thought he'd be more likely to go for the *Playboy* bunny type—young, blond, innocent-looking, but smart, with long legs and big tits.

Alma certainly didn't fit that description, except maybe for the innocent part. Actually, she wasn't even innocent, as Howland had found out the third time he'd taken her out. They'd gone back to her apartment and started out by watching a little TV, and the next thing he knew he was on the rug getting his brains screwed out.

The funny part was, he wasn't sure just how he'd gotten there, whether it was his idea or Alma's. The only thing he was sure of was that he had rug burns on both knees, his shoulders, and his butt.

Alma probably did, too, but he sure wasn't going to ask her.

The only problem with his relationship with Alma was, now that he was involved with someone for the first time in a long, long time, he was probably in imminent danger of losing his job.

The Chief was not pleased with Howland's progress, and he had called him into his office to let him know.

"I had a reporter in here the other day," the Chief said. "From the *Post*."

The Chief was wearing a dark gray suit that had set him back about five hundred bucks, a white shirt, and a dove-colored tie. He knew how to dress. Howland had to give him that. Howland, on the other hand, was wearing his rumpled navy job from Men's Wearhouse, a wrinkled shirt, and a tie that had an unidentifiable stain on it. He felt at a disadvantage.

"He was asking me about a rumor he'd heard," the Chief went on. "Seems he'd heard there was a link among some killings here in town."

Howland tried to smile, but he didn't quite make it.

"I guess we both know what he was talking about, don't we?" the Chief said.

"I guess we do," Howland admitted.

"So what are you going to do about it?"

"I'm working on the license numbers," Howland said. "I could go a lot faster if I had some help."

"No help," the Chief said. "It's already getting out. I was able to convince the reporter that the rumor he'd heard had no basis in fact, and he admitted that he couldn't confirm it. So it won't get into print. This time. Do you take my meaning?"

Howland took it. "Yes, sir."

"Then get busy. You've got two weeks."

"Yes, sir," Howland said. There wasn't anything else he could have said.

**He was sitting** in his office looking over the printout, an updated version that he'd gotten only the day before.

Just looking at it made him feel like shit. He was never going to get to the end of it, and even if he did new names were being added all the time. He was working alphabetically, and as cars changed hands, new names got on the list, some above where he was working, some below.

He shook his head. It was hopeless, and he had a week. Might as well turn in his badge right now.

Of course that wasn't what would happen. He would simply be replaced, probably given some harmless desk job as punishment, something that would bore him to distraction before he reached retirement.

He started reading through the list. His only chance was to find something by hunch or intuition, something that would lead right to the killer.

He knew it wouldn't happen. It might work for some cop on TV, or some private eye in a book, but it wasn't going to work for him. Things just didn't happen that way in real life.

He had another thought. Why not do a rapid scan through the list? Maybe some name would jump out at him. Maybe some connection he hadn't thought about would suddenly become apparent.

He started looking, running his finger down the list, waiting for something to happen, though he didn't have much hope.

Then something caught his eye.

Interesting, he thought. He kept on scanning the list, and he found something that was even more interesting.

**253**

Goddamn. Maybe amazing breakthroughs *did* occur in real life.

He had never looked all the way through the list like that before or maybe he would have noticed it earlier.

Or maybe he wouldn't have.

It was probably just a coincidence that he had noticed it now.

And speaking of coincidences, that was probably all he was looking at. Nevertheless, it was something that he thought he should check out. He looked at his watch. It was after five. He wondered if Romain would still be in the office.

Probably not. A lot of the people who worked regular hours, like Romain, had left early because there was a tropical disturbance in the Gulf, and it was threatening to make landfall somewhere down the coast.

It wasn't going to come in at Galveston, but that wasn't necessarily good news. It was going in to the south, which meant that Houston would be on the "wet" side. There would be a lot of rain, and it would come in a short time. Houston, being built on flat ground, on what had at one time been practically a swamp, was not known for its efficient drainage. There was a very good possibility of flooding. In 1979 a tropical depression had dumped more than forty inches of rain on Alvin, a small town about twenty-five miles from Houston, in twenty-four hours. Now *that* was a flood.

Howland walked down the hall to Romain's office and knocked on the door. Sure enough, there was no one there.

A plainclothes cop Howland knew slightly passed by, and Howland asked him about the storm.

"Not supposed to hit till later this afternoon," the

man said. "Maybe not until tonight sometime. They still think it'll go south of us, though."

"Yeah," Howland said. He realized that no one really knew where the storm would go. The weathermen always talked in probabilities. Hell, the thing might come right over the city. But that would be all right, better, in fact than if it went south.

Fuck it. Howland couldn't let the storm worry him. If it came, it came. He didn't want to be out in it, but he would chance it if he had to. He called Alma before he left.

"I have to check something out," he said. "Something about our case."

Alma liked it that he called it "our" case. She liked to think that she was doing something to help.

"Does it have to do with my dream?" she said.

"Yeah," Howland said. He didn't like being reminded of the source of his information. It took away a little of the excitement that he had been feeling. A coincidence mixed with a dream was really pushing it.

"Be careful," Alma said. "Can you come by later?"

They had been spending a lot of time together during the few hours Howland allowed himself to relax from his investigation.

"I'll try to make it," Howland said. "What's your part of town like when it rains?"

"It never floods," Alma said. Then she added, "Well, not much. Besides, it's not supposed to rain until very late. Maybe not even until tomorrow. Maybe not at all."

"Don't wait up for me," Howland said. He didn't have any confidence in weather reports. He could imagine himself stranded at one of the exits on the loop or somewhere equally unpleasant.

"I might," Alma said. "You try to come by."

"I'll try," Howland promised.

**255**

**The traffic was** terrible as he tried to escape downtown. He wondered why it was that people seemed to crowd up like that when a disaster was in the air. All he had to do was go down Main to the loop, but it was going to take forever.

He had not been in the car for more than five minutes when things got even worse. Several blocks in front of him, a man parked at the curbside opened his car door and the car in the lane beside him never saw it. The driver kept right on going and hit the door, tearing it off the car.

That stopped the traffic flow completely. Everyone had to spend some time rubbernecking the free show, which got even better when the man who had lost his car door started to argue with the man who had hit it.

The argument grew in volume and intensity, and before Howland realized how serious things had gotten, the man with the damaged car had opened the door of the other car and dragged the driver out into the street, where he proceeded to punch him in the mouth. The second driver, not wasting any time, struck back, and in seconds the two men fell to the pavement, yelling obscenities and locked together in a hold that the World Wrestling Federation would never have recognized.

Howland really didn't have time for this kind of shit, but since traffic was stopped anyway he got out of his car and threaded his way through the tangled vehicles to the struggling men.

When he reached them, he tapped the top man on the shoulder. The man turned a fiery red face to him, and Howland showed him his badge.

"If you guys want to fight in this fucking heat, that's fine with me," Howland said. "But you're gonna get your asses hauled off to jail if you keep it up."

It took a second for his words to sink in, but when they did the two men got to their feet and began to brush off their clothes. Both looked sheepishly ashamed of themselves.

It took Howland a few minutes to get things organized so that the second vehicle could pull off the right-of-way. By then, horns were honking and people were beginning to get restless. The show was over; everyone was ready to go home.

Unfortunately, Howland couldn't leave. He went back to his own car and radioed for a patrolman, but even the patrolman's arrival wouldn't help. Howland was a witness to the whole thing, and he would have to stay around to make sure another fight didn't break out when the two men began describing what had happened, since he knew that neither of them would be willing to accept responsibility.

He wondered if he would ever get where he was going, though somehow his sense of urgency was lessened. The wreck was real, with real men striking real blows and rolling around on a real street. What he'd been thinking of earlier was mostly supposition and intuition, nothing solid.

What did it mean that Romain's personal car had turned up on the printout, and that another Ford at the same apartment address also happened to fit the pattern?

Probably not a damned thing.

Romain had seen the printout, though. Why hadn't he said something about the license plate letters being similar to his own?

Because he didn't know them, that was why. How many people knew their own license plate numbers? Howland didn't even know what the numbers on his own plate were.

Romain would still be at his apartment when

Howland got there, even if it took a while, which it certainly would. Howland had gathered that Romain didn't have much of a social life.

So what did that mean? Howland put the thought out of his mind. He had to deal with the immediate problem of the wreck.

The traffic snailed its way along. Howland moved his own car over to the curb behind the two cars that had been involved in the wreck and waited for the patrolman to arrive. He got out and wiped the sweat off his face.

He hoped it wouldn't be a long wait.

# 37

Casey's phone was ringing when she unlocked her apartment door. Margaret ran to answer it.

"Buckner residence," she said, sounding very adult to Casey.

Margaret listened for a second in silence, then handed the phone to her mother. "It's for you."

"Hello," Casey said.

"Casey Buckner?" said the deep voice at the other end of the line.

"Yes, this is she."

"Very good. This is Dr. Jeremy Fallon. I'm the department chair in Languages at GCCC."

Casey knew what the initials meant. Gulf Coast Community College. It was one of the schools to which she had applied.

"I understand that you're interested in a part-time teaching position," the voice went on.

"That's right," Casey said, trying to keep her voice from showing the excitement she was feeling.

"I've looked over your vita, and I think you're well

**259**

qualified to teach in my department. I wonder if you could come by for an interview."

"Of course," Casey said. "I'd be glad to. When would it be convenient?"

"Ah, there's the problem. You see, school starts in less than a week, and I've suddenly been caught short. One of my regular part-time instructors called earlier this afternoon to say that he'd gotten a full-time job on another campus, and I've got to fill the position quickly."

"I could come in tomorrow," Casey said.

"Ah . . . that might be too late. Is there any possibility that you could come in this evening?"

Casey glanced over at Margaret. She could ask Rob to sit with her, but she hated to do that at the last minute.

"I have a daughter," she began.

"That's no problem, I assure you. You could just bring her with you. The interview will be very informal, and quite brief. I know that your qualifications are excellent, and all I really have to do is meet you and explain how my department works and what you'd be doing in your classes. Let you look over the texts. That sort of thing."

It sounded to Casey as if the man had already made up his mind about hiring her.

"How many classes would I be teaching?" she said. "If you hired me, that is."

"Three. All composition classes."

Casey didn't care about the fact that she would be grading papers almost constantly. Three classes was more than she'd hoped to get at any one school, and if the salary was commensurate with the load, she might not even need to teach anywhere else.

"I can come this evening," she said. "What time?"

"I have a few things to clear up here in the office first. Would nine o'clock be too late?"

"That would be fine," Casey said. She'd have time to bathe, wash her hair and dress properly if she hurried. She'd stayed at the pool with Rob a little later than usual after the others had left, and it was already nearly seven.

"Excellent. Do you know where the campus is?"

Casey said that she knew. It was just off the Gulf Freeway on the way to Galveston, and she had seen it when she and Margaret had driven down to the island with Rob.

"Fine. We're all located in one big building. My office is room 449."

"I'll be there at nine," Casey said.

"Excellent. I'm sure you're just the person I'm looking for."

When she hung up, Casey turned to Margaret. "Looks like we've got a job, kid. And you can go to the interview with me."

"OK," Margaret said. "Does this mean we're rich?"

Casey laughed. "Not exactly."

But it did mean that she wasn't going to be so dependent on the Asshole any longer, and that felt good.

"I'll bathe first," she said. "Then I'll call Rob and tell him I've got a job."

That was fine with Margaret.

**He hung up** the telephone with satisfaction. He had done it. They would both be there, and he hadn't even had to suggest it himself. He could eliminate both of them and the terrible marks they bore at the same time.

It was perfect.

He wondered whether he should record his success

**261**

on his computer disk, but he knew that this was not the time. He could do it later.

Later, there would be more to record. Much more. The thought of what he would do to them made his blood run hot.

He reached up with his right hand and rubbed at the scar on his own forehead, feeling the ridged skin under his fingers. A frightening thought occurred to him, something that he should have thought of long before.

*I have the marks too.*

He rubbed furiously, scrubbing the skin as if he could make the mark go away, take it from him and make his forehead as smooth as if the mark had never been there.

It was no use. He could still feel it, no matter how hard he rubbed.

He went into the bathroom and looked in the mirror that hung above the sink. The mark stood out from his forehead in sharp relief, red and angry. It seemed as he looked at it to writhe like a worm under the skin.

He slapped at himself with the heel of his hand, trying to kill it, trying to make it go away.

Nothing helped. In fact, everything he did made the mark stand out more, made it twist more wrathfully than ever.

He had to make it stop.

He reached into his medicine cabinet and got out a package of double-edged razor blades.

He slid a blade out of the plastic dispenser and took it between the thumb and forefinger of his left hand. He pulled it the rest of the way out of the holder, watching in fascination as the light reflected from its smooth, slightly oily surface.

He raised the blade to his forehead, knowing what he had to do.

A quick slice right through the middle of the mark, to kill it. He couldn't afford to let it get away.

Then more slices, faster and faster, until he had cut the mark into an infinity of slices so thin that each one was practically invisible.

The mark would be gone then. It wouldn't come back.

Would it?

He couldn't be sure. The only way he could be sure was to kill himself, then cut the mark off, the way he had done with the women.

The women.

They were the ones on whom the marks were evil, not him.

Wasn't it possible that on him the marks were a sign that he was an exceptional person, the one designated to eliminate the evil blood marks from the iniquitous women of the world?

Yes, he thought. That was it. That had to be it.

On him, the mark was there to show his unique purpose.

On the women, the mark was there for him to see, there to let him know they were the ones who must be cleansed.

And he would cleanse them.

He had raised the blade to his forehead. One edge of it was poised less than a centimeter from the scar.

He lowered his hand, looking steadily at his reflection in the mirror. Already the red was fading from the mark. It was quiescent now, not moving at all.

In fact, it was hardly visible at all.

He flipped the plastic dispenser over and stuck the blade in the slot for used blades.

He noted that his hand was completely steady. That was good. He would need for it to be steady later on; he was going to use something very similar to a razor blade on the woman and the girl.

He had bought it at one of the many huge hardware stores that dotted the city. It was called a package-opening knife, but it was really just a slightly beefed-up razor blade in a handle. It was supposed to be used for slashing open cardboard cartons.

He was going to use it for slashing something else. He thought for a moment about how well the smooth handle fit his palm, and he could imagine how the blade would carve through the smooth skin of their throats, severing the arteries and causing the blood to pour out.

He had checked out the parking lot at GCCC the evening before. It was well lighted, but there was an area near the entrance to the building that was deep in shadow. He would catch them there, as they were coming in. It would be getting dark by nine, and the evening was heavily overcast. No one would be there to see.

It would be easy.

He would wear the new plastic raincoat he had bought. He would have to be careful not to get blood on himself.

He smiled at the thought.

**Rob hadn't been** as excited as Casey had thought he should be about her job prospect.

"I don't know anything about this Dr. Fallon," he said. "Why would he want to meet you so late?"

Casey explained about the urgent nature of the situation.

"He sounded desperate," she said. "I don't see how I can miss. And it's *three* classes."

Rob thought that sounded good, all right. "But I still don't like the idea of your going out there at nine o'clock all alone."

"I won't be alone. Margaret's going with me."

"Margaret?"

"She wants to see where I'll be working," Casey said, stretching the truth defensively.

"I suppose it's all right, then," Rob said. "Do you want me to come with you?"

"No," Casey said, a little too quickly. "I mean, it wouldn't look right for me to have some man come along for protection. I don't want Dr. Fallon to think I'm scared of him."

Rob didn't like it. He had visions of a dimly lighted parking lot and shadows that were pools of deeper darkness.

"It's going to rain," he said.

Casey laughed. "I won't melt. Tell you what. I'll give you a call when I get back, and you can come over and help me celebrate."

"Well . . ." Rob said. Casey was right. He was being overly protective. He didn't own her. "All right. We can have peanut butter sandwiches."

"Peanut butter it is," Casey said. "I'll call you about ten."

"About ten," Rob said.

When he hung up, he wondered what was the matter with him. It wasn't like him to worry about anyone. His philosophy was to let everyone live his or her own life without interference. What right did he have to interfere with Casey, anyhow?

None at all, and it was a bad sign that he wanted to. It was a sign that he was more serious about her than he had thought.

Sure, he knew that he liked Casey. A lot. And he knew that they enjoyed one another's company. He liked Margaret, too, and he didn't usually like children all that much.

Uh-oh, he thought. I might be about to get myself in real trouble here.

**265**

But when he thought about it, it didn't seem so bad. It didn't seem bad at all, in fact. Suddenly he wanted to see Casey very much. Margaret, too. He wished it were ten o'clock.

**Casey dressed in** what she thought was a casually professional outfit, dark skirt, gray blouse, midheel shoes.

Margaret was another matter. Margaret insisted on wearing a pair of jeans, sneakers and a T-shirt with a picture of one of the Teenage Mutant Ninja Turtles on it.

Casey didn't know which of the turtles it was, and she didn't much care. She just hoped Dr. Fallon had some understanding of children. Or that he at least didn't hate them.

"You ready?" she said.

"Ready," Margaret said. "But you better get the umbrella. It's started raining."

Casey looked out the window. Margaret was right. It was raining hard. She hoped the traffic wouldn't be too bad on the freeway. The rain always caused problems.

Well, it couldn't be helped. She got the umbrella.

"Let's go," she said, and she and Margaret, standing very close together, ran across the parking lot to the car.

# 38

**H**owland thought he was never going to get away from the accident site.

The large number of rubberneckers caused a continuing stalling of the traffic, and the slowdown resulted in hot tempers, honking horns and—this was the part Howland couldn't believe—another accident before the patrol car had even arrived to write up the first one.

He shouldn't have been surprised. When the Houston streets got wet at the rush hour, the wrecks piled up; it was inevitable.

An impatient woman, her head bobbing to the beat of the drive-time rock station she was tuned to, tried to weave her way through the traffic and made the mistake of cutting in front of a pickup driven by a man who had no intention of yielding. He crumpled her front fender, without much damage to his own vehicle, and the two of them successfully blocked both outward bound lanes of the street.

Traffic was piled up for blocks since there was no way around the pickup and the car, not with the cars involved in the first accident already pulled to the side.

The patrol car arrived in time to help Howland get the two newcomers out of the traffic flow, but it seemed to take forever to get the homeward bound drivers moving again. Then, with Howland's assistance, the patrolman had to begin sorting out the drivers' stories and decide on who should or should not get the tickets for the two accidents.

Then it started to rain.

That was all Howland needed. He gave his information to the officer and went back to his car. He leaned back against the hood and let the warm rain trickle down his shirt collar. Maybe he should just go on over to Alma's, let Romain wait until tomorrow. Shit, Romain was a cop, even if he was a pretty weird one. He wasn't the type—

Howland brought himself up short. Hadn't Romain himself told him that *anyone* could be the type?

And wasn't Romain the one who knew all about serial killers? The one who could even think like a serial killer?

Wasn't it a possibility that Romain could identify with such men so closely, that he could almost tell how they thought, because he was one of them himself?

Howland didn't like what he was thinking. The Chief would shit a brick if the killer turned out to be a member of the department, but considering some of the troubles that the department had lately experienced with its own members, nothing was out of the question.

Howland shook his head. He didn't know why he was thinking like that. Romain, of all people.

Still, why not?

Who would be in a better position to know how to avoid the police? Who would know more about exactly what to do to avoid leaving any trace of himself at the scene?

The more Howland thought about it, the more sense it made, and he felt the urgency rising in him.

He looked around. It had gotten quite dark, the thick clouds lowering the sky so that you could almost reach up and touch it. The rain-slicked streets reflected the lights of the crawling cars and the flasher of the patrol car.

Howland went over to the officer and asked if there was anything else he could do.

It was raining harder. The patrolman had put on his slicker, and the rain rolled off to spill on the street.

The tickets had been written and the motorists were almost ready to leave. Howland wasn't needed any longer. He got into his car, his wet clothing sticking to his back and legs, and worked his way carefully into the traffic.

He didn't want to have a wreck.

**Casey Buckner didn't** want to have a wreck, either. She didn't like driving on the Gulf Freeway at the best of times, but this was really awful. The rain had increased in intensity ever since she had left the loop, and now her wipers were clacking furiously but to little effect as the water washed over her windshield.

Coming toward her on the left was a constant stream of headlights. Her own headlights seemed to be absorbed by the rain-blackened pavement and to provide very little illumination at all. In front of her were three unbroken lines of red as the taillights of the other drivers stretched endlessly down the freeway. There were cars on either side and close behind her. The roadway was slick beneath her tires.

Her hands gripped the wheel desperately. She felt only seconds away from a rending crash. The only good thing was that everyone was driving safely, which on the Gulf Freeway meant that they were actually driving under fifty miles an hour. On a normal day, sixty was the minimum speed, no matter what the posted signs said.

"Where are all these people going?" Margaret said.

"I don't know," Casey said, and she didn't.

She had often wondered the same thing. She knew why she was there, but what possible reason could everyone else have? Why weren't they at home, watching TV and digesting their dinners? They couldn't be commuters, not at this hour, unless, of course, the rain had slowed them down. That was a possibility. But it didn't make any difference. The traffic was always thick on the Gulf Freeway, no matter what time of day it was.

Casey gritted her teeth and watched the exit signs. It was still at least ten miles to where she wanted to go, but she had left early because of the rain. She was still going to make it in plenty of time. She hoped that Dr. Fallon was really going to give her the job. After this ordeal, she certainly felt that she deserved it.

It seemed to be raining harder than ever now. She could hardly see the road, much less the other cars. She slowed down, hoping that no one would rear-end her car. She hoped she could see her exit sign when she came to it. She hoped it would never rain like this again.

**He waited in** the darkness, thinking how well things were working out. The rain was something that he had more or less expected, having heard the weather forecast, but it was even better than he had hoped.

The evening was darker than dark, and the lights in the parking lot were practically obscured by the rushing water.

Water spilled down from the roof of the building, swirled an inch deep over the sidewalk, ran into his shoes. He didn't mind at all.

**270**

In the parking lot it ran like a river. That part bothered him. He hoped that Casey wouldn't just sit in the car and worry about her shoes.

He didn't think she would. She needed the job too much; he'd heard her say so often enough as they sat by the pool in the afternoons.

In fact, he wondered what had taken him so long to get the idea, but now he realized that it was just as well that he had waited.

He had found two days before, with a phone call, that the college had just finished its summer session and that the fall semester would not begin until the next week. That meant that there would be no one on campus during the day except for the administrators and their secretaries. At night, there would be no one there except for whatever security force a two-building college might have.

It wasn't much.

He had checked it out the previous evening. There were two men, as best he could determine, neither of whom ever came around to the outside front of the building. He had stood there in the shadow for two hours and watched both the inside and the outside. He saw both the men pass once, on the inside. They never even looked his way, though they would not have seen him if they had.

They were not expecting anyone to be there, and the decorative shrubs along the side of the building were quite adequate to conceal him.

He was in fact worried about only two things, other than the water flowing through the parking lot.

One was the unfortunate fact that because the security officers parked elsewhere, there was only one car in the parking lot.

His own.

He didn't think Casey would recognize it. That

271

wasn't what bothered him. The problem was the fact that the parking lot was deserted except for that one car. It was enough to worry someone who had a bit of a suspicious nature.

There was also the fact that the building was not well lighted. Oh, there were lights on inside, but only those used for the minimum illumination required when no one was there. None of the office windows showed a light.

He hoped she would think that Dr. Fallon's office was on the other side, that Dr. Fallon at least was working late this evening, eager to replace the defecting part-timer.

He would take Casey first, taking her hair in his left hand, pulling her head back, exposing her slender neck, making one smooth stroke with the razor blade.

He imagined the look of surprise on her face.

He imagined the rain carrying the blood away, purifying her as she died.

Then he would do the girl, just as quickly.

Pull them into the shrubs, remove the blood marks.

Drive away into the rain.

He felt a tightening in his groin, a hardening, a thrusting.

*Not yet*, he told himself, resisting the impulse to reach down. *Soon now, but not yet.*

He smiled in the shadows as the dark rain rolled off the plastic coat and swirled away across the walk.

*Soon.*

He felt the razor-knife in his hand.

His smile grew broader as he waited for Casey's headlights to appear.

# 39

Howland cursed the rain.

It fell steadily and hard. It squished in his shoes, and he had to keep wiping it out of his face. His hair was plastered to his forehead, and his clothes were soaked. He wished that he'd brought a raincoat.

He was having trouble finding Romain's apartment. All the groupings looked the same to him, and he couldn't see the numbers because of the fucking rain. Even the entrance lights burning by most of the doors weren't much help. He couldn't even find the manager's apartment to ask about Romain's location.

He kept on looking.

When he finally located the right number, he walked up to the door and started beating on it. He didn't even look for the doorbell.

There was no response, but Howland didn't even mind at first. He was in a small entranceway out of the rain. The small shelter was worth a hell of a lot. He wouldn't mind standing there for a while.

He wondered where Romain was, though. Why would anyone be out on a night like this?

He thought about that for a minute, and his mind wandered down strange corridors. It would be a perfect night for a murder. Potential witnesses would be hurrying along, heads down. No one would see anything, and even if they did, they wouldn't stop, not in this downpour.

He looked back out at the curtain of rain, listened to it swishing along over the walks and the roofs. No one would be particularly likely to hear someone scream, either.

He pounded on the door again.

To his surprise, there was the rattling sound of a chain being unhooked, and the door opened.

"Jesus Christ, Howland, what are you doing here?" Romain said. His reddish hair was tousled and his eyes were bleary.

"Damn," Howland said. "Were you asleep?"

Romain shook his head. "No. Yes. Maybe. I was tired. What difference does it make? Can't a man take a little nap?"

"Sure," Howland said. "Sure. Why not? Are you gonna ask me in, or what?"

Romain looked at Howland, noticing his condition for the first time. "Hell, you'll drip all over my rug."

It was true, Howland realized. Water was running down his pants legs in a steady stream and dripping off the sleeves of his jacket.

"I'm sorry," he said. "You got a towel or something?"

Romain left Howland standing in the doorway and returned shortly with a beach towel.

Howland took off his jacket and hung it on the doorknob. He dried off his pants and shirt as best he could. He also dried his face and hair.

"Can I come in now?" he said.

"I guess so. You never did say why you were here."
Romain turned and walked across the room to a sofa.

Howland followed Romain. Water squished out of
his socks as he crossed the room.

"You can sit there," Romain said, indicating a Nau-
gahyde-covered chair.

Howland tossed the towel on the chair and sat on it.

Romain looked at him. "You look like a drowned
rat," he said.

"I feel like one." Howland looked around the room,
wondering where the ashtrays were. The place didn't
even smell like smoke.

"So why wade through all the rain?" Romain said.
"You could've called. Or talked to me tomorrow."

"No. There was something I had to see you about."

"What?"

"Your car," Howland said. He explained about the
license plate.

Romain ran a hand through his already mussed hair.
"Jesus. You don't think—"

"I don't know what to think. You didn't say anything about having a car that fit the description."

"Howland," Romain said. "I'm a cop."

"You said anyone could be the killer. That it would
be a mistake to disregard anyone."

"I didn't mean *me*, for God's sake!"

"You'd know how to keep a scene free of clues.
You'd know—"

"OK. OK. But it's not me. If you want to examine
my car for blood traces, you can."

"There wouldn't be any," Howland said. "You'd
take care of that."

He was feeling like an asshole for ever having suspected Romain in the first place, but he had to go on

275

with it now that he'd slogged through the rain to get here.

"You can't ever remove all trace of blood," Romain said.

"You could've used another car."

"That would make your hypnotized witness completely useless."

"Shit," Howland said.

"Absolutely," Romain said. "But I'm really sort of proud of you. It took a lot of guts to come here and confront me like this. Shows you took what I told you to heart."

"Yeah. But I'll probably get pneumonia for it."

Romain smiled. He didn't want to encourage Howland. He was uncomfortable having another policeman in his apartment. He wanted to keep his private life and his job life separate, and Howland was interfering with that.

"There's one other thing," Howland said. "I feel almost stupid even to mention it."

Romain stopped smiling. "What other thing?"

"One of your neighbors has a car that fits the description."

"Who?" Romain said.

Howland told him.

**Rob Hensley was** worried. The rain was sluicing down and was obviously setting in for the night. The tropical depression was really cutting loose over them. He hoped that Casey didn't have any trouble.

He wished that he'd insisted on going with her. He could have sat in the car in the parking lot while she went for the interview. Dr. Fallon, or whatever, would never have known that Rob was there.

Rob looked at the digital clock on his VCR. It was almost time for Casey to be arriving. There wouldn't be anything wrong if he called to check on her, would there?

She wouldn't like it, naturally. She'd think it was a threat to her independence. But he didn't have to tell her that he'd called. He could speak to Dr. Fallon, ask him if Casey had gotten there. If she had, he could ask Fallon not to mention the call. Fallon would surely understand.

Casey wouldn't, though. Not if she found out.

It took Rob five more minutes to convince himself that she wouldn't find out. Then he got out the phone book and looked up the number for GCCC.

The phone rang for a long time. Ten rings. Maybe there was no one on the switchboard in the evenings. Rob was just about to give up when someone picked up on the other end.

"Gulf Coast Community College. Security."

"Uh, yes," Rob said. "I was trying to reach Dr. Fallon's office. Could you connect me?"

"Dr. Fallon?"

"Yes, the English Department chair."

"Nobody named Dr. Fallon here."

"But—"

"English chairman's named Chester. Dr. Gene Chester."

"You're sure about that? Dr. Fallon—"

"Sir, I been here eight years. Dr. Chester's the man in English. Besides, nobody's here tonight, except for me and Al. We're security. This place is closed for three more days. You want to talk to Dr. Chester, you call back on Monday."

"Wait a minute," Rob said. "I have a friend who's coming there for a job interview tonight. Are you sure—"

"Sir, it's like I said. Nobody's here but me and Al. Won't be nobody here till Monday. You call back then."

277

"But—"

"Thank you, sir. You call back Monday, you hear?"

The phone clicked down, the connection broken.

Rob stood for a moment, holding his own phone in his hand. What the hell was going on here? There was no Dr. Fallon. There was no interview. Had Casey lied to him?

No. She had been too happy and excited about the possibility of a job.

So what did that mean? Had someone called her out in the rain for some kind of joke?

Or for something much worse?

Maybe he should call back, see if the security guard would check on Casey. He would have done so had the guard seemed at all interested in helping him, but that had not been the case.

Rob slammed down the phone. All his earlier fears came rushing back to him, intensified.

He would have to go himself. And he would have to go now.

**"Craig Warley?" Romain** said. "I know Craig. He's not the type—"

He bit off his words as soon as he realized what he was saying.

Howland smiled.

"Anyhow," Romain said, "those letters aren't uncommon in this county, as you should know by now. And Warley and I bought our cars from the same dealer. He recommended the place to me. Said they gave good service. He was right, by the way."

Howland didn't give in. "I ought to talk to him, anyway. I'm not going to pass up anyone. I don't have much longer. The Chief is getting really antsy."

"OK," Romain said. He considered Warley for a minute, recalling some of the man's remarks around the pool. "In fact, the more I think about it, the more I see that he *could* be the type. Why don't I give him a call, ask him to come over?"

"Good idea," Howland said. "You got a bathroom I could use? All this rain—"

Romain pointed the way and reached for the phone.

**It was nearly** eight-thirty.

He wondered where she was. He'd thought she would be so eager that she might arrive early. Of course the rain might have held her up. It was certainly bad, and it showed no signs of getting better. There could have been an accident on the freeway, and if that had happened there was no telling how late she might be.

He looked back into the building. There was no sign of the security men. They were probably back in a cubbyhole somewhere with hot coffee and doughnuts, reading a skin magazine. He hoped they stayed there. When he'd checked the place out, they'd made their rounds on the hour, which would give him more than enough time with Casey and her daughter.

If only they got there on time.

He stared out through the streams of rain, squeezing the razor-knife, opening and closing his hand. Opening and closing. Opening and closing.

*Why didn't she come?*

**Casey was sitting** in her car, cursing under her breath. There had been an accident in the middle of the exit ramp, and she was three cars behind.

The wrecker had already arrived, and the cars would be cleared out of the way soon, but she was going to be late. Not too late, but late nevertheless.

"I hope Dr. Fallon will understand," she said.

"Understand what?" Margaret said.

She was actually enjoying the delay. The flashing

279

lights of the wrecker and police cars fascinated her as they reflected from the slick pavement, the shiny surfaces of the other cars, the glass of windshields. Having spent most of her life in Lubbock, where rainfall was as rare as diamonds, she was not accustomed to the effects of great quantities of water falling from the sky.

"Why we're late," Casey said. "I don't want him to think I'll ever be late to my classes."

"He won't care," Margaret said. "We'll tell him about the accident."

"I'll leave earlier from now on," Casey said, not sure that the excuse would be acceptable.

"Maybe you won't have to come at night," Margaret said.

Casey looked out at the rain, the wreck, the line of traffic backed up behind her.

"I hope not," she said.

# 40

**H**e's not there," Romain said when Howland came back into the room.

"Not there?"

"He went out," Romain said. "His wife doesn't know where he is."

"His wife?"

"It wouldn't be too surprising if the man you're looking for had a wife. Remember, we discussed that possibility. The man could seem perfectly normal to others if he wanted to." Romain paused. "Not that I think Warley is the man you're looking for."

"Well, you know him. Maybe I'm getting too excited about nothing."

"He could fool me, too, though," Romain said. "What bothers me is that Tina—that's the wife—told me that he frequently goes out without telling her where he's going. Just says something about business. Never says where he's been when he comes back in, either."

"So he *could* be the one I want."

"He could be."

"But you don't think so."

"I don't know," Romain said. "It's possible, I suppose. There was one talk we had by the pool, something about childhood abuse. He said that he'd been abused fairly regularly, I think. Something like that, anyway. He has a scar on his forehead."

"A scar?" Howland was very interested now. He sank back down on the Naugahyde chair. "That fits, right?"

"Not necessarily. It didn't seem to bother him. But he mentioned once that he'd noticed the scar on a woman at the table with us. Casey Buckner. It was so small I'd never noticed it myself."

"Let's talk to her," Howland said, his excitement mounting. "Maybe she has some kind of feeling about him. Maybe he's said something else to her."

"I don't know her number," Romain said. "She's fairly new here."

"Well, which apartment is she in? I want to talk to her. Now."

Howland was beginning to think that maybe he had gotten lucky. This might be the break he'd never thought he'd get.

"It's raining out there," Romain said.

"You've got an umbrella, right? Get it. I need this, Romain."

"It's pretty farfetched," Romain said. "I'm not sure—"

"Get the fucking umbrella," Howland said.

Romain sighed, but he stood up. He hated rain. It got all over his glasses and made it hard to see.

"All right," he said. "I'll get the fucking umbella."

**"I think it's** slacking up a little," Howland said when they were outside.

"The eternal optimist," Romain said.

The rain slanted in under the umbrella and soaked into their pants.

"Her apartment's over this way," Romain said, leading the way. They sloshed down the sidewalk, and Rob Hensley nearly ran over them as he came dashing out his front door. He hadn't seen them from under the rim of his large black umbrella.

"Sorry," Rob said, trying to dance past them. "Oh, hi, Dan. Didn't mean to run you down."

"Where are you off to in such a hurry?" Romain said.

"I'm looking for Casey," Rob said.

"So are we," Romain told him. "What's your rush?"

"She's not at home," Rob said. "I think she might be in trouble."

"This man's a police officer," Romain said, introducing Howland. The two men shook hands awkwardly. "What kind of trouble is Casey in?"

Rob explained as quickly as he could about the interview, his phone call, his fears.

Howland looked at Romain, their faces close together as they tried to shelter under the single umbrella.

"Did she ever mention in front of Craig Warley that she was looking for a teaching job?" Howland said.

"All the time," Rob said. "Why?"

"We don't have time to explain everything now, Rob," Romain said. "Where did you say she was going?"

Rob told them.

"I think you'd better go on back inside," Howland said. "Romain and I will look into this."

Rob looked at Romain.

"I work for the police, too," Romain said, noting Rob's surprise. "I'm a police psychologist."

"I see," Rob said.

"Show him your badge," Romain told Howland, who obediently got out his wallet and flipped it open.

"I don't understand," Rob said. "Why did you ask about Craig? What's going on?"

"Probably nothing at all," Howland said. "But let us check it out for you. No need for you to be out on a night like this. We'll drive out to the campus and make sure that Casey's all right."

"Well," Rob said. "If you think that's best."

"We do," Romain said. "Believe me."

"Call me as soon as you can," Rob said.

"Sure," Howland said.

As Rob went back to his apartment, Howland turned to Romain. "Let's go. My car's over here."

**Casey turned into** the deserted GCCC parking lot. The classroom building loomed darkly in front of her, and the lot's lighting seemed to be vacuumed up by the blackness of the sky. There was only one other car anywhere in sight; it was parked near the main entrance of the building.

"Where is everybody?" Margaret said.

"That's what I was wondering," Casey said. She wondered if Dr. Fallon was the only one who was working late.

Water swished beneath the tires as she drove across the parking lot. She wished that there were a little more light, and it would have been nice to see an office window glowing yellowly in the forbidding facade of the building. Maybe Dr. Fallon's office was on the other side, and anyway, there was light on in the large entrance hall. There would no doubt be someone in there whom she could ask about the whereabouts of Fallon's office.

She parked next to the other car.

"Slide over here by me," she told Margaret. "We'll both get out on this side, and maybe we won't get too wet."

Margaret looked doubtful, but she slid over.

Casey opened the door and stepped out, opening the umbrella as soon as she could get it clear.

Water flowed over and into her shoes, soaking the feet of her pantyhose.

"Shit," she said.

"Huh?" Margaret said.

"Never mind. Hurry up and get out."

Margaret joined her mother under the umbrella, and they started for the building.

**Two of them** at once! His erection throbbed as never before. He could almost feel the sweet flesh parting at the touch of his blade, almost see the writhing blood marks as they ceased their seething motion and died.

*Calm down,* he told himself. *Don't rush it. Wait, or you'll ruin everything.*

He forced his muscles to relax, but his mind continued to race. He knew that he was at the peak of his alertness. There would be no mistakes. It would be perfect. He could feel it.

**Casey and Margaret** were entirely unaware of the presence of a man in the shrubbery near the sidewalk. They were intent on remaining close together under the umbrella and getting to the entrance while there was still a square inch or two of dry clothing on them.

So they didn't see the dark shape that moved suddenly out of the shadow of the building into the faint light that spilled out from the long glass expanse of the entrance.

The harsh spattering of the rain on the taut fabric of the umbrella was all they heard. They did not notice the slight splashes made by the feet running across the walk toward them.

285

They did not see the upraised arm or the hand holding the knife.

They did not see the razor blade that streaked down toward Margaret's throat.

They were laughing at something Margaret had said when Craig Warley struck.

# 41

**D**on't drive so fast," Romain said. "You'd think we were on the trail of Jack the Ripper."

"Maybe we are," Howland answered, switching lanes at fifty-five and hydroplaning in front of a red Toyota whose driver honked indignantly.

Howland didn't notice. He was already intent on looking for another opening in the traffic.

The more Romain thought about things, the more he thought that maybe Howland had a point about Warley, though it seemed doubtful that Warley would actually try to kill someone who lived in the same apartment complex. If he were really going to do it, however, he might do it in the very way that Howland suspected—by luring his intended victim far away, to some place where he would not be a suspect.

If that were the case, and Romain still wasn't convinced that it was, Warley had planned things cleverly enough. Though Warley knew that Casey was looking for a job, if Casey had not told Rob Hensley about the interview, no one would have known exactly why Casey and Margaret had gone to the GCCC campus. Warley would have been completely in the clear. He probably would not even have been questioned.

Romain realized with a start that he was almost assuming that a murder had already taken place, and that Warley had committed it. It was possible, dammit. The license plate alone was very thin evidence, but when you put it in with everything else—Warley's childhood, Casey's scar, both of them missing—it all began to fall into place.

Howland dodged around an eighteen-wheeler, gunned down an open stretch and swapped lanes again, sliding in front of a black pickup.

This time, Romain didn't ask him to slow down.

**Warley would have** killed Margaret easily, cutting a gaping gash across her bare throat, if it hadn't been for the umbrella.

As his arm descended, dipping to move in, a strong gust of wind flipped the umbrella inside out with a loud pop.

The umbrella ribs grazed Warley's arm, and the sudden motion threw off his aim.

He still managed to slice open Margaret's upper arm, just where it came out of the sleeve of her T-shirt.

Margaret screamed, rain washed the blood away from the wound, and Warley brought his arm down a second time.

Casey, not quite realizing what was happening, swung the umbrella, striking Warley's arm. This time, he missed Margaret completely.

He yelled in frustration. The dirty bitches! This was not going at all the way that he had planned. His mouth twisted with hate as he struck again. He could see the blood marks glowing in the darkness, mocking him as they danced redly in the rain.

His face twisted grotesquely as he swung his arm.

Casey did not recognize him. He was nothing more than a black hulk in his plastic raincoat and hood. She jabbed out with the umbrella, not aiming very well because Margaret was clinging to her leg and screeching.

Had she been aiming, she might not have put out Warley's right eye. As it was, she hit it dead on with the tip of the umbrella just as Warley was thrusting toward her.

When the blunt point went into the eye socket, Casey was horrified to hear what she thought was a popping noise as the eyeball burst, but that must have been her imagination. Her stomach heaved when she realized what she had done.

Warley reeled back, his hands pressed to his face.

One hand still held the blade. Blood ran between his fingers and trickled down the backs of his hands before being washed away by the rain.

Casey and Margaret ran toward the light of the entrance, Margaret with her hand clamped on her arm. She was crying now, but she had stopped screaming.

The thick glass doors were locked.

Casey struck them with her fists and yelled for help. There was no response from inside.

Warley staggered into the light, one hand still over his eye, the other waving the blade.

"Bitches!" he screamed. "Whores!"

There was something about the voice, something about the shape of him that Casey recognized despite the incredible situation.

"Craig?" she said. "Craig Warley?"

"Shut up, bitch," he said. His hand flew away from his face and slammed into her head. She caromed off the door and he hit her again. She collapsed to the cement.

Warley reached for Margaret.

She ducked under his arms and ran back toward the parking lot.

**289**

Warley looked down at Casey and with an almost casual movement kicked her in the head. There would be time for her later. He ran into the rain after the girl.

**"There's the exit,"** Romain said.

"I see it." Howland shot across three lanes of traffic and took the ramp at fifty. He sailed onto the service road, across two more lanes, threw on his brakes and hooked a right at a red light.

Thank God for front-wheel drive, Romain thought. They would never have made that turn in a rear-wheel-drive vehicle. They would have fishtailed, the rear tires would not have held the pavement, and they would have slid across the lanes of oncoming traffic, through a fence and into the field across from them. The fence was covered with signs warning that the field had once been a toxic waste dump.

"How much farther?" Howland said.

"Not far," Romain said. "Half a mile to the next light. Turn right, it's another half mile. You could see the buildings if it were daylight."

Howland goosed the accelerator. The car jumped forward.

**Margaret looked over** her shoulder and saw the man chasing her, his right eye socket dripping thick fluid that he brushed away along with the rainwater that streamed into it. She veered to the right, not knowing how well she could run in the water pouring over the parking lot.

There was no sidewalk along the side of the building, nothing but shrubs and lawn. Margaret slopped along through the grass, her feet making sucking sounds as they lifted from the rain-softened earth.

Warley caught her quickly. He reached out and

**290**

grabbed a handful of her hair, jerking her backward, exposing her throat, white in the darkness.

But he did not kill her, not then.

He was going to kill them both at the same time. Dragging her along by her hair, he started back toward the entrance. Her heels kicked and plowed the ground as he pulled the struggling girl after him.

Casey was trying to sit up when Warley reached her. He jerked the bedraggled Margaret around to face her mother.

"Look," he said, pointing to Casey's scar. "Can you see it? See the way it twists and burns on her face? Well, it won't burn much longer."

Margaret had no idea what he was talking about. She tried to kick his shins, but he held her at arm's length.

"Little bitch. I'll do yours first, then."

He pulled her head back.

Casey dimly understood what he was about to do, but her eyes were not quite focused. Too, she had never in her life thought of doing violence to another person. Still, as Warley put the edge of the razor blade to Margaret's throat, Casey knew that she had to stop him.

Somehow.

The umbrella was under her leg. She reached for it and felt that one of the ribs had come loose from the fabric, the metal shield having slipped off its somewhat pointed tip when the wind had reversed the umbrella's shape.

She yanked the rib free and shoved it into Warley's side with all her strength, hoping at least to distract him.

She did more than that.

The thin rib slid through Warley's plastic raincoat,

**291**

pierced his cotton shirt and punctured the thin layer of fat under his skin.

Warley released Margaret and tried to turn to Casey. His lips were peeled back from his teeth, and his single eye burned with the ferocity of his hatred.

Casey shoved desperately on the rib, using the heel of her hand to push it in. Her own skin was punctured, but Warley was hurt considerably more.

The metal point struck a bone, slipped off and penetrated deeper into Warley's body.

Warley screamed like an animal, releasing Margaret and arching his back as the pain suffused him.

He slashed Casey in a fury, drawing the razor blade across her face. A thin line of blood jumped to the surface along a line running diagonally from just below her right eye, across both lips and down her chin.

Casey fell back, her head striking the glass doors with a dull thud.

Her fingers tore another rib from the umbrella as Margaret grabbed Warley around both legs, causing him to tumble forward.

Casey got the rib up just as Warley fell heavily onto it, with Casey trying to twist out of his way. The rib entered his abdomen, and he screamed again, dropping the razor-knife as he collapsed onto Casey.

Casey shoved his heavy body aside with disgust and got to her feet, leaning against the doors.

"Are you OK, Mom?" Margaret said, frightened more by the appearance of Casey's face than by what had happened. There was blood running down Margaret's arm, but she wasn't worried about that.

"I'm fine," Casey lied.

She looked down at Craig Warley as he moaned and twisted on the sidewalk. Her knees were weak and threatened to collapse at any moment. She could not believe what had just happened, still had no idea what was going on, but she knew one thing. She wasn't going to stay there to ask Craig.

"Let's get out of here," she said to Margaret. She hoped there was a hospital nearby.

As they walked back toward the parking lot, they saw the lights of Howland's car turning in.

**"There they are,"** Romain said as the headlights caught Margaret and Casey. He could tell that they were not walking normally. "They don't look so good."

"Is Warley there?" Howland said.

"I don't see him."

Howland skidded to a stop at the edge of the entrance walkway, and he and Romain jumped out of the car.

"Police," Howland said, showing his badge.

Casey and Margaret shrank back.

"It's all right, Casey," Romain said. "He really is the police. Are you two all right?"

"Yes," Casey said, recognizing Romain. Her voice was shaky. "Is there a hospital around here?"

"About a quarter mile down the road," Romain said, now able to see Casey's face. "Jesus. What happened?"

"It was Craig Warley, I-I think. He . . . tried to kill us." Casey's astonishment was evident. She still couldn't quite comprehend what had just happened.

"Where is he now?" Howland said, his hand under his jacket resting on the butt of his .38 Special.

"B-back there," Casey said.

Howland looked into the light and saw the figure squirming in front of the doors.

"What the hell did you do to him?" he said.

"I poked him with the umbrella," Casey said, just as another car pulled into the lot.

Rob Hensley stopped his car and ran up to them.

"I thought I asked you to stay at your apartment," Howland said.

"I know. But I didn't," Rob said. "I wanted to know about Casey. What happened here?"

"Something bad," Margaret said, looking back at Warley.

"Listen," Romain said, "as long as you're here, you might as well make yourself useful. Take these two to the hospital down the road. Get them sewed up, whatever they need. They can tell you what happened. But don't leave. We'll have to talk to them later."

Rob picked up Margaret in one arm and held her close. She put her arms around his neck. She was quite a load, but he didn't mind. He put his other arm around Casey and hugged her tight.

"I couldn't stand to lose either of you," he said. "Who did this?"

"Craig Warley," Romain told him.

"Warley? That bastard," Rob said. "I'll kill the son of a bitch."

"I don't think you'll have to," Romain said. "I think Casey may have taken care of that already."

**But she hadn't.**

Romain finally managed to get Rob to leave for the hospital by pointing out the urgency of getting treatment for Margaret and Casey. Then he joined Howland, who was looking at Warley, who seemed in no condition to speak coherently. He was muttering about bitches and blood marks and how he would cut them all to pieces. His hands were clasped tightly over his abdomen. Romain still found it slightly hard to believe that it was really Warley who was lying there.

"What do you think?" Howland said.

Romain tried to wipe the rain off his glasses with the tail of his shirt, but all he succeeded in doing was smearing the lenses. He bent down and looked into Warley's face. Then, as best he could under the circumstances, he examined the two steel ribs sticking into Warley.

"He'll probably live, unless he gets tetanus. I don't think anything vital's been hit. His eye's gone, too, but that's not fatal."

"Good. That's good. But will he talk?"

"He'll talk," Romain said, knowing that he was right but sharing none of Howland's enthusiasm. His voice was tired. "Once they're caught, they always want to talk."

"Great!" Howland started tapping on the glass door with the barrel of his .38. "You think they've got security here, or am I going to have to shoot down the fucking door?"

**"It's after two** in the morning," Alma said. "And you look like somebody tried to drown you."

Howland was standing in her doorway wet as a water rat. "Yeah. I know. So can I come in, or what?"

Alma laughed. "You can come in, I guess. Don't let the cat see you, though. You might scare him to death."

Howland stepped inside. "Our case is solved," he said. "Thanks to you. It was the license number that did it."

Alma clapped her hands together. "It was? You'll have to tell me all about it. As soon as I get you out of those wet clothes."

She started unbuttoning Howland's shirt, then leaned over and licked his chest.

"Well," she said, "maybe not *that* soon. There might be time for something else first."

Howland smiled. "Yeah. Maybe there will, at that."

**Romain lay in** his bed and stared at the black ceiling above him, wondering how he could have missed it.

295

Craig Warley. A man that he had seen every day.
And you think you're so fucking smart, he thought.
But it could have been anyone.

It could even have been me. Howland thought it was me.

It wasn't, of course. No way. The job had gotten to him, but he wasn't crazy. Yet. And they *had* gotten the killer off the streets, finally, thanks to a rather sizable assist from Casey Buckner.

Romain and Howland had talked to Casey at the hospital after Warley had been taken away. Casey was a strong young woman, and Margaret was just like her. They would heal quickly, and it appeared that they would have plenty of help from Rob in doing so. There would be no permanent effects on either of them as a result of Warley's madness, except that both of them would have new scars. Casey's probably wouldn't be visible under makeup. Margaret's was a little deeper, and she would carry the reminder of the attack for everyone to see on her arm.

Romain thought again about how tired he was of dealing with killers, trying to think like them, trying to live inside their twisted heads.

He thought about how Warley had been right there under his nose all along and not been noticed.

*I can't quit now,* he told himself. It wouldn't be right.

He had to keep on, just as Howland would keep on, working on the next case and then on the one after that, trusting to their skills, and hoping for a little luck.

Maybe that would be enough.

After a while, Romain slept.